THE
GLARE

THE
GLA

RE

MARGOT HARRISON

LITTLE, BROWN AND COMPANY
NEW YORK BOSTON

Copyright © 2020 by Margot Harrison

Cover art: digital glitch texture by The7Dew/Shutterstock.com; broken glass texture by yourasasin/Shutterstock.com; girl photograph by Aleshyn_Andrel/Shutterstock.com; falling numbers by gaihong dong/Shutterstock.com; title font by Laralova/Shutterstock.com. Cover design by Jamie Alloy and Neil Swaab. Cover copyright © 2020 by Hachette Book Group, Inc.

Little, Brown and Company
Hachette Book Group
1290 Avenue of the Americas, New York, NY 10104
Visit us at LBYR.com

First Edition: July 2020

Little, Brown and Company is a division of Hachette Book Group, Inc. The Little, Brown name and logo are trademarks of Hachette Book Group, Inc.

The publisher is not responsible for websites (or their content) that are not owned by the publisher.

ISBNs: 978-1-368-00565-4 (hardcover), 978-1-368-01483-0 (ebook)

Printed in the United States of America

LSC-C

10 9 8 7 6 5 4 3 2 1

To my mother, Sophie Quest, who
showed me how to imagine

1

The sun is just up in the desert, the mesa red against the violet sky, as I watch my mother use the Glare. Mom huddles between the coop and the supply shed with her right hand raised to her ear, her shoulders hunched like she's holding a live grenade. She doesn't know I'm awake and spying on her from the window, but she hides the Glare-box with her body, just in case.

I'm not fooled. I've seen her break her own rules before.

The first time it happened, I was fourteen. It was a morning like this—barely dawn, still cool. When I saw those tense shoulders and the flash of metal in Mom's hand, tears of rage pressed hard and hot against my eyes. For a second I was so angry I wanted to scream, *I can see you! It's going to get inside you, too!*

A few days later, while Mom was out helping a goat deliver a kid, I went through the purse she only uses on our trips to town.

Under a false bottom I found a smooth clamshell of metal. I pried it open just long enough to glimpse the flicker of Glare inside, then clapped it shut. Later, I wasn't sure if I'd felt a humming vibration or just imagined it.

In those days, I still half believed the energy in that metal chunk could get inside me and make me hurt myself. It had happened to the girl in the story I grew up hearing: a girl who had so many screens, too many screens. The screens were full of Glare, and the Glare wormed its way inside the girl's head and possessed her. When she realized what was happening, she put drain cleaner in her eyes so she wouldn't have to see the screens anymore. But it was too late. As the EMTs carried the girl away on a stretcher, with the red lights flashing and her mom tight-faced and her little brother sobbing, the girl screamed at the top of her lungs, "I can still see it! I can still see!"

The facts of this story are true. It happened to my babysitter when I was six years old in San Rafael, California; Mom wasn't the first one to tell it to me. But I know now nothing's so simple, and it's how we interpret those facts that matters.

Now I give Mom's Glare-box its proper name—cell phone. I know she's probably just talking to Dad, telling him stuff about my trip she doesn't want me to hear. That's why she didn't use the phone in the kitchen with its sticky black cord.

And the tears that blind me today are tears of tenderness, because tomorrow I'm going back to the world of Glare, the world where I was born, and I'm not afraid.

. . .

Mom doesn't let me clear the dinner dishes. She pours us both more watery iced tea and sits down opposite me in the sweltering desert evening, under the motionless ceiling fan that needs a new motor. "Hedda," she says, "I know you're going to be testing the boundaries at your dad's."

Think fast. Is she threatening to cancel my trip? My hands start shaking under the table. Flies tap the window where the scorching sun swells it amber, their drone drilling its way into my brain.

She can't keep me here. Not when I'm so close to getting away.

I've been carefully monitoring Mom's moods ever since I started plotting my escape from this ranch—ever since the call came from Australia. Mom's childhood best friend in Melbourne had been diagnosed with stage IV breast cancer. She has no family, and Mom started talking about flying out there for a few months to take care of her.

It took me nearly two weeks to persuade her to let me stay with Dad in California. First Mom wanted me to come with her. Then she suggested sending me to New Genesis, a place run by her friends in Nevada where people wear white robes, obey rules set by a Council of Elders, and don't use electricity or running water, so she could be sure I wouldn't look at Glare-screens. I let her know that was an over-my-dead-body scenario.

Because yes, okay, maybe I am testing the boundaries. My plan is to get Dad to let me attend school in San Rafael, then use that as leverage to convince Mom I should go to school here. And if she still says no...well, that's when I'll tell Dad I want to live with him. Or threaten to run away.

There's only so long you can live twenty miles from everyone and everything before you get left behind.

"If you know exactly what I'm planning to do on this trip," I tell Mom, keeping my voice level, "then you must also know you can trust me not to take it too far. I'm not a little kid anymore."

"I hope I can trust you."

The stress she puts on "hope" makes me tense. "What makes you think you can't?"

Trust me not to stare, she means. Trust me not to get addicted like those girls I see at Walmart who are so busy on their Glare-boxes that they barely raise their eyes long enough to check out. When I was little, every time we went to town, Mom used her body to shield me from anyone who was smoking or using the Glare. Nowadays she seems to realize a single accidental inhale won't turn me into a two-pack-a-day addict, but she hasn't gotten any less paranoid about screens.

"Let's not get into the blame game again, Hedda," Mom says. And then she reaches under the table and brings out her secret cell phone and plunks it on the worn oilcloth between us.

I stare at the phone, blood pounding in my temples. Should I look surprised? Betrayed? Is she trying to trick me into admitting I touched it?

"I know," I say because it's too late to pretend I'm the girl she wants me to be, the girl who wouldn't have gone looking for that phone.

"I know you know." She looks straight at me, her eyes enormous and indigo in a strong light, just like mine. "And you've probably guessed I have it for emergencies, in case we break down on the way to Phoenix to see your dad."

For the past decade, I've seen Dad exactly once a year when he buys me a fancy dinner in Phoenix on my birthday. He has a cell phone, too, of course—probably a dozen of them—but he's not allowed to use it in front of me, not even to show me a picture of my half brother, whom I've never met.

"So we both know you don't follow your own rules," I say. "What's your point?"

Mom opens the phone. I wince—can't help it—but the screen is dinkier and duller than I remember. It's nothing compared to the brand-new phone that belongs to Shannon, a girl I see sometimes at the county fair. Hers is perfectly smooth and flat, with a screen that lights up in colors that remind me of hard candy or the costume jewelry at the dollar store.

"It's just an old flip phone. Touch it if you want." Mom pushes the phone across the oilcloth to me.

I shake my head automatically. I may not be scared of her "flip phone," but I'm not going to get myself in trouble now. "No thanks. I can do without the Glare just fine."

Mom keeps staring at me. We look alike—wiry bodies, unruly black hair, intense eyes—and we have matching tempers, too. Today she's holding hers back, and not just because we're separating tomorrow for the first time in ten years. She wants something from me.

"We both know you've had your fill of looking at screens," she says. "I've seen you with that girl at the fair, the one in the ridiculously short shorts, staring straight at her phone."

Blood rushes to my face, and my vision blurs. "I was curious."

I wanted our last day together to be special, a throwback to the days when I was little and we'd work all day and then Mom would brush my hair and tell me stories about a crew of happy cactus mice who lived deep in the desert on insects and rainwater. But here we are having the old fight again.

"The important thing is, I'm fine. Nothing happened." I muster my resolution like a clenched fist. "The Glare doesn't actually make people put drain cleaner in their eyes. I mean, you know that, right?" *Please tell me you know that.*

Mom keeps looking straight at me. "When I worked at your dad's company, I was exposed to the Glare at least seventeen hours a day. I have a very good idea of how it affects people."

"I *know* that." When we lived in California, Mom designed games that people play in the Glare. The goal is to get the players addicted; the goal of everything in the Glare is to addict you, to unstick you from reality, and you never know you're unstuck until it's too late.

But getting addicted or unstuck isn't the same as getting possessed. The babysitter's story still makes me sad, but it no longer sends shivers down my spine.

Mom goes on. "And you haven't forgotten the things that happened to *you*, have you?"

"The Glare knocked me off-kilter. I know. But I barely even remember that stuff, Mom. I just know what you've told me."

She's told the stories so many times they're emblazoned on my brain: How I screamed when she took my Glare-screens away. How I climbed out my window and sat on the roof. How I switched on the gas burners so the whole house could've burned down. Bad, scary, unmanageable Hedda, who had to be taken away for her own good.

But I haven't been that little girl for so long.

I rise and brace myself on the edge of the table, frustration simmering in my gut. "Whatever I did when I was six, I'm not unstuck from reality now, as you can see. And I don't ever plan to be."

This argument never ends well, but I keep going, my voice rising: "You need to get it through your head that you can't control me forever, and I don't give a flying…freak about the Glare. I don't want the Glare. I don't *need* the Glare. All I want is not to spend the entire rest of my life in the middle of nowhere taking care of goats."

Mom doesn't snap back. I can see to the blue bottom of her eyes.

"Hedda," she says, "you're sixteen now. If I thought I could control you, here or in California, I'd be stupid. So that's why I'm begging you—don't tempt fate. You've seen the Glare for yourself—now let it alone. Or if you have to use it occasionally, use it carefully, the way I do. Control *yourself.*"

She closes her secret phone with a neat clap. I turn around, blinded by tears, and stumble outside into the August heat to do my chores for the last damn time.

Just an hour ago, the knowledge that I'm leaving was a pool of brightness inside me. Now I want to kick everything—the red dirt, the feed bucket, the dusty stalls, a stray hen.

Instead, I take a deep breath and start the routine that keeps me grounded, day after day. When I'm done feeding the goats, I pet them, feeling sorry for what I said about them earlier. They butt against my hand longer than usual, staring at me through their alien horizontal pupils. The chickens ignore me, too busy having peck fights and pulling up grubs.

The scrubby red desert stretches like a basking lizard to where Wedding Cake Mesa slices the horizon. As far as it's concerned, I'll be back here tomorrow to throw feed for these hens, and the day after and the day after that, till the sun has turned my face to leather. How could someone like me ever come unstuck?

I could've said more. I could've challenged Mom to prove the Glare had anything to do with my bad behavior—or with the babysitter hurting herself, for that matter. I could've picked apart the logic that made Mom bring me here to live on the ranch she inherited from her uncle, twenty miles from the nearest town, where she can homeschool me and keep me safe from screens.

I could have pointed out that normal people don't even call it "the Glare." That was my word originally, something I cried out in waking nightmares when we first came here. Whenever Mom left me alone in the house for more than a few minutes, she says, I'd run to her saying the Glare was after me—sneaking through the cracks, creeping along the floor, looming on my bedroom wall like an intruder. It had got the babysitter, and now it would get me.

We both had plenty to be scared of back then—the desert silence, the snakes. But little by little, as we fixed up this run-down place, it started to feel like home. I'd read to Mom from instruction manuals, sounding out the big words, while she fumbled underneath the water heater or the solar generator, muttering (usually) sanitized curse words.

The first time we helped a nanny goat birth her kids, we broke out the sparklers like it was New Year's Eve. We learned to milk, to make cheese, to slaughter and pluck chickens, to plant the garden, to fix the roof. We turned a wreck into a ranch with tidy outbuildings and beds of chard and kale and rioting tomato plants.

It's still so quiet, though. Sometimes, like now, I close my eyes and stretch my inner sensors out and out in every direction like insect antennae, looking for someone or something to connect to. All they ever report is echoing emptiness.

I open my eyes to the dazzling horizon, then examine my calloused fingertips and the sludgy white scars on my inner arm. I got those when I was six, climbing a cottonwood tree and falling in barbed wire.

Everything here is rough, dangerous—no playgrounds carefully designed to be kid-friendly. I'm not complaining. But after all the hard work we've done together, all the things we've both given up, all the years without friends or a father, she has the gall to tell me to *control myself.*

Well, I can—but not because she says to. From now on, I make the rules for me.

After chores, I finish packing and take a long look at the stuff I can't take with me: the rock collection, the snake skins, most of the books, the stuffed animals, and the long scrolls of paper that unfurl across the robin's-egg-blue walls of my room.

Soon after we got here, Mom found twenty paper rolls in the crawl space under the porch—from an old accounting machine, she said. For years afterward, I filled them with cartoonish images of the home I'd left behind: a brown-shingled, gabled house on a tree-lined street. There's Daddy with his curly black hair and his Glare-box, Mommy with her wide smile, and me in a red shirt with my own Glare-box. There's the babysitter with her tattoo of a blue flower. I drew her with sparkly eyes, the way she was before she hurt herself.

There are my two best friends and neighbors: Ellis with his freckles and shy smile, and Mireya with her glossy black hair. Ellis was the babysitter's little brother, and in the pictures, we're always happy and having fun. At the beach, on the playground, in school, at Mom and Dad's office. On my ninth birthday, I filled a yard of paper with the party I dreamed of: friends, a sparkly dress, fireworks, a movie. For the movie, I drew blue light exploding from a black rectangle.

Blue light. That's all I really remember about the Glare in my life before.

Blue light bathed me as I sat beside Ellis at Mom's desk, pressing keys. Blue light bathed the babysitter as she stared at flitting shapes on a screen. "Don't look, this isn't for kids!" she snapped, but I kept looking because I wasn't a baby.

Then the blue light was gone, disappearing somewhere in the red dust, and the desert drew a clean line across my life: before and after. And here I am, still reaching out toward something I lost.

· · ·

I'm having the dream again.

A girl walks through a vibrant green forest flecked with autumn reds—lush and moist, nothing like the desert. Dead leaves carpet the ground. Blue sky stretches above a square black tower.

The girl is me. Someone whistles, and she turns to find a boy with freckled cheeks—my friend Ellis. "They're coming," he says.

Fear rockets down the girl's spine; she hears *them* slithering through the leaves. "Let's go!"

The boy runs, and she runs after him as the wind rises. A sickly blue light bleeds through the trees. Together they wriggle inside the tower, where a stink of old burning sears their nostrils. The tower is a smokestack rising to a ring of bright sky, and that brightness is the Glare. A *good* Glare, a light that will never hurt them.

But now clouds film over the sky, forming a shape like a grinning skull. The girl shivers.

The boy releases her hand. "You have to leave, Hedda. You're already dead—did you forget?"

How can he say that? How can he abandon her? "I'm not!" she yells.

A wind swirls up from nowhere and drags the girl outside, away from the boy. She screams, but his back is turned.

The storm rips leaves from trees as the girl runs helter-skelter, looking for a tree with a safety rune on the trunk. Stray twigs sting her cheeks. A massive branch falls in her path, and she staggers backward. A high keening splits the air. *They're here.*

All the trees are one tree, the leaves thrashing above and the deadfall crackling ominously below. Something stirs under those leaves, slithering toward the girl, and she tries to run, but her legs won't work. Something perches on a branch above her, crouched to spring, and she screams and screams—

And I cry out and wake to my room, starting to lighten with the new day.

My heart's racing, my body drenched in sweat. I throw off the blanket and breathe deeply until everything slows down to normal. The nightmare is as familiar to me as the lines on my palm. Ellis always deserts me in it, though in real life I was the one who left him behind.

Dawn creeps over the creek and the cottonwoods, the sky violet again from mesa to flat horizon, and I need Mom.

When I think of how we fought yesterday, a ragged void opens inside me. The two or three months we plan to be apart might as well be forever.

I tiptoe down the hall and ease the door of her room open. She doesn't stir, a dark lump under the covers, her jaw swollen with the mouthguard that keeps her from grinding her teeth all night.

Part of me wants to creep into bed with her like I did when I was six and had the black tower nightmare, and part of me is pretty sure she'd scream bloody murder. She solves the dilemma by opening her eyes. At first they widen with panic, but then she wakes for real, her face becoming the calm, patient one she always had when she bandaged my scrapes and reassured me there were no monsters under the bed.

As she yanks the mouthguard out, I say, "I'm sorry."

She holds out her arms, and I sink onto the bed and into the hug. Her breath is soft and even, raising fine hairs on the back of my neck as she says, "It's a big change for us both."

And I can handle it, something whispers deep inside me, still rebellious, but I stay still and let the warm cliff of her body protect me one last time, knowing that tonight I won't sleep in the bed I woke in.

I'm going home. And when—*if*—I come back here, I won't be the same.

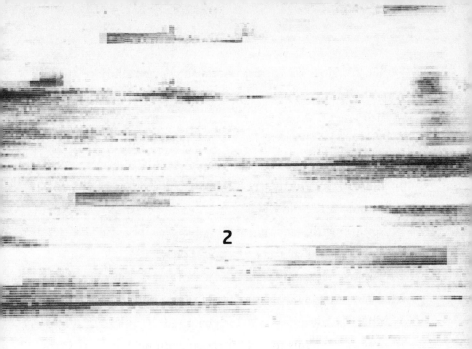

2

The airport has acres of stainless steel and mirrors and clanking conveyor belts. Boxes of bluish Glare flicker everywhere—bolted to posts, on people's laps, in people's hands, on people's wrists. Even children have them.

Is California like this? My experiences at Walmart, the feed store, and the county fair haven't prepared me for this *level* of Glare.

It's not the Glare that really fascinates me, though; it's the girls my age. I've read every book in the town library about them: *Carrie* and *The Runaway's Diary* and *Go Ask Alice* and newer books when I could find them. I know never to go anywhere with a stranger you meet at a bus station, never to assume a cute guy is also nice, and never to trust popular girls. I even know what texting and friending are, in a vague way, and how to hold a phone.

But *these* girls—they're real. They wear ponytails and pin-striped shorts and frilly blouses and leggings and headwraps. They stretch out their long, tanned legs and yawn as if everything bores them. They tap on their phones like it's the most natural thing in the world.

I know how to avert my eyes from the Glare so Mom won't think it's sucking me in. But how can I be friends with girls like this without using the Glare?

Mom must be noticing my furtive eyes, because she says, "You're okay, Hedda. You know you're okay."

"I know." I try to keep the sarcasm out of my voice. She's already scrutinizing me for signs of losing control.

It hurt saying goodbye to the goats and the chickens. It hurt driving away, smelling the familiar blend of moist clay and gritty sand and animal dung. And it hurts as we stand at the gate and she folds me in her arms.

"Maybe you'll find Raggedy Ann," she says as we come apart.

She's told me the story a hundred times: When we were half-way to Arizona, I wailed because I'd forgotten to pack my favorite doll. Dad promised to bring her to our first birthday dinner, then claimed he couldn't find her.

"Maybe." I think of those girls again, how they'd roll their eyes and maybe call me a freak. *I'm not a child. Stop wishing I were.*

"Your dad understands everything. He promised he won't give you culture shock."

"Okay."

Mom's crying, her eyes too bright in her wind-burnt face, the ranch's scent clinging to her fleece. As her arms wrap tight around me, I feel cold, like she's already gone, and I whisper, "I love you."

14

. . .

It's harder to ignore the Glare on the plane, where it's right in my face. The back of each seat has a tiny screen embedded in it, and the instant the lights blink on, so do the screens. Their sharp-edged jewel brightness draws me in: winking, twitching, flashing. Like they're trying to send me signals.

Did Mom know about this? Presumably not.

If my senses reached out into the desert and found only emptiness, here they're overloaded. My stomach flips over, and for an instant I forget the Glare is no more dangerous than secondhand tobacco smoke. Probably less. Mom's books disagree on what exactly glowing screens do to people's brains, but lung cancer isn't involved.

Mom gave me a pill to take in case my first flight made me nervous. I didn't mean to use it, but now I reach into the front pocket of my backpack, pull out the dusty-rose tablet, and swallow it dry.

Once I get to California, every conversation with Dad will be crucial. For the past ten years, he's obeyed Mom's rules around me, never even openly questioning them. If I want to go to school, if I want to avoid a future of New Genesis or growing old with Mom on the ranch, I need to show *him* I can control myself, too.

Two rows ahead of me, a girl with a purple streak in her hair taps on a book-sized Glare-box. She looks calm and confident, like she's flown hundreds of times.

I close my eyes, waiting for the pill to kick in. The plane rolls, the engines whining, the oil stink making my stomach shrivel.

Cheerful, tinny voices from everywhere yell about seat belts, exit rows, and oxygen masks.

Not real voices; they're in the Glare. I think we're *supposed* to look.

Control yourself. My head's starting to feel fuzzy, my ears refocusing on the vibrations beyond the cabin. The engines roar. The plane shivers with eagerness to fly, then wheezes and rockets across the tarmac.

When we leave the ground, my stomach drops away. I open my eyes, hoping to see Phoenix shrinking below us, but my seatmate has lowered the shade.

The Glare-screens have gone mute, but their shimmer still draws me, and I let myself drink in some of the moving pictures. A tanned, toned couple in bathing suits perch above the ocean, toasting each other with glasses full of fruit and flowers. The colors sear my eyes, the shivery-precise images like winter and spring at once.

I close my eyes again. *Think goals.* I need to be nice, to show Dad and his new family how adaptable and grounded I am. I need to talk about the Glare as little as possible, making it clear I'm not greedy for their shiny devices but I'm not judging them, either. Instead, I'll talk about school and how much I love learning.

Kids pick on kids who are different. Girls might give you a hard time, even call you a freak. That's what Mom's been saying ever since I turned thirteen and started begging to try out real school. I tell myself that if I can face down rattlesnakes, I can face down meanness, but it's hard to be sure what you can do when you've never been tested.

At least my stepmother doesn't seem mean—in Dad's Polaroids, she's young, pretty, and smiling. I imagine her taking me out to buy stylish clothes, then hugging me as we drink those elaborate whipped-cream coffees together. Dad will listen intently as I tell him about my latest read (Richard Feynman on quantum theory), and then he'll say, *I don't care what Jane thinks. You need a real education.*

Light keeps moving behind my eyelids, and before I know it, I'm looking at the Glare again. Without the sound, it's a jumble of images telling a story I can only guess at. Each time the scene shifts, the screen flashes, and I blink. *Woman in bikini laughing. Fingers intertwined. Man and woman kissing. Pineapple. Cocktail shaker. Waves on sand.* DIRECT WEEKDAY SERVICE TO ISLAND DESTINATIONS. Then, after only a slightly harder blink: *Ship on dark water. Rocket blazing across sky. People running. Buildings exploding.* THE WARTIME EPIC OF THE DECADE—

Next comes something about weight loss, and then something about a family living in space, and my head pounds, pounds, *too many questions*, and I return to my private imaginings, but they've become wilder now, brilliant and exciting.

I'm at a party with an older version of Mireya, dancing in an off-the-shoulder top, checking a phone and laughing. I'm back with Mom, only I'm taller and tanner with amazing silky hair, and she's frowning and saying words I can't understand because my new life is a train taking me away from her, faster and faster.

An amplified voice mutters in the distance. I float in grayness, soft and peaceful, all the images swept away.

Wind rises in the forest, and with it come a slide and rustle like a snake in gritty sand. The sound caresses each of my vertebrae, pricking my spine like a high-voltage station.

You're dreaming. Wake up.

Ping. My eyes open on the Glare. Cold, chalky fingers snake themselves around my left wrist and hold on tight.

I scream and rear up, my other hand reaching across my body to thrust the attacker away. The seat belt yanks me back down, but there's nothing to fight anyway. No one there but my seatmate, whose hands are busy knitting.

I try to catch my breath, but there's nowhere to look but into the Glare, and every single screen shows me the same thing:

A jagged white face made of sky and clouds. A skull.

A skull grinning down at me.

Warm hands press my shoulders against the seat—a flight attendant with a blond ponytail and navy pantsuit. "Deep breaths," she says.

I'm on a plane. I'm safe. I take deep breaths. The colors of the world, the air in my lungs—nothing feels real. Was the skull a dream, too?

"You're all right," the flight attendant tells me, but she doesn't let go. I crane my neck around her restraining arms, trying to catch a glimpse of the nearest screen.

A family on vacation, riding a roller coaster and eating cotton candy. All sun and happiness and rollicking adventure. *It wasn't real. Not real, not real, not real—*

"She was just having a bad dream," says the grandmotherly woman beside me. "Weren't you, honey?"

I nod, my cheeks burning as I return to reality—canned air, someone's perfume, the rumbling engine. The girl with purple-streaked hair has turned to look at me, white cords dangling from her ears. She stares the way you do at someone who's *off-kilter* in public. I want to die.

The two other flight attendants bustle around, coaxing people back down with maternal whispers. The one who's taken charge of me brings me water and asks if I take any calming medications, if I need something now.

"No thanks." *Please let this be over soon. Please don't let me mess up again.* "Just a bad dream."

"Well, we're about to start our descent. Buckle your seat belt. I'll check on you when we're on the ground."

My grandmotherly seatmate promises to keep an eye on me. More deep breaths.

Less than two hours away from Mom, and I've already called dangerous attention to myself. The memory of her skeptical voice, her steady stare, makes my fists clench.

Control yourself. But that doesn't mean avoiding screens, it just means not letting them freak me out. If I want to be normal, I need to get used to normal things. I need to get used to the Glare.

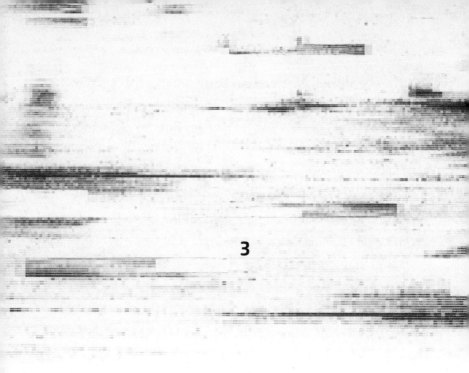

3

The flight attendant follows me up the Jetway and past the ticket counters. "I'm really okay," I promise over and over. *Please don't talk to Dad. Please go away.*

When we reach the arrivals lounge, she says, "Stay safe, hon," and strides briskly on. I look frantically for a restroom where I can calm my wild hair and dab my raccooned, red-rimmed eyes, but it's too late—here's Dad.

How does my face look? Is my smile normal, or crooked? Do I seem *off-kilter*?

To my relief, his hazel eyes are calm behind his rectangular glasses with thin wire rims. Then I'm being pressed against his sport coat, smelling his cologne, feeling the slight paunch that pushes out his crisp button-down. Often he wears cartoon-character T-shirts to my birthday dinners, and then Mom teases him: "When are you going to grow up, Mike?"

His face is still serene as we come apart. "Flying sucks, doesn't it? At least you had a short one."

"Yeah," I say. "It wasn't bad at all."

Mom likes to say Dad's ability not to notice things is practically a superpower. To me that never seemed like such a bad thing. He didn't *need* to notice us, because he always won at chess and knew everything about everything. He was benign, distant, and self-possessed, like a wizard in a book.

But there were things I didn't notice about him, either. Without Mom here to counterbalance him, I spot the sweat glistening at his temples, the nick where he cut himself shaving. He's life-sized now, and one of the things he's no longer hiding from me is his connection to the Glare.

As we wait for the baggage carousel, Dad excuses himself, takes three paces from me, and pulls out his phone. He doesn't use it long, but as we step outside into the crisp, springlike air, it buzzes again.

"I'm sorry, Hedda." He ducks inside the concrete taxi shelter. "This won't take a second."

"I don't mind." I have plenty of distractions, starting with the cars zooming everywhere. Already my feet ache from walking longer on pavement in a single day than I usually do in a year.

Dad's car is sleek, bone-white. When we're buckled up, he touches something, and the interior comes to weird, quiet life, a Glare-screen flickering on the dashboard.

My eyes dart away, and I feel a strange tingling at the back of my thighs, part queasiness and part yearning. I half expect to see that skull again, but there's only a map.

Queasy or not, I need to practice looking. According to Mom's books, screen addiction comes from interaction, and I'm not doing that, am I?

I wonder how Dad feels about being addicted as he accelerates onto an enormous freeway that groans with traffic. My eyes dart from the screen to his face. How long until I can start asking him about school? The rush of the wind gives me confidence; it's not a question of wanting or wishing, but of willing, because now that I'm free, no one can put me back in the cage. Does he feel free in this life, too? I think he does.

We rocket toward a clump of skyscrapers on the horizon, the engine whirring in ghostly quiet, our speed like an optical illusion. "This is a Tesla," Dad explains. "Fully electric."

As the highway snakes through the city, I almost stop breathing. Western light gilds towers of glass and steel—are there really enough people to fill them? From a distance, all I see are cars.

I could live here. After college, I can live anywhere I want.

As Dad points out Twin Peaks and Golden Gate Park, I wonder what he remembers about me, what he expects. For every birthday, he gives me a couple of fat books that serve as a conversation starter for next year. We hardly ever talk about my life on the ranch, Dad's new family, or his job in the Glare.

The arches of the Golden Gate Bridge, the color of dried blood, etch themselves in the sky. The air over the bay shimmers like a diaphanous veil.

So beautiful. So unreal.

On the other side of the bridge, in Marin, we exit the highway in a city where date palms frame adobe facades as clean and smooth as cake frosting. There's an old-time movie marquee and a gleaming Mission-style church. Everything looks like set dressing for a dream, barring the occasional grimy basement window or mean-eyed seagull.

"Is this San Rafael?"

"You don't recognize it?" He sounds disappointed.

I thought I remembered my life here, but it looks different now. I've always known that Dad has money. But as the near-silent car floats up a street lined with graceful, glittering cottonwoods, I see what money can buy. Before the goats and the chickens and the rusty, airbag-less trucks, this was how we lived. This light-filled place is what I lost.

We slow before a house that seems to tower in the tree branches, shielded from the street by a steep flight of stairs. The brown-shingled house. My first home.

The watery forms of memory coalesce into solid things. The central gable. The three sets of cream-colored pillars that frame the door like piping on a uniform. The picture windows on either side.

I climbed up on that roof once—so high! My room was in that front gable.

"It's the same." My voice quavers, and abruptly tears bulldoze my composure, coming so fast and hot I can't blink. For a few seconds, crying feels like vomiting, like drowning.

I'm home.

"You do remember," Dad says. He reaches out and clasps my hand in his.

4

By the time we're inside, I've managed to sniffle back some of the tears and wipe my face. Which is lucky, because she comes to meet us—thick black hair in a messy ponytail, black-framed glasses, curvy upper lip. Dad's new wife, Erika Kim.

We hug but pull out of it quickly. Feeling Erika's eyes follow me as I move around the living room, I can tell she *does* notice things.

She looks so young and earnest in her jeans and T-shirt, more like one of the geology students who spent a month digging up our old creek bed than a vain stepmother in a book. But there's also something wary about her that puts me on guard.

"You look so much like your mom," she says. "I was going to make tea—would you like some?"

"That would be great." *Control yourself. Smile. Be normal.*

On the way to the kitchen, something goes *tick, tick, tick,* and I stop short.

"Isn't it gorgeous?" Erika pats the grandfather clock's oak cabinet. "An heirloom from your great-grandfather, and who knows how much further back it goes."

"I remember." The clock pauses solemnly after each metallic tick, as if holding its breath. And now I also remember that when I was little I always thought it was saying, *Tsk, tsk,* disapproving of me.

As we reach the kitchen, I'm holding my breath like the clock, though I don't know why. It's straight out of a home-improvement magazine: glittering granite and stainless steel with older dark paneling on the walls and door frames.

"You redid most of it—not the floor, though," I say. The tiles are dingy pink gray, just as I remember. A dark splotch draws my eye like a vortex. *Drain cleaner. Blinding. Blood.*

Stop being silly. The babysitter didn't hurt herself in our house. I sink into a chair, my T-shirt suddenly sticky, my heart thumping.

"Floors are next on the list," Erika says, shoveling leaves into a teapot. There's still a tension in her spine, a watchfulness, as if my presence has changed this beautiful house for her and she's not sure why.

When she clicks on the gas burner, something clicks in me, too. *Hedda, what were you thinking? This house could have burned to the ground!*

It's Mom's voice. I close my eyes, shocked by the waves of

guilt that fill me along with a rush of memory. The whiff of gas in the air is pure shame. *I did it. I turned on the burner and let it hiss. Mom was so angry.*

"This house is so old," I say, fighting my urge to jump up and flick off the burner. "I didn't remember that."

"Craftsman, 1909." As Erika brings us a steaming tray, Dad launches into a lecture about their latest renovations.

My face stiffens into a mask: nod and smile, nod and laugh. I want to be happy for real, but it's all just too new, and the stakes are too high.

"Are you going to pick up Clint?" Dad asks Erika.

My nine-year-old half brother, a complete stranger to me. My heart thuds at the thought that he might look at me for the first time and see a freak, an intruder.

"Conor's mom's giving him a ride," Erika says.

"Where does Clint go to school?" I clasp my hands to stop the trembling.

That turns out to be the right question to ask; Dad and Erika rhapsodize about the nearby elementary school with its "holistic curriculum." "They grow their own lettuce and feed chickens," Erika says.

Do they slaughter, pluck, and stew chickens? I know all about that. But I smile back—*normal*—as she says, "We've heard good things about the high school, too."

Dad clears his throat. "Not that you'll be going there. I assume you brought your study materials."

Fortune favors the brave, right? "I'd love to try out regular school, actually. I'm curious about AP classes."

Dad looks confused. "Jane said—well, you did bring your

homeschooling stuff, right? At schools around here, kids use computers, and—"

"You can get special accommodations to learn however you need to. I read that in the *New York Times*."

The doorbell rings, and Erika springs out of the kitchen.

"You'd really want to enroll in school here?" Dad asks.

I feel light-headed, like I've snuck beer from a discarded can at the fair. "It's just an idea. That way Mom could stay in Australia as long as she needs to. And it wouldn't cost you anything if I went to public school, right?"

"Cost's not the issue."

But before he can continue, Clint shuffles into the kitchen. He looks like a mini Erika with Dad's wavy, tousled hair, and his eyes are glued to his phone.

Erika whispers in his ear. Clint lowers the phone and solemnly says, "Hi."

"Hi." I grope for something he and I could have in common. "Is that your bike in the garage? Pretty cool." My own rusty bike was barely adequate for getting around the ranch, but it gave me distance from Mom when I needed it.

Clint speaks in a drone, eyes back on his screen. "It's a mountain bike. I got it for my birthday, and I can't ride it yet, because we don't have time to go to the mountains."

When his mom releases his shoulder, he bolts, his footsteps pounding upstairs.

"He's shy," Dad says.

"We're working on his social anxiety." Erika clears her throat. "Maybe we can hit the trails before school starts. You could help teach him."

If Mom were in Erika's place, she'd keep Clint close and not let me near him. Erika's shy, too, but she's reaching out, almost like she's lonely. I feel a sudden rush of gratitude toward her.

She follows Clint upstairs, and my dad excuses himself to make up my room, so I set out to see how much of the house I remember. The living room has been renovated into magazine perfection, but I recognize the narrow, sun-flooded passage running along the back of the house, and the little room beyond— Dad's study. Once his sacred domain, now it's a storage space crammed with packing boxes. The desk is dominated by a giant flat Glare-screen, but it's not lit up.

The walls are clean and white, yet half-formed memories darken them like smoke blurring a landscape. I wasn't supposed to go in here. I did something bad—what?

I bend over the desk, where Dad has lined up framed photos: Mom and me, just me, him and Erika, him and Clint and Erika. None of him and me. Those two sun-faded people must be his parents, whom I've never met. They're barbecuing on a cement-block porch, the man raising a Budweiser. Beside that is a photo of a small boy, fishing pole in his hands, caught in the glitter of sun off a lake. A hand rests on his shoulder, but the rest of the image has been sliced away. I lean closer.

"Hedda?"

I back away like Dad's caught me at something. "I wanted to see how much of the house I remember."

"Let me show you the rest."

He shows off the tiny but breathtaking bay view, then ushers me up the majestic, dark-paneled staircase. "Your stuff's already in your room."

Fizzy sounds echo in the hallway, and Clint's half-open door reveals an enormous Glare-screen. Bizarre shapes in wild colors flit over it, making me blink but not look away. That's control, too.

Dad pulls the door closed. "He's in a pretty serious gaming phase. Erika was worried about his screen time, but the one he's most hooked on is recommended by his school for the educational content, so we're letting it slide for now."

Hooked. Addicted. I want to tell Dad I understand what he's talking about, having read newspaper articles on the "screen time" debate, but before I can find words, I'm standing in my room. *My* room.

It's different. The toys that used to cover the floor have given way to the staid maturity of a guest room. The princessy purple-and-gold bedspread and curtains are gone, replaced by crisp cream-and-green cotton.

But the gabled ceiling still slants over the bed, making it feel enclosed and protected. The window still looks out on the street, with its shimmering cottonwoods so close together they could be one continuous tree. Towering built-ins still hold my stuffed lions—a pair, male and female—my unicorn figurines, and—

"*Oh.*" I fall to my knees to leaf through my childhood books. Each illustration strikes bells in my memory: the twelve dancing princesses discarding their worn-out slippers; Mr. Toad joyriding in his motor car; Hugo Cabret working the gears of the gigantic clock.

Dad kneels beside me, looking over my shoulder.

"I never read these to you," he says as I slide *D'Aulaires' Book of Greek Myths* back on its shelf. "I was working insane hours in those days. One of the things I regret."

He cares. I say, "Me too," rising and plopping my backpack on the bed.

Dad's voice wobbles. "Hedda…"

"What?" I glance at the door. No sign of Erika.

My father takes a deep breath, then fixes his eyes on mine. "Hedda, what did your mom tell you about why she brought you to Arizona? Or maybe you remember?"

I sit on the bed and hunch into my hoodie, drawing the sleeves down to my fingertips. If I use the word "Glare," he'll think I'm still six. "She said—well, there was that thing with the babysitter, and then I got scared of screens, so Mom took them all away, and I…" *Freaked out. Went off-kilter.*

Dad winces. "That poor Westover girl. Jane liked her a lot, and she never quite recovered from what happened to her."

To the babysitter. Not to me. Does he not remember the bad things *I* did, or is he just being polite?

Or did Mom not tell him?

Dad's still talking: "That's when your mother decided screen culture was hurting people, especially young people. Me, I've always believed technology reflects us. It can hurt or heal or be completely neutral, depending on what—"

"I know. I've read all about it." It's an enormous relief to be honest with someone. "I know Mom isn't the only person who thinks screens are dangerous." *The devil. Crack cocaine.* Those are just two of the things parents compared the Glare to in an article I read called "Silicon Valley's Elite Are Shielding Their Kids from the Tech They Created." "But most of those people…they worry about *young* kids. Not teenagers."

Dad cocks his head. "And do *you* feel like screens are dangerous?"

Being asked for my opinion brings a flush of warmth to my chest, then to my face. "I don't really know," I say in a small voice. "But I think I could manage the Gl—screens. I don't think they can make someone hurt herself. Not without help from her own brain."

Dad fumbles in the pocket of his sport coat. "I realize your mother can be...adamant, Hedda. But she does love you, and you're sixteen. I told her I'd keep your tech exposure to a minimum. I even installed a landline so you can talk to her."

My heart sinks—then does a roller coaster loop as I see what he's holding out to me on his palm. A sleek sliver of metal—a Glare-box! No, a phone.

"But—"

"But this is for you." He places the phone in my palm—smooth, heavy, *alive*. My pulse thumps so hard it's a struggle to focus. "It's strictly so I can find you if you go missing. I've set it to block all numbers but mine and Erika's."

I stare at the shiny dark screen, knowing from watching other people that one press of the single button will light it up. *Control yourself.* "You don't want me to...use it?"

Dad's face is serious, but there's laughter in his voice. "Do you know how?"

I blush again. "No."

"Hedda." His smile creeps out now. "You're acting like I've asked you to disable a bomb. All you have to do is carry this every time you leave the house. If we call you, you'll see a flashing light.

Press the button on the screen that says accept. And if you're lost and need to get in touch—well, I'll let Erika show you the rest. There's a data plan, but you won't need it."

I'm holding a cell phone. I've seen how other people cradle theirs, like it's their most precious possession. My mouth goes dry as I realize he's trusting me with the Glare.

"Thank you," I manage to say.

Dad touches my shoulder. His eyes are so different from Mom's and mine, layered with green and gold like trees starting to turn. "This isn't a license to break all your mom's rules. But sooner or later you'll need to make your own choices, won't you?"

My fingers close around the phone, hard. "I want to go to college. That's why I asked about school—because I want to be like you someday."

"All these years," Dad says in a low voice, "I've thought of you out there in the desert, Hedda. Leading such a different life from us, like an early settler on the wild frontier, wiry and strong and tanned and fearless. Sometimes I've wished Clint could have that life. Sometimes I've envied you."

I let out my breath, afraid to break the spell. Not knowing how to explain that I don't feel fearless or enviable today.

He bends to hug me. "Maybe I didn't know you as well as I thought. Maybe we can do something about that now."

The phone is caught between us, and I swear it hums in my palm. I don't pull away.

When he's gone again, though, I don't know what to do next. The phone thrums almost imperceptibly with the power it carries.

It wants to harvest signals from the air and connect, connect *me*, and I don't know how to be connected. I want to be, but—

I hide it on a shelf in the walk-in closet under a pile of sheets and pillowcases. If it hums or flashes now, I won't know. It can call to me all night—I don't care.

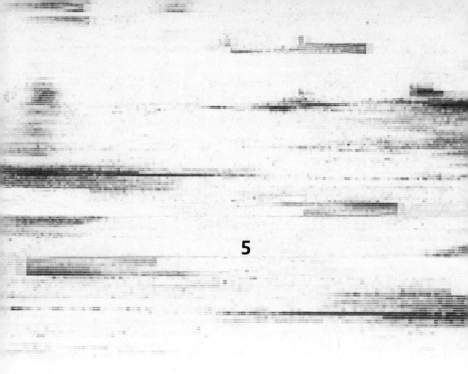

5

Something's moving in the closet.

The sound hovers on the edge of awareness, like tree branches rubbing in the wind. I sit upright in the pearly-blue Pacific dawn, staring at the half-open door. I woke several times in the middle of the night, thinking I heard the Glare-box ringing like our phone at home, but it wasn't, of course.

I rise, the hardwood cold on my bare soles. The closet is dead still now. I lift the sheets to check the phone, but it's a silent, shiny brick.

I kneel to explore the narrow crawl space at the back of the closet, where I find a shoehorn, vacuum cleaner hoses, and—something soft. A Raggedy Ann doll in a dirty-white pinafore.

Found you. For ten years she's waited alone in the dark for me. I lift my abandoned doll into the light, remembering her soft weight, her heedless thread smile—and freeze. Her button eyes are gone, leaving only snips of thread.

A chill goes through me, and I almost drop her. Did I do that?

Maybe it was just wear and tear. Her face has a dark patch around the mouth where I used to feed her (or try to), and I certainly don't remember cutting her eyes off. But the more I stare at her, the more I think I was trying to do to Raggedy Ann what the babysitter did to herself. To shield her from seeing something terrible.

. . .

I stow the phone in my backpack with a sweater and hoodie on top to muffle any sounds. Then I bring the backpack down to breakfast—which is lucky, because Erika asks for the phone to "show me the basics."

When she presses the button at the base, I tingle all over, but I don't look away. *This is part of control.* The screen is hard under my fingertips, yet it responds to my touch like something alive. Erika shows me how to enter a password. When I get it right, the screen blooms with all the colors of the rainbow. Tiny birds fly to roost, then turn into pictures like heraldic coats of arms.

Magic. It's Christmas morning and Fourth of July fireworks rolled into one, and I'm shaking, staring, doing my best to concentrate as Erika shows me how to call her or Dad. It's almost a relief to put the thing away again. Seeing someone else's screen is one thing, but there's something about touching *my* screen, giving it commands, that I could get too used to.

The dizziness doesn't go away until Erika takes Clint and me to the downtown farmers market, where I breathe in straw and overripe berries and frying tortillas. I stop at a stand where a girl my age in a sundress is selling leafy greens, tapping on a phone.

I pick up a bunch of chard, admiring the red veins, and ask her about planting times and mulching methods. She answers me, the phone alive in her hand the whole time, and I want to ask how she manages to live in both worlds, but I don't dare.

"Look at these," I tell Erika, pointing to the speckled heirloom cherry tomatoes. "With those serranos, they'd make a great chili."

She smiles in a sly way I haven't seen before. "Are you offering to cook?"

"Could I?" Itching for chores to do, I grab a paper sack for the tomatoes. "I make it at home all the time."

"I was kidding!" Erika swivels to keep an eye on Clint. "But if you actually want to, I won't say no."

After the market, we spend the afternoon at the beach. Clint complains when Erika makes him leave his Glare-box—a tablet, it's actually called—in the car.

When he walks out into the surf, I follow at a distance, still trying to get used to this vast watery commotion I loved as a kid. It smells *fishy*. I pass a girl in a glossy peony-pink bikini and wonder how that would look on me. Or maybe the leopard print? No, something in between.

Clint walks backward toward me. "You won't drown. I used to be scared, too."

"I'm not *scared*." His face closes up, and I change my tone. "Can you show me how to ride the waves like you do?"

Now he looks earnest, just like Dad. "Watch me."

By four, we're both salt-caked and sunbaked, and my brother has smiled at me once. He seems to have decided I'm not a bloodthirsty ogre, and that's a start.

Back home, Clint actually skips up the steep steps from the sidewalk, humming under his breath. At the top he stops abruptly and says, "Hi, Mireya. Why are you here?"

Mireya? At the ranch, I imagined this moment over and over—what I'd be wearing when I saw her again, what she'd be wearing, what we'd say. Now it's all happening much too fast, and my throat cinches shut, leaving me speechless.

Mireya steps out from behind a porch pillar, raising her sunglasses. Her hair is gorgeous, glossy black, falling well below her broad shoulders. "Hey, Hedda."

Behind me Erika says in a low voice, "I asked her to come by one of these afternoons; I meant to tell you. Hope it's okay."

I nod a little too hard. "Of course, but how did you...?"

"How'd she know about me?" Mireya says. "I watch Clint sometimes. Erika said you were coming, and I told her how tight we were in kindergarten and first grade. How I gave you the rock candy you lost your first baby tooth on."

Warmth floods my chest as I remember a little girl with satin ribbons streaming from her barrettes, laughing wildly and dominating every conversation. I always hoped she'd remember me, too, but I'm not sure I believed it. *I had a real life here. I was real.*

Erika unlocks the door and shoos Clint upstairs to take a shower. "I'll let you girls reconnect," she says. "Can I get you iced tea or something?"

"I'm good." Mireya has a forthright, forceful way of

talking—nothing like Shannon at the fair, who made every sentence into a question. It scares me a little, because forceful people make quick judgments. What if she decides I'm a freak?

We sit down awkwardly in the living room, Mireya stretching out her legs, which are athletic with no shaving scars. Her T-shirt is faded and ripped, but everything else about her—eyeliner, earrings, even her brand-name flip-flops—makes me feel sloppy. She's holding a phone.

"So," she says. "Your dad and Erika told me you were out in Arizona, but not much else."

That's an invitation, I know, but all I can do is laugh nervously. "There isn't much else. I mean…" What can I possibly say about the ranch? "We're off the grid. We make cheese. And preserves to sell. We raise goats."

This is not going well. She's staring like I just told her I live in New Genesis. She wants to know what regular things I did in Arizona, like dates or parties or high school debate team, and the answer is zero regular things. "I'm homeschooled," I add.

"That's so cool." She nods like she's trying to think so, fidgeting with her phone like she might abandon the conversation at any minute for something more interesting.

I take a deep breath; this has to be faced head-on. "Did, um, Dad tell you about my mom and her rules?"

Mireya's hand closes over the phone protectively. "Erika did. I'm sorry, I wasn't thinking, I—"

"No!" It comes out too loud, and I modulate my voice. "I mean, I don't mind, I'm totally fine. My mom has the issues with technology, not me."

"Oh!" Mireya seems to take a moment to absorb this before

flipping her hair back, eyes wide in her light brown face, her posture relaxing. "That makes more sense. Erika told me you don't go online, and I was trying to imagine it, but I couldn't. When we were little, you never went anywhere without your tablet. It was like a third arm."

I visualize myself with a third arm—a monster. If Mireya remembers me going *off-kilter*, she's giving no sign of it. "I barely know what a tablet is now," I admit. "Or what you do with one. I haven't used a computer in years."

"No? Really?" Her frown is back. "Well, maybe you're better off. Anyway, you used your tablet to game—hard-core, racking up levels. You always had the best games 'cause of your parents."

"I played Dad's games?" I wish I could remember; it would give Dad and me more to talk about.

"Your mom's, too—she was an awesome designer. My friend Rory says she designed phone games that were, like, cutting edge back then. It's too weird that she gave it all up." A wistful look softens Mireya's face. "That's actually how I started designing games myself—I saw your mom doing her work, and I figured, hey, this stuff isn't just for boys; maybe *I* can do it."

Mom's energy can be inspiring when there's a project to do, but the thought of her inspiring Mireya or anyone to design Glare-games sends a shudder down my spine. The old memory comes back: the babysitter sitting in blue light, telling me to look away from something that wasn't for children.

To hide my reaction, I stand up. "Want to see my old room?"

Upstairs, Mireya's voice echoes stridently off my walls. "This place totally takes me back." She picks up a sparkly-horned unicorn from the bookcase. "We used to fight over this one—who got to do his voice. Remember?"

"Of course!" I've basically admitted I don't remember the Glare, but I don't want her to think I have full-blown amnesia. "Remember that time your dad was away, and you were sad, and Mom made us a tea party?"

"Yeah, my dad was away a lot. Now he's away permanently." Mireya plunks herself down on the bed and grabs Raggedy Ann. "She was at the tea party, too. You stained her poor mouth."

My hand darts out before I can stop it, as if to grab Ann back. I let it drop quickly, hoping Mireya won't notice, but how could she not?

"Wait, wait, what happened here? Who de-eyed her?"

I shake my head helplessly, but before I can come up with an explanation, Mireya flips Ann over, rucking up her pinafore. "And what's *this*?"

She peels off the pinafore, revealing writing on Ann's cloth chest. Sitting down beside her, I see a childish ballpoint scrawl, a string of disconnected letters and numbers followed by a period and the word "onion." Beside it is a crude drawing I recognize instantly: a square black tower.

I can't breathe. The tower has to be the one from my dream. The writing is mine, too, but why? It's pure nonsense, like someone speaking in tongues.

"I don't remember doing any of that," I admit. "But it must have been me."

I'm so sure suddenly that Mireya's discovered evidence of something hideous I did, something forbidden, that it takes me a few seconds to absorb the words coming out of her mouth:

"Why were you on the Dark Web?"

"The dark what?" The words evoke oily black strands strung between gnarled trees, a giant spider waiting for unwary travelers.

Mireya smooths Ann's pinafore and sets her back on the bed. "Onion addresses are on the Dark Web, the part of the internet where innocent little children aren't supposed to go." She whips out her phone. "But I'm not an innocent little child, and I have Tor, and I'm going to find this address for you—if you want me to. If you're curious."

Address? Foreboding sneaks up my spine, but I *am* curious, and a little excited. "You could do that? It won't be dangerous?"

"You're so intense!" She gives me a teasing shove. "Just like old times. Trust me, whatever's out there, I can handle. When I do find it, I'll text you—wait, can you get texts?"

"I have a phone." But I don't know how to text, or even my own phone number. How can I admit that? Heat rises to my cheeks, and for a moment I want nothing but my mother, want to throw my arms around her and say, *I need you, I was wrong.*

The moment passes. I stiffen my spine. "It's new, so I haven't memorized my number yet. Can you give me yours?"

6

"How's it been?" Mom asks when she's done telling me about the prodigious flowers and spiders at her friend's house in Melbourne, and I've told her about Erika and Clint and the home renovations—but not about Mireya, the phone, or the doll.

"Fine." I curl up on a kitchen chair with the cordless receiver that Dad and Erika call a "landline" against my ear. "There was way more Glare flashing in my face on the plane than there is in this house."

"It's not making you anxious?"

Mom's voice, wispy and tentative with distance, brings it all back—the trickle of the creek, the stink of red clay. I try to think about that instead of the phone in my backpack, or the conundrum of how to receive messages from Mireya, which *is* a little anxiety-making.

"No. It's kind of funny, actually, to see Clint walking around the house with his nose in a Glare-box. This morning he bumped into the kitchen island and changed direction without looking up."

Mom chuckles. Feeling encouraged, I say, "And Dad—it's on his wrist, in his ear, in his car. He keeps twitching like he's getting these invisible signals, and out of the blue he'll say stuff that doesn't mean anything."

She outright laughs now. "He sounds like a secret agent."

We go on that way, making fun of the behavior of Glare-mesmerized people, me silently reassuring her I won't get sucked in.

But through it all I hear Mireya saying, *Maybe you're better off*, and I hear the doubt in her voice, and I'd rather be laughing with her. I'm the girl defined by the things she wasn't allowed to have, the girl being *smug* about the things she wasn't allowed to have, and who wants to be friends with that girl?

. . .

My chili is a hit, and Dad asks for seconds. I jump up to fill his bowl, my cheeks flushing, while Clint and Erika argue about whether Clint's too young to watch a movie that combines Frankenstein's monster and vampires.

"When I was your age, I wanted to read *The Exorcist*, but Mom wouldn't let me, so I read *Frankenstein*," I say, hoping to end their stalemate by suggesting an alternative. "The monster isn't scary once you get inside his head."

Clint looks blank, like the book's not on his radar, while

Erika says, "You read the original *Frankenstein*? Pretty heavy, isn't it?"

"Hedda's always read way above her grade level." Dad digs into his chili. "What were we discussing on your last birthday—*Crime and Punishment*?"

"I don't have much to do on the ranch besides read." I droop my head to hide the blush spreading from my face to my chest at my dad's praise.

"Maybe you'll be a lit professor. I can just see that—you in an office lined with books."

His phone vibrates on the table, and he starts tapping it, while Erika says warningly, "Mike..."

"I know, not at the table, but this is Verdon. Big game studio exec," he says in my direction, and continues tapping. None of us speaks. Clint's knee jiggles the table leg.

Finally, Dad darkens the phone, finishes his chili in three gulps, and stands up. "Back to the salt mines. Can you folks hold down the fort? Erika, do you have a plan for that, uh, block barbecue thing? It's potluck, right?"

Erika nods too quickly. "On it."

"Awesome." He pats her shoulder, blows a kiss at me and Clint, and grabs his briefcase from beside the door. Then, just as quickly as he arrived forty-five minutes ago, he's gone.

Clint immediately pulls out his tablet. Erika says in a tired voice, "We don't use our devices at the table."

"*He* did." Clint pushes his tablet away. "All I want is to get to the next level."

He's playing games, just like I did. "Games are all about

getting the players hooked, right?" I ask Erika. "Mom says she felt like a drug pusher when she worked at Dad's company."

Erika ruffles Clint's hair, looking a little uncomfortable. "Games give the players incentives to keep playing, yes. As you can see from Exhibit A here."

Too late, I remember that Erika herself works part-time marketing Dad's games. I change the subject. "Do you know if a boy named Ellis still lives on our street?"

"Ellis Westover? I see him out mowing the lawn. Was he a friend of yours?"

"Yeah. His sister was…" I trail off, realizing I don't know what became of the babysitter after she blinded herself with drain cleaner. It's like asking what happened to Snow White after happily ever after—or, in this case, horribly ever after.

"I didn't know he had a sister."

Erika must not have been around then. "He did—does." I'm not going to walk up to Ellis's house and knock, but Mireya must know him. Maybe she can help—if I can figure out how to "message" her.

"Erika," I say, "I can cook stuff for the block barbecue. I *like* cooking. But I'm wondering, could you maybe help me with my phone?"

Erika gets up and starts clearing. "What kind of help?"

Dusk has fallen, and I smell grilling from the neighbors' yard. While Clint runs upstairs to play his game, I hold out the palm where Mireya scrawled her contact info—a phone number, but also some kind of address. "Mireya says I can text her or reach her this way. She doesn't like to 'do voice.'"

Erika examines the palm. Her expression is neutral, but I sense the tiniest opening and relaxing, as if she no longer sees me as such a frightening unknown.

"Your mom would want you to call Mireya on the landline." Her voice is neutral, too, not a hint of sarcasm, but I can tell she doesn't think much of Mom's rules.

"Yeah." There's no point in lying. All of a sudden I feel a desperate need to get this over with so I don't have to spend my life wondering what happens if I take a single puff of the metaphorical cigarette.

I look straight at my stepmother. "Mom says the whole reason she let me come here is that I have to start taking control of my own life. Making my own choices." It's not a lie.

"But…" Erika seems confused. "Mike said the phone was just for emergencies. He said you wouldn't want to use it."

"A phone's just a tool, right?" I remember what Dad said about the Glare. "I can use it a few times without getting hooked." I lower my eyes. "And…Mireya wants to send me something tonight." *Something I need to know about.*

When I glance up again, Erika's face is still quizzical, but it's not a brick wall. "Learning might be tough on the phone. I have a spare laptop you can use. But don't tell your dad just yet, okay?"

I zip my lips.

. . .

The laptop's screen is harmless, glossy black. Erika presses a button, and something sizzles—the Glare springing to life.

The humming glow makes me quiver, but I don't look away,

46

trying to make sense of the colored blotches on the now-blue screen. They're tiny, dimensionless pictures that, like Mr. Toad's driving goggles or Hugo Cabret's clock, summon memories from deep, muddy parts of my brain. A slip of paper with a folded corner, a briefcase, a trash can, a black arrow.

And I know what to do, my pointer finger sliding over the smooth panel below the keyboard. I move it, and the arrow moves.

It's magic, and at the same time it's as natural and familiar as riding a bike. My eyes flick from the screen to the closet door to the bed to the window. The goal is not to get sucked in. I need to skim over the surface.

I always imagined *going online* would be like taking the ramp to the freeway, everything speeding to a blur, but instead it's like looking out a window with a view of a thousand places at once. Too many pictures, too many things to read, too many invitations to knowledge and adventure, and my eyes skittering to take it all in.

"Want to search something?" Erika asks, and my stomach flips over. *Too many choices.*

I gaze down at the old scars on my forearm, the ones that look like blurry letters if you squint: an *N*, a *T*, an *E*. I reach for my center, the place where I have control. Imagine my bedroom at the ranch with the paper scrolls on the walls.

"I just want to know how to send Mireya a text or a message," I say.

As she shows me, I feel my inner antennae reaching out and out, just like they did in the desert—shy and sensitive and eager, seeking a connection. And this time they find it.

. . .

Hey! You awake?

The robotic *boop* wakes me from a light doze, the sound seeming to come from everywhere at once. It takes me a few minutes to trace it to the laptop. I used it to send a text before I went to sleep, but somehow I didn't expect Mireya to respond till morning.

Yes, I'm here. I mean, this is Hedda.

You're adorable. Anyway, so it worked! Your onion link. There's a page with a file to download. I did a bunch of scans, but no viruses or malware, so I opened it.

Viruses. Malware. Download. I sort through the mystery jargon, searching for the kernel that matters. *What did you open?*

A game. First-person shooter. It's called the Glare.

The darkness presses around me, suddenly too dense. My stomach clenches like it did the night I ate fried Oreos at the fair and rode the Scrambler and puked on the way home—my head out the car window, promising myself I'd never do anything that stupid again.

Hello, still there?

My mind is still struggling to fit itself around what she just said. How can a game be called the Glare when the Glare is the light on every screen? It's like naming your boat *The Ocean*.

You're sure? That's what it's called?

Why would I make that up?

She can't understand, because she doesn't know the Glare is a word I invented when I was six to represent all my fears. At least, that's what I thought until now.

Is the name just a coincidence, or could the Glare be real? Something specific you can find, something you can play?

Gotta sleep now—work in a.m. But if you come over tomorrow after the BBQ, we'll play this thing. I'm rly freakin curious. Check this out.

The next thing that pops up on the screen is a picture.

I'm staring into a forest. The vibrant green trees are flecked with autumn yellows and reds. A black tower rises in the distance.

The image is frozen, yet I hear the leaves shivering. I hear the insects keening—are they insects? Wind rises, ruffling my hair, and I hear Ellis saying, *You're already dead,* and I jump up and shove my chair back and lurch away from the screen as if it could bite me, as if it could suck me in.

Dizzy, I sink down on the floor and hold tight to the chair legs like I'm on a ship that's pitching in a gale. I stay there for a while, trying not to think at all, before I realize I need to be outside.

It's real. I tiptoe downstairs, through the kitchen, and out the back door, wincing at each tick of the grandfather clock as if it might watch me and report to Mom. *The dream is real. The Glare is real.* And I used to know about it.

On the lawn, with the grass cool on my bare soles, I almost trip over Erika. She's sitting in the dark with a cigarette in her hand.

She stubs out the red ember. "I shouldn't be doing this—it's a nasty habit left over from college. Mike would kill me."

I flop down beside her. "My lips are sealed. Light another."

"Oh, no! I only do it when I'm stressed."

"Just sitting here's nice." I dig my toes into the dirt, smelling the cedars that separate our house from the next one, knowing that if I close my eyes I'll see that ghostly forest again. Maybe hear it, too. *Stay here.*

"It's weird how I feel like I need an excuse," Erika says.

I remember how Mom and I used to sit for hours on the screened porch or the ridge watching the stars. "Did your parents do that? Sit outside and smoke, I mean?"

Her laughter is soft in the dark. "My dad would with his friends sometimes. I'd smell it through the screen door. But Mom didn't even like me to hang out with girls who lit up. Well... forbidden fruit, right?"

"So you tried it, and then you quit?"

"Mostly." She shrugs. "Having a kid gave me the push I needed."

I wonder what she'll tell Clint about smoking when he's old enough, if people are still smoking then. Maybe new kinds of forbidden fruit will be invented. "Thanks for helping me tonight. I won't overdo it with the laptop—I know how to control myself."

"I can tell that about you," Erika says.

I wiggle my toes in the cool earth. I don't close my eyes. I promise myself the first thing I'll do when I go back to my room is snap the laptop closed, *without* looking.

But for now, the dizziness has receded; the ground is solid. We stay there for a while, side by side, finding the constellations through pale ribbons of haze.

7

From the top of our front steps, I watch the block barbecue. Smoke rises through the cottonwoods from grills manned by dads with gleaming white teeth. Skinny moms in gauzy tops flit from yard to yard carrying casserole dishes. Kids shoot hoops and ride bikes in wild circles.

I've spent my second full day in California making potato salad, two kinds of cookies, and brownies. The sparkling-clean, well-equipped kitchen is now *my* spot in the house, while Clint plays his game upstairs and Erika types on her big Glare-box in the guest bedroom she uses to "telecommute." Dad came back late last night and disappeared again before I got up, but Erika insists he'll have a day off soon.

The laptop has stayed closed, the phone dark. If Mireya is

sending me messages, I don't know about it, but she said she'd be here.

Clint appears beside me, downcast without his game and hugging the plate of brownies. "Mom says we have to take these over to the Moretons'."

"I'll go with you." I dash inside for the potato salad.

Back outside, the hum of the barbecue closes around us, classic rock blasting from invisible speakers. A football whizzes inches over my head. A shirtless young guy catches it and yells an apology. I scan each group for Mireya, but don't find her.

Five houses down, we deposit our food on a communal buffet and share a sterile smile with the hostess. She tries to hug Clint, who turns to a statue till she releases him.

So he's not just shy around me. I trail him as he trudges back toward our house, his whole body a homing system for his precious game.

"Check it out!" I point out an ancient cottonwood whose trunk cants toward the sidewalk, begging someone to climb it. "Wouldn't you like to sit up in that fork and look down on everybody?"

Clint gives the tree a glance. "That's dangerous."

"Your game's dangerous, too, I bet. Just not the same way." All games are dangerous, right? Because you can lose. A shiver grips my shoulders.

Clint keeps considering the tree. "Maybe it would work. With a belay harness like we use at the climbing wall."

Something sizzles on a nearby grill, the urgent fragrance of browning beef chasing nightmares back to the realm of sleep. A deep voice calls, "Hey, Clint, you hit level nine of *Infinity Hatch* yet?"

"I'm almost on eleven."

"You're a freakin' ace. Just like your dad."

The boy playing chef is tall and strong-jawed, wearing an apron printed with cartoons. One hand holds a can, covering the label, while the other flips a burger. Lank coppery hair tumbles in his bloodshot blue eyes.

He notices me and grins. "Those are sweet boots."

"Thanks." I step closer in my red cowboy boots, a little wary. The boy stinks like the beer tent at the fair.

He winks and indicates a cooler sitting in the manicured grass. "My folks are doing a benefit in the city, so they left me manning the grill. Got some hoppy IPA—help yourself."

"Um, thanks. I mean, no thanks. But thanks." No older than me, he doesn't seem worried about anyone catching him drinking.

"Hedda," Clint says behind me, "I'm going back now."

The boy's grin melts like a mask, and his hand freezes, the burger on the spatula left unturned. "Hedda? That's you?"

"Yeah." His eyes are shiny as fish scales, long-lashed and oddly naked. "Wait, are you Ellis?"

Grease pops on the grill, catching him in the face, but he doesn't seem to notice. "Yeah. You probably don't remember."

"No, I do!" There are too many things I want to say. Does he have freckles? In the shade, I can't tell.

"Been out in Arizona, right? Back for a visit?"

"Staying for a couple months." The Ellis I remember hides his eyes during scary movies and has to be reassured that zombies aren't real. This boy drinks beer and has fancy names for it. I feel about twelve. "We, um, played together a lot, right?"

"Yeah." Ellis picks up the spatula. "When my parents were

53

dealing with the Caroline situation, I was over at your house all the time."

Caroline—the babysitter. His sister. Somehow I'd forgotten her name, and my head is suddenly full of grisly images. "I'm so sorry about what happened to her."

The grill spits grease again. Ellis winces. "Yeah. Well. She got most of her vision back in one eye eventually. You were my lifeline back then, Hedda."

Was I? "I'm glad I helped," I say around the lump in my throat.

"Me too. I missed you when you left. Sorry for laying the heavy shit on you when we haven't seen each other in ten years." He gives me another look—brief this time, but blowtorch blue, with a ghost of a grin that weakens my knees a little.

Beneath the grin, though, in the unsmiling eyes, I see remnants of my shy, scared Ellis. Ellis running to the black tower; Ellis saying, *You're already dead.* Does he know about the Glare game, too—or if not, why's he in my nightmares?

"You gonna give me a burger, Westover, or just keep throwing your eyeballs out of joint?"

It's Mireya, wearing a sundress printed with cherries with cherry-red lips to match, scowling at us both. Guilt clutches at my throat—has she been sending me messages all day that I ignored?

Ellis scowls back. "You didn't put in an order, Rios."

"Not entirely sure I want my cheeseburger with a side of beer breath." Mireya takes my elbow. "Hey, Hedda, wanna go check out the desserts?"

Wanting to stay with him but not wanting to let her slip away, I smile apologetically. "Hey, Ellis, it was nice to see you again."

"Same here. Hey, Hedda—" He leans forward, tossing his bangs out of his eyes. I step closer, my heart suddenly thumping.

"Can I follow you?"

Follow me? Why would he ask that when he could just ask to come with us? My face goes hot, my hands cold as he looks at me as if his request were completely normal—and then I get it. He doesn't mean now. Erika mentioned something about how you can "follow" people online.

"Um—yes!" But now I've waited too long, and it's clear I'm the *off-kilter* one. I'll have to go home and figure out how to become someone people can follow, assuming he ever wants to have anything to do with me again.

"Cool!" Ellis raises his beer, sloshing it, as I back away. "I'll see ya, Heady Hedda!"

When we're clear of the Westovers' lawn, Mireya releases my arm. "Oh my God, was he hitting on you?"

"I don't think so." At least she doesn't seem to have noticed how weird I was just now. "We were just catching up."

"I'm not saying he's a date rapist or anything, but ever since he grew six inches in six months and joined the track team and started going to keggers every weekend, he kind of acts like his old friends don't exist. So be careful with him, that's all."

"I understand." I brace myself, then dive in. "You know about his sister, right?"

"Oh God." Mireya shudders. "It was horrible. They say she did it in her dad's basement workroom. Ellis found her and called the EMTs."

This whole time Caroline's been more of a cautionary tale for me than a person. I can't begin to imagine what finding her did to Ellis. "I didn't know."

"He was in therapy for, like, ever. We all used to tiptoe and whisper around him. Ugh." Mireya sighs. "I feel bad now for saying what I did about him."

"It's okay." Remembering Mireya's face when I told her about my life in the desert, I wonder if Ellis rejected his old friends because they pitied him. Pity is only a step up from contempt. "Why'd he call me Heady Hedda?"

Mireya snorts back a laugh, more embarrassed than amused. "Back when we were kids, you were intense. My friend Lily Chen and I used to call you that 'cause you were always off in your head somewhere. Guess Ellis picked it up." She cuts her eyes to the pavement.

The name Lily Chen brings up an image of Mireya whispering and giggling with a girl in a purple coat, but I don't remember them calling me anything.

"I'm sorry I didn't answer your message last night," I say, hoping there weren't too many of them.

"That screenshot? Dude, it was late. I went to bed right after that." I hear her draw in her breath, a studied pause. "But did it look familiar or anything?"

Light bounces off picture windows, car roofs, wind chimes, making me dizzy again as I try to match up past and present. I don't answer yet, though, only say, "Mireya, do you remember me when I left back then? Was I acting weird?"

"Weird like what?"

"Mom always said I was freaking out about the Gl—about screens. Because of Caroline Westover, I guess."

When Mireya looks at me again, there's a guilty pinch to her eyes. "Something happened before Caroline—you must remember this. Lily and me, we got tight, and there was some silly birthday party fight, and then—oh God, it was so stupid. I'm sorry. Kids can be such little jerks."

"What happened?" My fists tighten, nails biting my palm.

"We just...we made a couple of posts about you. With pictures. Using filters to give you a huge head and horns and bulging eyes, calling you a snob and a bitch, which was the worst word we knew, and oh God, it was pathetic, and your mom saw them and came over to our house and screamed at my mom, saying you were doing crazy things, all because Lily and I cyberbullied you. I felt so bad that day, Hedda, I wanted to curl up and die."

The fuzzy fingers of a larch shade our faces. She looks miserable, but I feel oddly...not bad. I feel in control.

The Glare is real. The Glare is a game. *Just* a game, something I must have turned to after my friend rejected me. It all feels so much smaller now than it did in the desert, when imagination molded my fractured memories into monsters.

"You really don't remember," Mireya says.

I shake my head, not wanting her to feel bad. "I mostly remember the good things about living here. Or maybe I just don't remember...screens. Anything connected with them."

"That's so weird. I know people selectively remember things, but I've never heard of anybody forgetting the whole internet."

I laugh, because I've just admitted to something *off-kilter*, and Mireya hasn't run off in terror. She thinks I'm weird, which is...good?

"Hey," she says, "so you want to come over tonight and try it? Play this Glare thing? I'm hella curious."

No, says a deep part of me, but those are night thoughts, and the sun is so bright, glinting on the leaves and her gleaming smile, and before I know it, I'm saying, "Sure."

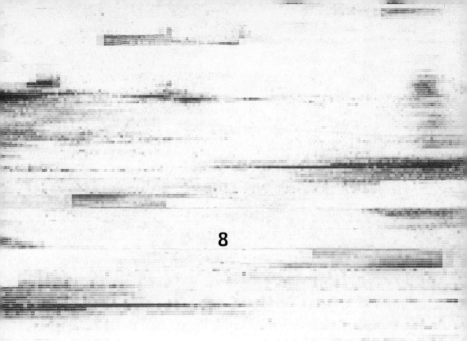

8

At my desk again as the twilight creeps in, using Erika's laptop, I stare at the image of the forest and the black tower till it turns to a meaningless swirl of colors. I don't hear any noises this time. Satisfied that I overreacted last night, I make the window tiny and search Ellis Westover's name, looking for places where we can "follow" each other.

Within a few seconds, I'm reading an encyclopedia of Ellis: his life documented in words and pictures. It starts in the present: Here he is on the beach, shirtless. Balanced high in the girders of a suspension bridge over a raging river. Leaping off a cliff into the ocean. Half passed out and draped over a laughing blond girl. And—is that just an American flag he's wearing, posed in front of a brick building with a beer in his hand? The comments mention an "epic prank" and "suspension."

In most of these pictures, he has the sloppy, indolent grin I remember from the barbecue, when he drew it over his face like a mask. But as I keep scrolling, the pictures take me back to Ellis's childhood, and the grin disappears, along with the height and broad shoulders. At twelve, he's a small boy with a tentative smile. Here he is with his dad. With his mom. Even younger, he wheels his bike up our street, his coppery hair catching the sunlight.

He looks bashful, almost sweet. Here he is with Caroline, back before she hurt herself. She has a squinty smile, piercing blue eyes. Now here they both are with a skinny, dark-haired little girl, and wait, that's *me*.

I click on my name, and then I'm reading the encyclopedia of the life I thought I remembered, the Glare filling in all the fuzzy details. Here I am with Mom on the beach, her holding the camera and beaming. Here I am riding a merry-go-round. At my fifth birthday party wearing orange—not pink, as I'd thought. Playing chess with Dad. There's only one picture of my parents together: They stand arm in arm on the porch of a rustic cabin accented with spiny bark.

Six years old, and now I'm making my own posts. These I don't remember at all: a blurry photo of a Glare-screen to celebrate a high score on a game. Videos of fuzzy kittens and ducklings. Pictures of my own face with a silly mustache, of Ellis's face with horns.

Mireya said she and Lily posted pictures of me with horns and bulging eyes. I search for the offending posts, but they must have been deleted.

This was my life. This was me. The desert severed me from it, a line drawn between six and seven, but the more I click, the more comes back. The sting of ocean spray. The rush of warmth and safety as Mom rubbed me in a towel. The shy way Ellis ducked his head in the days when I was louder and more confident than he was. The ache of my shoulders after hours of playing a game.

Imagine if I'd had all this on the ranch. Instead of drawing pictures on a paper scroll, I could have been following Ellis's and Mireya's real lives on a screen. I could have been looking up books and recipes and the names of flowers and birds. Finding people who cared about the same things. Never feeling alone.

I make accounts in the places where Ellis posts most often now. I follow him and Mireya. But then I feel stupid, sitting there and waiting for my clicks on the keyboard to mean something.

The laptop pings with a text from Mireya. *Wanna come over?*

"I'll be back in an hour or so," I tell Erika on my way out, hoisting my backpack over my shoulder.

Mireya lives in a duplex just past the first cross street. Her room is way pinker than I expected, with a big mirror and gauzy scarves knotted around the bedposts, but her computer desk, with its huge Glare-eye, is all business.

"I followed you," I say like I'm confessing something.

Mireya laughs, but not in an unfriendly way. "I noticed that," she says, sitting down in the rolling chair. "I just followed you back. Don't be so tense, okay?"

Is it that obvious? I sink down on the edge of her bed. "I'm okay. A little weirded out, I guess. Whatever this game is, I feel like I should remember it."

"The mind's a weird place, Hedda. But I've played some

pretty twisted games, and this one's just your basic survival horror. Probably still in dev—all the levels look the same. There are no cutscenes, the background graphics are crazy detailed, and the monsters are super rudimentary." She touches her keyboard, and all the windows on the screen disappear except one.

It's the forest again, with the black tower in the background—over to the left this time. On the closest tree trunk, there's a piece of graffiti, not words but a symbol I've never seen before. Its eerie blue radiance sends chills inching over my scalp.

The window's foreground is crowded with the cartoonish image of a metal cylinder in a human hand. It's a gun from the shooter's perspective, I think, but I can't focus there. My eyes flit around the landscape, scanning the treetops and the carpet of fallen leaves for—what?

Furrows. Broken branches. Signs of movement. *They're here. I know they are. The instant it unfreezes, they'll start keening, and then they'll come, and I can't possibly make it to the tower—*

Fingers are being snapped in my face. "Hedda. Hedda!"

I blink and recoil, the bedsprings creaking under me. The screen is just a screen again. The forest is just a picture made of tiny flecks of light.

"Are you okay?" She kneels beside me, a pleading look in her eyes. "You don't have to play, you know."

I blink again, hard. *Control yourself.*

And the screen shrinks to manageable size. I'm not scared, just giddy, like someone standing on the ground and watching a roller coaster mount its highest loop. Feeling ready to ride.

"I dreamed that." If I tell her how often I've dreamed it, she'll think I'm *off-kilter.* "I mean, I had a dream that was like that place. Once. Maybe I was remembering this. So, how do I play?"

Mireya presses more keys, and the forest disappears. "That was my saved game. I'm going to make you your own avatar."

She pulls a second chair over to the desk and pats the seat. "You have to come close enough to use the keyboard."

Feeling like an idiot, I sit down beside her. The Glare is asking for username and phone number. Mireya types *Heady* over my shoulder, and I try to laugh, but my throat is too tight. "Why does it need my phone number?"

"It wants to send you texts, I think. Don't worry, I've scanned it for malware."

I pull the phone out of my backpack—sleek and perfect and utterly unused—and try to look like I've entered my password a million times, but my finger trembles as if the screen burns it. "I still don't, um, remember my number."

Mireya grabs the phone and starts tapping the screen, while I resist an impulse to grab it back. *Mine.*

"Here we go." She reaches around me to type again. "Your phone's set to silent mode with most of the numbers blocked. I'm going to turn vibrate on and unblock everything, okay?"

I nod. The forest is back, seething green and red, with the tower in the distance. The gun in the foreground has returned, too, accompanied by the words LEVEL 1 and a black bar.

"You use the keyboard to move yourself around, and the mouse to turn your head, aim, and shoot. Here, like this."

She reaches out her hand, but mine is already on the keyboard, going straight to the *W*, *A*, *S*, and *D* keys. Forward, left, backward, right—it's awkward, but it works.

When I look up again, Mireya's staring at me. "You do remember."

"I guess my hands do." I click the mouse, and a bolt of light bursts from "my" gun, startling me backward from the screen. "What do I shoot at?" We were always running from something in the dream, but I don't know what.

"You'll see. Try to get to the tower before your gun powers down—the bar shows your power level. You can hide behind any tree with a symbol carved on the trunk, but only for five seconds. Ready?"

I nod, and the game comes to life.

At first nothing happens. Leaves quiver in an imaginary breeze. Clouds drift over the tower, which looks about as far away as Bent Rock from our ranch. I hear cicadas to my left, distant birdsong to my right. My head whips that way—is it real or in the game?

"To the tower!" Mireya hisses.

She points out the speakers on either side of me. I work the keys, moving my second self across the screen in clumsy jerks. When I collide with a tree, my real body recoils, and Mireya giggles. "It's okay, Hedda. Not real."

Not real. As I backtrack around the tree, toward the tower again, something white flickers in the corner of my eye. A stray reflection? A high, thin sound bleeds from the speakers to my right and left—keening. It vibrates through me, tensing every muscle; I'm primed to react to that sound. *They're close.*

I speed up, working the keys more deftly now, and dodge the next tree in my path. A flash of white above.

This time I ignore it—until it solidifies and slithers off a tree bough and drops to the ground in front of me. It's human-shaped, but it has no clothes or sex or face, like the little walking person that tells you to cross the street.

Mireya shrieks, "Shoot at it!"

Too late. The blank person swells to fill the whole screen, its eyeless face right up against my game self's face, its long arms raised as if to hug me. The keening is deafening. The whole image judders and flashes, then goes ghostly white like a photographic negative. I clutch at my throat like I'm being throttled—and maybe, in the game, I am.

Not real. Not happening. I draw a deep, shaky breath as the screen turns completely white, then black, and Mireya says, "You're dead. Want to try level one again?"

When I don't answer, she bends over me, a steady hand on my shoulder. "You okay? That's a lot to take in."

"What *was* that thing?" I can't stop imagining how the fingers of the almost-person would feel around my neck. Cold and slimy—no, dry and chalky, like the dust inside a long-untouched vault. Like the hand I thought grabbed me on the plane.

"A monster. I call them Randoms because they're animatics—sketches without details. The designer probably meant to go back later and make them scarier."

I think they're scary enough, but I can't chicken out now. "So as soon as I see one, I aim and shoot."

"That's my girl—they're easy kills. Ready to go again?"

And I do go—again and again.

I follow my instincts, like the one that told me the keening signals the arrival of Randoms. The first time I manage to reach the tower, I hold my breath in anticipation of something miraculous, but find only a dark funnel open to the sky. Following Mireya's instructions, I step into the circle of light and watch the power level on my gun ratchet up, just like fueling a car.

"You're getting better at this," Mireya says as I exit the tower and plug the Random that was waiting for me. "You're sure you don't remember playing it?"

"I don't know. Maybe." When I reach down deep, I find a memory of a shape that could have been a Random, looming immense on my bedroom wall and making me freeze in terror. Maybe it was just Mom's or Dad's shadow as they stepped into my room. Or maybe that shape wasn't actually on my wall; it was on my screen.

On level 3, Randoms start coming at me two at a time—one from the east, one from the west, or one from a tree branch, one from the deadfall. Sometimes my movement keys stop working, the leaves flurrying wildly, the screen darkening like I'm being dragged underground. Once that happens, there's no way to save myself. I'm in the middle of a particularly nasty death like this when a buzzing noise from the wrong direction—behind me—makes me jump.

As I catch my breath, Mireya hands me my phone. I'm back in my body again, feeling everything I've been ignoring: shaky hands, stiff shoulders, beads of sweat trickling down my temple.

"Erika's calling you." Mireya peers at the big Glare-screen. "Oh shit, it's two in the morning."

The phone slips from my hand to the carpet. I was supposed to be back in an hour—what happened? I feel like only minutes have passed since I started playing. I feel like I've been trapped in that forest for months, dying over and over.

And the weirdest thing is, I don't want to stop.

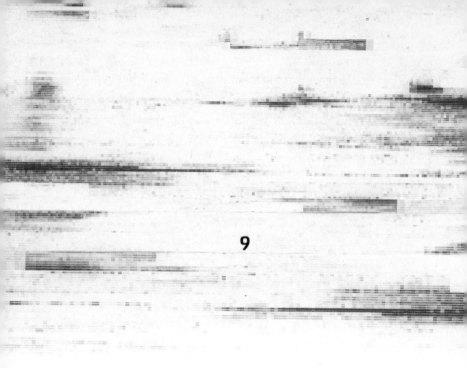

9

Mom says, "You sound tired."

"We went biking yesterday in this amazing park. I ache all over." I go on, detailing how Dad almost wiped out on a downhill, and we spotted wild turkeys and maybe a bobcat, and even Clint forgot about the Glare and acted like a regular kid. I don't mention the real reason I'm tired, which is that Mireya and I stayed up late last night playing the Glare. Again.

It's been the same routine for the past five days: We bike or hike or go to the beach, and then Erika and I make dinner and drink tea and talk, and then, at night, I go to Mireya's and play. My eyelids are crusty from lack of sleep, yet somehow each morning the Marin light gets me up and ready to restart the cycle. Maybe I'm making up for lost time.

I'm getting better and better, Mireya says. Granted, she's on level 12 while I'm on level 9, but I can handle Randoms coming at me from three directions now. Mireya says the game's "ultra basic" because the levels all look the same, and often she zones out on her phone while I play, but I can't seem to stop.

During the day, to balance things out, I stay away from the Glare except when Mireya messages me. I don't look up random things on my phone the way she does, even when I want to. *Control.*

I wish I could tell Mom how good it feels.

She says, "You sound happy, too. Like you and Mike are really reconnecting."

"I think we are." I do feel happy, deep down in my bones, though Dad's occasional appearances don't have much to do with it.

Just for a second, I teeter on the edge of spilling everything: *I know what scared me. I understand so much better now.* I want her to know that I'm connected now, free of that echoing emptiness. She must remember the feeling of being linked to other people herself; she can't entirely hate it—

"What's that noise?" she asks sharply.

Damn it. I left my phone out on the table beside the landline, which is on speaker, and a text just came in. "Clint was using the electric pencil sharpener."

"Kids still use pencils?" she asks while I check my phone.

There are no words in the text, only a picture of an ash tree with a smattering of red leaves and a symbol glowing on its trunk—one of the "safe trees" from the Glare. Adrenaline sharpens my focus, and my pointer finger twitches, reaching for a mouse that's not there.

It's the fourth text I've received like this since I started playing. Mireya hasn't found much online info about the Glare, but she thinks the game uses the texts to "nudge" us to come back, like it's saying, *Where are you? Connect with me.* She says that makes it an "alternate reality game," though I'm not sure how a text is more "real" than anything else on a screen.

I'm grateful for the nudge now, because it's stopped me from being dangerously honest. "I got Clint into drawing with colored pencils. Mine were still up in my room." What Mom doesn't know won't hurt her.

. . .

I know all the names, faces, and pronouns of Dad's employees from his website. Kai, the receptionist, is barely older than me and so cool that I feel like I'm still covered with ranch dust. They have spiky hair dyed midnight blue, a tattoo of peonies above their plunging neckline, and a silver lip ring.

When I introduce myself, they give me a big smile and say it's cool to meet me, but then they peer at their screen and frown. "Is Mike expecting you?"

"No." Once I figured out how close Dad's company was to home, I decided to come and surprise him. His so-called "days off" are just brunch or dinner or an outing with us, after which he disappears again. Plus, I have an ulterior motive: I want to ask him about school, which starts on Monday.

I pull a plastic container from my pack. "I just made snicker-doodles, and I thought I'd stop by and give him some." It seemed like a good plan at the time. But the office's decor—perfectly sanded maple walls and floors and ceilings, interrupted only by stark black-and-white photos and framed awards—makes me feel like an intruder.

Kai's eyes light up. "Oh my God, can I have one of those? I just let Mike know you're here."

I peel open the container. "Please do."

Ten minutes of waiting on a hard maple bench later, Dad joins me, phone in hand. He wears a sport coat over his T-shirt, which I've learned (from Erika) means he has meetings today.

"How did you get here?" He looks genuinely surprised, as if I've trudged ten miles.

"Walked." I hold out the cookies again, hoping for a reaction like Kai's. "It's ten blocks. These are fresh-baked."

Dad sits down and takes a cookie absentmindedly. He tenses as his phone gives a brief buzz, his eyes flickering to it—then returns his gaze to me. "I'm sorry, honey. Just having a full day. We've got a few things to submit on deadline, and meetings...."

"No problem!" I keep my smile big and fixed—trying to look as cheerful as the full skirt I'm wearing, which is printed with sunflowers and borrowed from Erika. "I should've checked ahead. I was wondering if you've thought about—"

"Well, of course you should see this place. I should have given you a tour days ago. Maybe Kai can..."

He whips his head in Kai's direction, and I take the opportunity to change the subject: "School starts Monday. My friend Mireya says she'll show me around, if I could maybe just enroll, even for a month—"

Dad is abruptly beaming, but not at me. "This cookie is amazing!" he says, as if he only just realized what his mouth is full of.

My fingers claw at the edge of the bench. "Thanks. Just sugar, flour, butter, cinnamon. Anyway, I—"

The phone buzzes again. Dad does some intense swiping and tapping, then gives me a big smile as if we were never interrupted. "If college doesn't work out, you could be a pastry chef on one of those baking shows, Hedda."

"Thanks, but—"

"Joke. I know you're all about the academics." His hazel eyes meet mine at last. "So you've made a friend."

"Mireya Rios—you know her." He looks blank; maybe he doesn't. I start to tell him how Mom's career inspired Mireya to design games, but halfway through, his phone demands attention yet again.

This time, instead of answering right off, Dad glances at it guiltily, looking remarkably like Clint when he knows he's not supposed to be using his tablet at the table.

"It's okay!" All I really want now is not to be here taking up space, in his way. I want to be back at my desk playing the Glare, which Mireya's just downloaded to Erika's laptop for me so I can keep conquering the levels while she's at her summer job.

I get up and smooth my sunflower skirt. "You're busy. I should be getting back."

Dad darkens the phone with a snap of his thumb, like he really means it this time. "Hedda, I do hear what you're saying. How about we talk tonight? Would that work?"

"Fine. Totally fine." *If you're home tonight*—but I manage not to say the words aloud.

Dad gets up, too, his eyes flitting from me to the dark screen and back, and pulls me into a hug that feels like a Band-Aid slapped on an oozing wound. "Tonight, then. Maybe we can get out the old chessboard. You sure you don't want Kai to call you an Uber?"

"No! I like walking!"

And I smile stiffly at Kai and march out on the perfect maple floor, past the perfect photos, keeping my head high, until I reach the watery sunlight and the bay breeze and let the stupid tears flood my eyes.

You're stupid. You're boring. He doesn't even care whether you go to college or not; he just pretends because he's supposed to. I tell myself that's not true, that he'll be home tonight, that he mentioned the chessboard because he remembers teaching me to play, that I'm an important part of his life. And then I tell myself *I* don't care if he cares about me, because as long as he enrolls me in school and pays for college, I'll be fine. But the whole time it just replays in my head: how he kept glancing from me to his screen, like I was less real than whatever he found there.

. . .

You excited about the party? Mireya texts as I walk back.

I send back a face with heart eyes, relieved for something else to think about. She's invited me to a beach party day after tomorrow, and I've been researching on my phone, stuffing my head with her friends' names and hobbies and hair colors and favorite songs and movies. If—*when*—I go to school, they could become my friends, too. No more hanging out with the goats.

Not that I never miss the goats. Sometimes I even imagine snapping them with my phone and putting them online with personality profiles: *Buttercup, two and a half, in a relationship with my stallmates. I enjoy eating petunias and will hurt you with my horns if you're not careful.* But that would mean reconciling Mom to my new self, my phone self, and that's unthinkable.

The phone buzzes again, calling me out of my gloomy thoughts, connecting me. *What about school?*

Working on it.

. . .

I'm losing to Dad at chess. Just like old times.

We're playing on the deck in the aftermath of a grilling extravaganza, while Erika cleans up inside. The sun has sunk behind the trees, Mount Tamalpais a notched blue wedge in the flamingo sky. I spend five minutes mulling over the consequences of moving a pawn, then give up and randomly nudge a knight.

Dad captures the knight with his bishop.

"Why do I suck so much at this?" I ask.

"You don't suck. You're just out of practice."

I still remember what he said when I was six and he taught me to play this game: *You catch on like wildfire!* He seemed so happy, so proud, but later he must have figured out I wasn't a prodigy, just good at memorizing which pieces do what.

I'd do anything to beat him, just to put that glow on his face again.

"You need to concentrate." He sounds a bit smug now. "Stop pushing. Let it flow."

I wonder if he said the same thing about video games. He or Mom must have taught me to play them, and when I try hard, I

74

come up with a fragment of memory: *Blue light glancing off Dad's glasses, his hand guiding mine as I try to shoot aliens, but never fast enough!*

I wish I could tell him about the Glare, but he'd probably start harping on Mom's rules again.

"I can't concentrate." I zip my bishop slantwise and capture Dad's pawn, no doubt laying myself open to another attack.

Dad rests his chin on his hand. "Let's slow down, then. You wanted to talk about something this afternoon."

"Yes!" I run through all the possible openings in my head, but before I can choose the best one, he says, "School. You want to go to school."

I lean forward, all my nerves suddenly jangling with the intensity of my need to convince him. "It starts Monday, and Mireya would drive me. She says you need AP courses for a good college. Erika says she'd do the enrollment stuff." I know he hates having extra paperwork. "All you'd have to do is sign."

Dad inches his queen toward my bishop, his brow furrowing. "You know *I* wouldn't stand in the way of that. I think you'd benefit from a month or so in school. But your mother left you in my care, and I promised her I'd—"

"Follow her rules. I know. I know." Bitterness rises too quickly from my stomach, choking me. It's always about the damn rules. He's always shifting responsibility, but I can't let him do it when I finally have a chance to change things. I need to confront the problem head-on, even if it makes him uncomfortable.

"What are you afraid will happen if you don't follow the rules? If you let me near a computer or two? Are you afraid I'll go off-kilter?"

Dad blinks hard, then takes off his glasses and wipes them. "I'm not sure what you mean, Hedda."

"That's what Mom always says, that screens threw me off-kilter." I think of the half-formed memories I've had in this house. "I got scared or bullied or something, and I acted out. Is that what you're afraid of?"

Dad peers at the board, not meeting my eyes. "You were six then."

"I know!" I push my laggard rook off his home square, struggling to control my voice, to scrub the anger out of it. "When you gave me the phone, I thought you trusted me. I hoped you did."

"This doesn't have anything to do with trust." His own voice has gone very quiet.

"What does it have to do with, then? I know you let Mom take me away; I know you trusted her to do the best thing for me." *And maybe you shouldn't have.* I let the words hang in the air before I go on. "But you can't just let Mom decide who I am for all time. She acts like there's this...darkness inside me that I need to control. Like I'm broken and can't be fixed. Do you really believe that?"

My hands shake; I can't look at him. *Please say you don't.*

Dad's fingers hover over a pawn. When he speaks again, it's in a rhythmic voice I recognize as his storytelling mode. "When I was a boy, my parents used to send me every summer to stay with Grandpa Frank up in Shasta County. Grandpa lived in a rustic log cabin in the woods, not far from a military base. Some nights he'd sit on the porch with a shotgun between his knees, swigging whiskey, and when I asked why, he said, 'I can hear them out there, rustling. Coming closer.'"

Hairs prickle on the back of my neck. He's not answering my question; maybe he's even trying to change the subject, but I can't help asking, "Who were 'they'?"

"That's a question Grandpa Frank chose not to answer, except by introducing me to his stack of books about aliens, conspiracies, Area 51, and secret government mind control. I think he thought they were hosting aliens on that military base, and a few had escaped. Once when he was deep into a bottle, he told me 'they' could take many forms, and they wanted to drain our blood until only dry husks were left."

I use my bishop to block his pawn's path to my queen, starting to get an inkling of how this story might be relevant. "Did you believe Grandpa Frank?"

"When I was too young to know better." Dad nudges his queen deep into my side of the board. "He was a dark person, my granddad, and when we were alone out there, his darkness infected me."

Alone out there—like Mom and me. What is he saying? If Mom is the one with the problems, if her problems "infected" me, then why isn't he taking my side?

"Even after I stopped believing, I still had nightmares about 'them,'" Dad says, his voice calm as if he doesn't sense the turmoil inside me. "Elaborate ones, all through high school and college. Until, when you were about five, one night the dreams just stopped."

"Why?" I try to figure out where his queen's headed, block her with a pawn.

"Maybe I finally realized I was responsible for a child now, so I needed to give up childhood fears. Maybe I'd learned to wall off my dark places. For whatever reason, I haven't had a nightmare since. Anyway, I think that's check and mate."

Sure enough, his queen has cleared a path for his bishop. Maybe the whole purpose of the spooky story was to distract me.

But I'm playing a different game now.

"Dad," I say as he sets the chess pieces back in their box, "I need to find out what a college-prep curriculum is like, because I *am* going to college. Right?"

He's backlit now, his expression unreadable. "I hope so, but that's up to you—"

"Up to *me*, right. Not up to Mom. She doesn't want me to leave her, Dad, ever."

I remember my fitful attempts at rebellion on the ranch: looking at Shannon's phone, stealing the truck keys and trying to teach myself to drive. But mostly I've been good, too good.

Dad just keeps fussily arranging the pieces, setting each upright, and I say, "Mom's not a bad person. She wants to protect me, but she can't always do that, and I wish you weren't scared to break her rules. I wish you'd give me a chance with school like you did with the phone."

Dad turns to face me, his spine straightening, and again I feel that desperate yearning to impress him, to make his face light up.

"I am not *scared*, Hedda," he says in an almost cold voice. "Not of your mother, and not of you. I'm trying to do what's best for you. To keep the peace."

Peace. It's what he needs to do his work. What Erika, Clint, and I are supposed to provide by staying out of his way.

Not this time, though. Check and mate.

"If you're not afraid of Mom," I say, "then you'll tell her I need to try out school. Maybe even stay here for the year, if I like it and Erika doesn't mind. Unless you really think I'm in danger from computer screens because of stuff that happened back when I was still scared of monsters under the bed."

I let him absorb the words, calling his bluff. After a long, long moment, Dad says, "Okay."

"Okay? I can go?" My whole body tingles, and I have a sudden impulse to throw myself into his arms, but he's staring at a spot on the deck to my right.

"I'll sign your forms, yes." At last a small smile curves his lips, and he says, "I've never in my life seen a kid so eager to go to school."

10

This freaking level 13.

Erika took Clint off to some school orientation program, and I've been playing all day and into the night. I breezed through levels 10 and 11, only dying about six times each. Level 12 was tough—about ten deaths. Now, though, the Randoms won't stop coming.

They hide in the trees, but not the safe ones. There, on the knotty spruce, I spot a glowing blue rune like a stick-figure drawing of a horse. There, on the towering ponderosa pine, a greenish squiggle. If I hug either of those trunks, I'll be safe, but only long enough to catch my breath. Sometimes the Randoms flicker away. Sometimes they wait for me.

They can grab you from above, from below, by your neck, by your hair. And when several come at you at once, quick as lightning, you can't fight. You can't run. The movement keys go useless, dead, as the screen turns to a negative image and the keening rises to a roar, your whole world coming apart. When I'm in the zone, a death is just an annoyance. But later, when I'm half-asleep, I'll imagine a Random wrapping a ropy arm around my windpipe or forcing a cold, fleshless fist down my throat.

Speaking of which—oh damn. I'm dead again. That makes twelve times.

I should stop.

I text Mireya, but she doesn't answer, and for a moment, sitting at my desk before a frozen screen, I'm inside that echoing emptiness, that certainty that I'll never connect to anyone. I was used to it in the desert, but now I want to push it away, to stop feeling it on me like icy fingers, to stop hearing the breathy whisper in my head: *You're alone, alone, alone.*

One touch of the keyboard, and I'll be connected again. One more try at level 13.

It's after midnight. I should just go to bed. Or finish the letter to Mom that I started drafting hours ago, trying to erase the lie I told her last time we talked:

Dear Mom,

You've always encouraged me to overcome challenges. To be adventurous. To be brave. Together we took on the desert and even the snakes, and we made the ranch work, and I'm proud of that.

But you've also taught me to limit myself. Not to trust myself. To be afraid.

I know now what the Glare really is. It's a game. I'm guessing I found it and played it when I was a kid, and I'm sure it scared me back then, but

But what? If I'm not scared, why'd I stop just now?

I'll probably never send this letter anyway, but it feels good to get the words out. My fingers still itch to work the WASD keys, to click the mouse. I feel so much clumsier in the real world, trying to please two parents who couldn't be further apart, one of whom wants to control me while the other barely notices I'm there.

C'mon, one more, just one more before bed.

I touch the keyboard and bring the laptop to life. Something about all this feels familiar, weirdly right, maybe because of, oh, the hundreds of other times I've restarted.

If I can just beat this level, from now on I'll spend my nights reading weighty Russian novels and drafting college application essays.

Then the forest zings to life, and everything else disappears.

Making it to the tower takes a good five minutes of heavy fire this time, with several breaks behind safe trees. The fear of running out of power before I get there makes me pause the game to wipe sweat off my brow. My posture's giving me cramps. Once I'm refueled, I make a mad dash at the three waiting Randoms, holding down the mouse for continuous fire.

They don't bleed when they die, just crumple into white rags and fly away. Sometimes they blink out altogether. There they go, fluttering through the blue sky like filthy butterflies, lost behind the dark cone of a fir, and wait, right there, what's—

Shit. SHIT.

I'm dead. I knew to do a three-sixty perimeter check, and I didn't, and now I'm pissed at myself. RIP, Heady. But I feel like I'm starting to see patterns in this level, anticipating the Randoms' movements, and it's time to try again. *One* more freaking try, just one—

My head snaps back to the screen.

The forest isn't back. The game isn't restarting. Just white words on a black screen: YOU HAVE DIED THIRTEEN TIMES ON LEVEL 13. THIS IS THE END FOR YOU. THANKS FOR PLAYING.

Seriously? Can it do that to me? I try starting again. Quitting the browser, even restarting the computer. But returning to my saved game triggers the exact same message every time, and I refuse to start from level 1 again.

I message Mireya: *IT WON'T LET ME PLAY ANYMORE.* Then erase it and send the same message without the caps lock.

No answer—maybe she's asleep. She'll know how to dig myself out of this dead end, unless this level 13 thing is a cosmic sign that I need to stop playing. Maybe I couldn't win, so I needed to lose, which sounds annoyingly like something Mom would say.

Maybe now I can try all the other games Mireya says are so much better, more sophisticated. Except I don't want to. I want to kill Randoms. I want my forest. I want level 14.

The dark screen distorts my face, jutting cheekbones framing sunken eyes. Or is that just how I look after hours in the Glare? My face ghostly, as if my flesh is dissolving, my eyes stretched wide with the hunger for more.

I pull the paper toward me and finish my letter:

but a lot of things scared me when I was six. I must have been
pretty freaked out by what happened to Caroline, and that
made me vulnerable, and I acted out and started blaming
everything on "the Glare." I wish you'd understood that, but
it's okay that you don't.

I'm not scared anymore. Please don't be scared for me.
Love, Hedda

Something sighs faintly in the bowels of the house. The desk lamp flickers.

Wind has risen outside, and a branch scrapes the window, reminding me of the strange noise I heard on my first morning here. My screen tells me it's nearly one. The laptop was sleeping a second ago; my hand must have brushed the keyboard and woken it.

I pull out an envelope and address it.

When I reread the letter, it sounds childish. What if Mom jumps on a plane and comes straight here? I imagine her sitting on the edge of my bed in the dark: *You can still leave, Hedda. Come back to the ranch and learn to control yourself.*

But I can't keep lying to her. I need to make a break before this school thing distracts me, before I lose my nerve. Once we've talked through it, maybe I can get her and Dad's permission to stay all semester. Or to enroll in Arizona, so she won't have to lose me.

The level 13 frustration has sharpened all my senses to a point, filling me with the need to do something daring and decisive. If I wait for tomorrow, I'll probably end up stuffing the letter away in a drawer.

I stick a stamp on the envelope, slip my phone in my hoodie—in case Mireya texts back—and creep downstairs barefoot, already familiar enough with the house to find my way in the dark. The fancy fridge rattles, making ice. The porch light casts a coppery wedge through the window in the front door.

Outside, streetlights throw ghostly orange pools on the pavement. My bare feet are almost silent. At the corner, the mailbox beckons with the finality of its tight slot, its steel clang.

When Mom and I talk again, I need to say no and no and no to her. And I will, even if that means excavating dark parts of my past and exposing her half-truths to the glare of day. Even if it means saying a final goodbye.

I open the mailbox. Slide the letter in. Close it.

As I return under the rustling cottonwoods, the moon gives a sheen to ragged fringes of cloud and Japanese maples. My phone vibrates against my hip like a promise.

Before I can pull it out, a wind rises. In the neighbors' yard, the low branches of a juniper bush jerk back and forth, not with the wind but against it. Maybe their cat's fighting with a skunk or possum.

Something catches my eye off to the right, on a privacy fence—a flash of white. I walk faster, gripping my phone like an anchor as it buzzes a second time.

My feet hammer up the porch stairs. Inside, I lock the door and press my back to it, feeling ridiculous. I check the phone.

An image fills the screen—a little girl's face de-faced with bulging, red-veined eyes and horns jutting from her forehead. This must be what I was looking for earlier—Mireya and Lily's monster version of me. But who has it, and why would they send it to me now—with a message? *Ur pathetic,* it says.

Cold hands close around my throat. Mireya wouldn't send that. I rock back and forth, staring at the image, swimming in a familiar sea of shame. But who would?

I sit there for what feels like forever, my eyes glued to the phone, till I realize that's not all. I'm looking at the second text of two, both from the same restricted number. The first text is just an image.

At first it looks like a random pattern of light and dark, sun and clouds. Then I hold the phone farther away from me, and it becomes a skull.

S omewhere, in a dark room, a girl has just lost a game.

Why won't it let her play anymore? She slaps the edge of the desk in frustration, then sees it's nearly four in the morning. When she's running on empty, any stupid distraction can derail her for hours.

She sets her alarm, turns out the light, and pulls the covers over her head.

Something hisses, close to her ear, and she sits straight up. Oh, it's her phone buzzing.

There's no message, only an image that's somehow familiar and mysterious at once, until she realizes what it is—a skull. Sent from a restricted number.

As she puts the phone down, her temples pounding—*did* he *send that? what's wrong with him?*—it buzzes again.

What she sees on the screen this time makes her burn with rage.

It's that *photo, the one she sent him only after he begged, the one he's not supposed to show anyone. Why was she so stupid?*

With the photo comes a message: Ur pathetic.

It's an unmistakable threat, but he wouldn't post that pic. He wouldn't! She fires a text back: You are SICK, Liam, STOP.

She still remembers how she felt when she sent him that photo—mischievous and light-headed and in love. Burning with shame, she hurls the phone away and rolls over.

The phone doesn't buzz again. When she's half-asleep, something brushes her ear, gentle like her mother's hand, only colder. A faint radiance, like phosphorescence, bleeds through her eyelids.

Very, very far away, she hears a familiar keening.

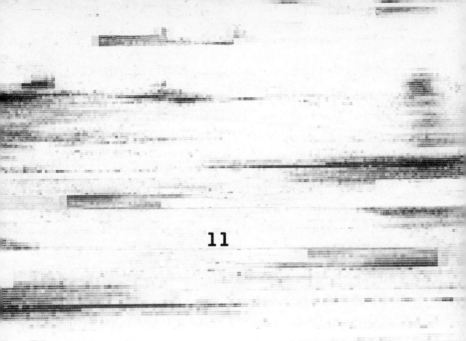

11

Mireya pulls up to our house in a rusted Corolla with the windows all the way down. She opens the passenger door and leans out, wearing gigantic sunglasses and a polka-dotted halter top. "Ready for a rager? I like your hair."

"Thanks." Erika showed me how to pull it back with a sparkly barrette.

Mireya's car is reassuringly cruddy like the trucks we had at the ranch, littered with power cords and Trader Joe's snack bags. I was excited to tell her about Dad's big yes to school, was waiting to do it in person, but now I don't know what to say. I haven't looked at those texts since last night, even to delete them. I don't want to believe they're real, or that she could have anything to do with them.

She fiddles with her phone in its dashboard cradle as we

approach the freeway entrance ramp. "Sorry I didn't answer your text last night. I got into a marathon texting session with Anthony"—her boyfriend—"and then I was wiped. What do you mean, the game won't let you play anymore?"

My frustration at not being able to play the Glare seems so trivial now, so childish. I rush through an explanation of how the game cut me off.

"Huh," Mireya says, switching lanes to pass an eighteen-wheeler, her hair streaming like black ribbons. "Remember how I said the Glare feels like a rough draft? Maybe this copy doesn't go past level thirteen."

"Maybe." And then I jump to the part that matters, the part I can't hold in any longer. "Something happened later, after I sent you that text. I got two texts from a restricted number, and—"

"What?" She shoots a worried glance at me. "You look really scared."

I'd rather keep it secret, but I have to show her. I have to hope she'll laugh and offer me an explanation that makes sense in the light of day. I wake my phone and pull up the latest texts.

There's *Ur pathetic.* There's the strange image that looks like a skull from the right distance. But the image of child me with horns is gone.

I scroll furiously, desperately, trying to make it reappear. I quit and relaunch. Could I have deleted the pic by accident, or accidentally on purpose, my finger twitching without my mind's consent? But no: That picture and *Ur pathetic* were the same message. They *were.*

I spent at least five minutes last night staring at the mocking image of me, immobilized by shame. How can it suddenly be gone? Could I have hallucinated it?

"Hedda, what's wrong?" Mireya looks really disturbed now. "What's this text?"

"Nothing. It's not important." I darken the phone and shove it in my bag, hands still shaking. "Just one of my standard newbie phone mistakes."

If I tell her what I thought I saw, she'll not only think I'm *off-kilter*, she'll think I have issues with her. Who else would or could send that photo? I grope for a safe explanation of my mood. "I'm just kind of pissed at my dad. We talked, and I got him to agree to enroll me in school—"

"No way!" Her whole demeanor shifts, her smile radiant beneath her blowing hair. "That's awesome, Hedda! We're going to have a blast."

"I know!" I make myself smile back. "I just wish I hadn't had to practically force him. I wish he wasn't so hands-off my entire life, letting Mom decide everything. It makes me feel—"

"Like he doesn't care?" Mireya sighs, but at least she doesn't look unsettled anymore. "Hedda, my dad's a tech guy, too. He's not great at dealing with the real world, so basically he slithers out of the hard stuff. He slithered out of his parenting responsibilities, and he knows any attempt to take them back this late in the game will piss my mom off. I'm guessing your dad's a slitherer-outer, too."

"I guess." It's not pleasant to realize you're part of your parent's definition of the "hard stuff," like a tax form or a root canal.

"It doesn't mean he doesn't love you, just that he's...limited.

91

Don't take it personally. You got what you wanted; that's what matters."

"That's what matters." I try to believe it.

. . .

By the time we reach Muir Beach, fog has rolled in, bringing a chill. At the base of a wooded cliff, Mireya's friends huddle around a fire pit, hoodies draped over their trunks and bikinis. The sweet aroma of weed mingles with the bite of liquor. A hypnotic beat drifts from speakers propped in the sand.

Mireya takes a drag off someone's joint and offers it to me, but I shake my head. She goes around the circle introducing me, the names flying by too fast as I try to match people to their photos.

Here's Mireya's boyfriend, Anthony, a freshman at Berkeley who likes Malcolm X, punk music, AeroPress coffee, and piercings. He has a boxer, Moxie, who is cute in a hundred different poses. Here's Lily Chen, who likes to snap pictures of herself in the mirror. Her girlfriend skateboards, and I've seen her latest injury in bloody, glistening detail. Here's Anil, who mountain bikes and is allergic to peanut butter.

Off on the edge of the surf, two boys are tossing a Frisbee back and forth. The taller one laughs in a loud, uncontrolled way, and with a start I recognize him—Ellis.

I shrink into myself so he won't notice me, not that there's much danger of that. Not a word from him since the barbecue, so apparently he's not as nostalgic about our shared childhood as he let on.

I turn to Mireya, hoping for a scowl of complicity—*What's*

he doing here?—but she's already grabbed Anthony and is pulling him into the surf with her. Her friends return to their conversations, muffled by the moist air. Sitting on the edge of the circle, I watch their bodies appear and disappear, their slick heads bobbing above the fog.

Near me, two girls languidly argue about where in San Francisco's Japantown to find "the best mochi outside Tokyo." They have curtains of salt-frizzed hair and long, dangly earrings. I consider googling "mochi," but I'm on a Glare break.

I try to make eye contact with Lily Chen, but suddenly she's busy sucking face with a girl with a crimson plume of hair jutting from her forehead, apparently the skateboarder.

Lily's just a stranger now. She probably doesn't even remember mocking me. And the photo I thought I saw—it must have come from the darkest recess of my imagination.

Still, I don't feel comfortable with these people. At least thirty feet up, on the edge of the cliff, shaggy black spruce carve out the soupy sky. If I were up there leaning against a trunk, breathing in the sharp scent and staring out to sea, nobody would be able to point me out as the weird girl who's sitting alone.

I close my eyes and see the forest of the game—pine, spruce, yellow aspen, an oak dotted with red, moss, dead leaves. I miss it.

"Hey, nice boots."

What is it with boys and boots? I roll over, and the boy adds, "I'm Rory."

Rory is slight with a pompadour of cotton-candy hair—pale pink and blue—a tiny nose piercing, and horn-rimmed glasses. He offers me a flask, and because why not, I take a swallow.

We're near a speaker, so I have to say my name three times,

but then he leans closer and says, "You're the one with the Fuchsia Groan avatar. I was obsessed with those books freshman year. I love how her hair's described—like a pirate's flag."

"You read the Gormenghast books?"

Suddenly we're having a conversation like two strangers who just discovered friends in common. Sparks fly from the red-tinged flames as we debate whether Fuchsia's feelings for Steerpike were her downfall, or whether an angry teenage girl locked in a castle is always headed for disaster.

As dusk falls around us, the reek of alcohol thickens. People chase and splash in the black waves, their shrill cries distorted by the fog. Lily and her skateboarder are two humps under a blanket. One mochi girl has disappeared; the other sits by the fire, busy with her phone.

Branches stir on the cliff edge, making heads turn. Laughter and curses drift down from above. Over Rory's shoulder, I see a boy raising his phone to film the cliff. Something white darts on the screen.

My muscles lock, my breath wheezing in my throat as all my game-honed reflexes say, *Random.* The camera's flash blinds me. When my eyes clear, there's a boy in a white T-shirt hanging over the cliff edge. He's clinging to a root with one hand, his long legs dangling and kicking.

"What the fuck, Westover?" somebody yells from down here. "You're gonna break what's left of your head open."

Ellis again. Did he lose his footing on the edge, or is he there on purpose?

"Nah." Ellis's voice drawls like a slowed-down record. "Went to rock-climbing camp, dudes. 'M fine. Levi, you're gonna owe me a case of Lawson's."

"If he's doing that on a bet, he's trashed out of his mind," Rory mutters.

A handful of girls gather below, whispering and giggling as Ellis creeps his way down the cliff face, somehow finding footholds and handholds in the sheer stone. I catch phrases like "so messed up" and "still hit that."

"It's like Westley in *The Princess Bride*," I say because he *is* a good climber, or else just extremely desperate and strong.

"Awesome movie," Rory says.

"There's a movie?"

He looks at me like he hopes I'm kidding. A cheer goes up, and I glance back to see Ellis leap the last six feet or so to the ground. He staggers across the sand, suddenly looking much drunker than he did up there, back-slaps a few guys, and stops in front of me.

The cocky grin slides off his face. "Hedda."

Something clenches inside me as I remember our awkward goodbye at the barbecue, but I force myself to smile. "Hi, Ellis."

"You're using a phone." He says it like an accusation, his eyes narrowing. "I saw you walking down the street with your face in one."

My face burns. Why was I so clueless when he asked to "follow" me? But I did end up following him, and he even followed me back.

Behind me Rory says, "Ellis, chill out."

Ellis laughs derisively but doesn't look at Rory, his eyes still fixed on me. "Don't you miss the desert? It misses you."

Then, before I can say a word, he lopes off toward the surf, yelling something about washing the sweat off. I hold my breath until he's gone.

"Dude is messed up," Rory says as a dripping Mireya collapses beside us. The mochi girl winces out of the way, then leaps up as her phone buzzes. Frowning at it, she steps out of the circle of light.

"We're going to start the corn!" Mireya hands us both ears to shuck.

Rory kicks a speaker farther into the sand so we don't have to shout. "Mireya, Westover's being a dick to her. You should kick his ass."

I protest, while Mireya says, "She can handle him."

"Speaking of weirdness," Rory says, "do you have any idea who designed that shooter with the black tower? Mireya says it came from you."

The fire blinds me for a second, the world jerking on its axis. *No one else should know about the black tower. Only Ellis and me.*

Then I understand. "You mean the Glare? You're playing it, too?"

Passing Rory the aluminum foil, Mireya says, "I sent him the link, Hedda—hope you don't mind. Rory's my shooter guru; you should see him slay those Randoms!" She mimes firing a rifle.

"Yeah, well." Rory tears off a sheet, not looking at me. "It's a pretty basic game, but the text alerts were probably hot stuff back in the day. Gives it this whole alternate-reality angle. While you play, you're looking for those runes, so when you see them in a text, you get triggered and start jonesing to play again."

If he's such an expert, maybe he can explain what happened to me last night. "Have you gotten to level thirteen yet?"

"Not yet, I—"

A scream tears the air in two.

We turn our heads just in time to see her—a girl running. A girl in midair with legs flailing like she wants to keep racing right over the whitecaps. For a fraction of a second I think she will. But she's not falling like Ellis at the end of his precarious climb; once she left the cliff edge, she had no control. Wind shear tips her, and she lands in the sand with a dull thump and a sharp crack.

"Caleigh?"

"No, that's Emily!"

The fog and the sophistication and the alcohol-weed miasma peel away, leaving a bunch of scared kids running around in the dark. My head spins, and I keep hearing that cracking sound.

Phones light up in people's hands. A couple on the cliff edge yells down frantically. Rory runs for the cliff, and I follow, my legs unsteady.

This isn't supposed to happen. This is a party. Our interrupted conversation mixes in my head with what I'm seeing, making me dizzy. *Safe trees. Black tower.*

Lying in the sand, the girl cries in long, frayed moans. It's the mochi girl, the one with a slim aqua streak in her long, perfect hair. Her arms thrash against the chest of a boy who keeps telling her to stay still, the EMTs are on their way. Ellis is suddenly there, too, pressing her shoulders down, whispering to her.

"Don't move her!" somebody yells. "I think she hit her head."

The girl keeps trying to raise her hand with something in it—her phone. "Just kill me!" she moans. "Please!" Her right leg is contorted as if a giant picked her up and corkscrewed it, showing a white flash of bone.

I turn and face the luminous fog over the sea, fighting nausea. *Unstuck. Off-kilter.*

"Kill me!"

The raw fear in the cry makes me whip back around. People keep aiming their phones at her—will this moment be posted for everyone to see?

"I saw her get a text," someone says behind me. "How much you want to bet it was from that asshole Liam?"

See? Mom says in my head. *She wasn't at home in reality. Her feet weren't on the ground. Words pushed her over the edge.*

"Totally batshit. What'd she take?"

The girl keeps moaning, begging for death, and the clammy air presses into my pores, weighs down my lungs. I stumble toward the surf, its lacy patterns stark white against the dusk.

A hand reaches for mine—Rory. He's shaking, but his voice is steady. "It's okay. Just breathe. She must've slipped."

But I saw what happened. She didn't fall. She ran like something was chasing her.

12

The parking lot swarms with flashers, the air gritty with the EMTs' radio chatter. We watch as they load the girl—Emily—onto the stretcher and sedate her, silencing her screams at last.

A couple who were hooking up on the cliff tell the cops and everybody else how Emily sprinted up the path and crashed through the trees, past their hiding place, and kept running. "I saw her face," the boy keeps saying. "Something scared the shit out of her."

The cops detain a few of us, the ones caught with something stronger than alcohol, and shoo the rest away.

Driving home, we shiver in the chill that sets in here at nightfall, our skin goose-pimpling. Mireya doesn't close the windows. For the first time, California seems to press around me like a living thing, a vibrating darkness pocked with neon. The edge of a continent, where people do things I can't fathom.

Maybe there is no normal. No on-kilter. I wish I could go home tonight and feed the goats and shoo the chickens into the coop and say good night to Mom, but it's too late for that.

When Mireya pulls up in front of my house, neither of us makes a move to leave. She seems subdued, smaller.

"It sucks that your first party had to end that way," she says. "I'm sorry. My friends—they aren't usually into the hard stuff."

"You think it was drugs?"

"PCP. Some heavy shit like that. You don't run off a cliff because your boyfriend dumped you."

So she saw, too. "She was scared." The cottonwoods in front of Ellis's house rustle, showing the pale sides of their leaves.

"She was high."

I don't want her to think I'm a total innocent, so I change the subject. "Can you ask Rory about the Glare? Why it won't let me keep playing?"

"Sure, but you could ask him yourself, you know. You know how to do this stuff." Mireya picks up her phone and taps on it. "I should get going. You won't tell your dad you were there tonight, will you? It might make the news."

"My dad?" I try to imagine him waiting up for me, worrying, asking me how the party went, and before I can stop it, a contemptuous laugh bubbles out of me. I still feel the sting of that visit to his office. "He might ask about something like that if he cared enough to be home."

Her hand finds mine in the dark. "Oh, girl. Like I said, don't take it personally. Stay strong."

I squeeze her hand back, feeling deep inside me the outlines of that six-year-old who ached to impress her daddy. Even now, I can't help hoping things will be different now we've had that talk. He wouldn't have told me about his nightmares if he didn't trust me.

Meanwhile, I don't want to slither out of the hard stuff myself. I want to be a good friend. "Are you doing okay? Emily's your friend, right?"

Mireya checks the phone again; it turns her face tangerine. "Yeah. I'm checking in with our friend Cheyenne at the hospital. What about you? I know you're not used to dealing with, well, situations like this."

The words ring like a challenge. I stiffen my spine and open the door. "Is anybody? I just need some sleep."

. . .

Something goes *plock* against my window, like hailstones. My eyes pop open.

How late is it? The cup of mint tea Erika made for me sits on the bedside table, half-full and cold.

Plock. I slide out of bed and go peel back the curtain.

And stagger away, my heart cantering, at the sight of a face. White in the darkness, pressed right against the pane, staring at me.

I clap a hand over my mouth just in time to stop the scream, because the face is attached to a lanky body that's gesturing at me to open the window. Ellis Westover crouches on the roof, clinging to a corner of the gable like a flying monkey that somehow got separated from the Wicked Witch's retinue.

Trying to breathe normally, I force the balky window up and jiggle the screen. Ellis shakes his head and whispers, "Just come down, okay? Need to talk."

You'll break your neck! But before I have a chance to say so, he scrambles down the shingled roof on all fours, grabs the edge, swings his legs over it, and disappears. I stand soaked in sweat with my mouth open, wondering if I dreamed what I just saw.

Still drowsy, I creep downstairs, already well aware of which steps creak. I hesitate before opening the door, because Ellis is obviously still drunk or otherwise *off-kilter*. Mireya said he wasn't actually dangerous, but I'm on my guard.

When I step outside, he's sitting on the porch rail, straddling it with a jagged grin on his face.

"You could have just messaged me," I say. Has he come to apologize for what he said earlier?

As I sit down opposite him, he draws his knees to his chest, shivering in the crisp night air. He stinks to high heaven of something stronger than beer, but he sounds reasonably coherent as he says, "Wanted to be sure I'd get your attention. Look, I'm sorry about before. I wanted to talk to you, and I told myself I'd leave you alone, and then I just—well, it came out mean."

There's a pulsing urgency to him, like he's one of those angry drunks you avoid on the midway. My face heats up. "I don't understand."

"Look, I was gonna steer clear of you until you left. Nothing personal, but it was just too much...heavy baggage. I like to travel light."

"Okay." The word comes out sounding sarcastic.

"I didn't mean it that way, Hedda. Promise." He pulls a phone from his jeans. "But we have to talk now. The skull. You saw the skull?"

"The what?"

The pounding in my head rises all at once as I stare at the picture he's showing me. It's distorted, staticky—a photo of another screen. A dark cylinder encloses a blinding-white circle, the sky seen from the bottom of the black tower. The clouds form a face: empty eye sockets, jutting jaw, bared teeth.

It's the exact same skull text I got last night. From the game.

Cold sweat beads on my temples. "Who—where did you get that?"

"Emily's phone. Somebody sent it to her right before she jumped, from a restricted number. You remember, right?"

"Remember what?"

"The game."

Adrenaline pumps through me, heat spreading to my toes and fingertips, blotting out the chill of the night. A twig snaps in the flowerbeds, and I rise and hover on the edge of the porch steps, surveying the lawn. "The...game?"

"The Glare," Ellis says. "Did Emily play it? Did you give it to her?"

"No!"

Nothing but stillness, stars glinting through the cottonwoods and the bay pricking my nostrils. But everything—the dark trees, the neat lawns and bushes—is menacingly alive in a way it wasn't a second ago.

Liquory breath wafts closer as Ellis comes up behind me. "Hedda, you must remember the Glare."

Mireya and Rory say that word so casually. In Ellis's mouth, it has thorns, and I wrap my arms tight around myself, not wanting to admit I've been playing it. "It's a game on the Dark Web. It scared me when I was a kid."

"It scared *us*." His voice has dropped to a whisper. "The first time you got a skull alert, the game said this was the end for you. Or that's what I remember, anyway—we were so scared. For years I thought I imagined most of it."

"We played the game together?" Of course we did. That's why he's in my nightmare.

The boards are cool under my bare soles. The streetlight washes Ellis's T-shirt, leaving his face in shadow, as he says, "The woods. The black tower. The wind. The keening when *they* come."

"For so long, I thought I dreamed it all," I say. "I dreamed about us playing."

"You were so good at it. Me, I could barely use a keyboard back then. I didn't *want* to play, but you dared me. Said I was chicken."

For a second I wonder if he's really as creeped out as he seems or if he's playing one of his stupid drunken pranks on me. But I remember how he used to hide his eyes during the scary parts of movies, and cold rushes on my skin like a wind rising.

"I haven't said a word about this for nine or ten years, because people would laugh me out of town. They'd say it's an urban legend. But everything got freaky after that skull text." Ellis scrubs his fingers through his hair, like he's worried I'll laugh, too. "You made me come over one day—you were so scared. You were writing all over the walls of your dad's study with a Sharpie."

"I don't remember." But that explains the creepy feeling I got when I explored Dad's study on my first day back, like something bad had happened there.

"You kept getting that skull text on your tablet," Ellis says. "That same damn creepy picture, over and over and over. You said *they* were after you."

Leaves stir above us, a puzzle breaking and reforming around the stars. That cold sense of recognition keeps sweeping over me, like a fire driving sparks in my face. When I got stuck on level 13 last night, when it told me this was the end, it wasn't the first time.

"In my dream," I say, "you tell me I'm dead."

"That's what you used to say after you started getting the skulls. That you'd died for the last time and now you were going to die for real."

Control yourself. Don't get unstuck.

But I'm not. I'm getting to the bottom of things, sorting them out. "That's a horrible thing for a kid to say."

Ellis nods. "We were both in a weird place back then, because of Caroline. You got the game address from her—that's what you told me, anyway."

The babysitter sits at a desk, outlined in blue computer glow. She tells me not to look, this game isn't for kids. "I don't think she would have given it to me. I think maybe I stole it."

"Maybe." Ellis sinks down at the top of the porch steps. The way he mentions Caroline, I can tell her story is a heavy stone around his neck, weighing him down the way Mom's fears and warnings weigh me.

"All I know is, you said it came from Caroline," he says. "You said maybe the Glare was what...hurt her, and maybe if we played it, we'd figure out how to fix her. Like magic."

Sitting down beside him, I think of the Randoms slithering through the trees. Jumping on me, throttling me. What kind of little kid would want to play that game, let alone convince another kid to play it? "Oh, Ellis. I shouldn't have done that."

"It's not your fault. I wanted to believe. I found Caroline the night she did it—you know that, right? She was supposed to be watching me." He presses his forehead against his knees. "I heard something in the basement, and I went down there and Caroline was sitting and moaning with her hands over her eyes. She was like Emily, only less frantic, like she was a mouse cornered by a cat and waiting for it to pounce. And she just kept saying, 'They're still here. I still see them.'"

I can still see.

I gingerly touch his hand. He shudders, then grasps back hard, weaving his fingers through mine. "My folks didn't want to discuss any of it. Caroline was 'sick.' She had a 'breakdown.' They sent me to a shrink, obviously, to express all my feelings in a safe space, blah blah, but I wasn't going to talk about that night with a stranger. So I talked to you. My house was a nonstop funeral, people whispering behind closed doors, and I'd run over here, and you'd be your normal self. You were never bored, always off on a new plan or obsession. Never scared of anything."

"Until the Glare," I say.

His fingers grip mine so hard I nearly gasp. He's pulling me *off-kilter*, into some wild, erratic orbit that could end with me crashing into the sun, but I need to hear this, need to know.

"And after the skull texts, you started doing freaky things, just like Caroline did. You played that game to beat the Glare, to save her, but it ended up taking you away from me, too."

I breathe evenly so he won't feel me trembling. *Never scared of anything.* "But Caroline's better now, right? You said she got some sight back?"

"Yeah. She was in this fancy clinic on a shit ton of drugs, and then she went to a halfway house and my parents were convinced she was good as new. They started talking about college. We had a couple of family dinners with her, super awkward—she just seemed so brittle—and then she flew the coop. Vanished. That was five years ago. My folks even hired a private detective to try and find her, but she obviously didn't want to be found."

"I'm so sorry," I say.

"Me too. I guess it's all just coming back to me. What happened tonight, how freaked out Emily was, and that skull…"

His breathing is ragged, his fingers loosening around mine. The breeze moves the treetops, and I feel a million miles from the desert. Wonder if Mom, in the Southern Hemisphere, could feel half this far away.

"You didn't give Emily the game, did you?" He sighs. "But you couldn't have, right? You don't even know her."

"No." But Mireya could have, and I need to know.

I reach down into myself, searching for the fearless, stubborn little girl he remembers. Searching for logic, for grounding, for courage. "Ellis, I don't know what really happened to Caroline back then, or what happened to Emily tonight. But the Glare's just a game. Mireya and I have been playing it. I even got one of those skull texts, and I'm fine. It's a rough draft, Mireya says, and the designer—"

Ellis yanks his hand from mine. His face twists, and for a moment I think he's going to shake me until I admit the Glare caused Emily's accident. Or until I spew forth the recollection of those months he remembers so well and I don't, when I was a girl who made up stories about dark magic, stole forbidden games, and dared boys to play them.

Instead, he stands up, staggers down the steps, and vomits into a bush.

When he speaks again, his voice is hoarse, and he pauses between the words. "How the fuck could you play it again? Or let Mireya play it? Did the desert bleach your brain or something, or did you really just forget? Look up the Glare, and then come back and tell me that skull text doesn't mean anything. And stop playing it *now*."

13

Mireya comes to the front door in a plaid bathrobe, phone in hand. She looks smaller somehow with no makeup and dark circles under her eyes. "What happened? You look like zombies were chasing you."

"Ellis," I whisper as we tiptoe upstairs.

My body is still taut from his parting shot. After he staggered off into his own backyard, I texted Mireya and then ran all the way here.

I sink onto the bed, focusing on the warm light of the lamp with its rose-colored scarf wrapped around the shade. Nothing here can hurt me. I need Mireya to assure me that Ellis is *off-kilter* and a game had nothing to do with what happened to Emily or Caroline.

"Just breathe." Mireya looks promisingly fierce. "What did

Westover do? If he messes with you, I'll drag him till he's sorry he ever saw you."

I ball my fist in the daisy-patterned bedspread and take a deep breath. "Why did Emily get a text with a skull?"

She just shakes her head, looking perplexed, and I say, "Ellis showed me the text she got. You didn't give her the Glare, did you?"

"No!"

"You gave it to Rory without telling me."

Mireya swivels her desk chair toward me, her face turning stony. "Rory's a gamer. He's the only person I gave it to. Tell me everything Ellis said."

Ellis's half-coherent story pours out of me, and Mireya listens with a scowl, swigging from her energy drink. When I get to the part about me writing on the walls, I slow down, and she interrupts.

"Wait a second. Do *you* remember any of this?"

"Some of it! Well…" I think I remember how it felt to write on the study walls, black ink spilling from the Sharpie like blood from a cut. And I remember seeing Caroline play *a* scary game, though I can't be 100 percent sure it was the Glare. "Mireya, Ellis told me to 'look up' the Glare. You said you googled it and didn't find anything."

Mireya's silent for a moment, blowing a strand of black hair off her forehead. Then she types something on her keyboard and hits enter. "I didn't want to say anything before, because I knew it would scare you. You have to understand, this is a thing, just not an actual thing."

How can something be a thing and not a thing? She's beckoning me over, so I bend to read what's on her screen:

The Glare on the Dark Web: Real or Legend?

It lurks in the internet's dark places. It has a level no one can beat. And if you try thirteen times and fail, you will die in real life.

I break off and turn to her, my chest so tight my head seems to be floating off like a balloon. "You knew about this?"

She doesn't meet my eyes. "Just read the rest."

If you spend enough time on gaming forums, sooner or later you'll hear some version of this story about a first-person shooter called the Glare. You may even have viewed images that people claim they received as text alerts from the game server—text alerts that have supposedly been linked to crimes, suicides, and self-harm. But did the Glare ever actually exist?

The story starts nearly a decade ago with an anonymous post on the horror-gaming forum Charybdis from the user "L13Survivor." *I am the only person to get past level thirteen of the Dark Web game called the Glare*, it began. *If you don't know what I'm talking about, you are lucky. If you haven't started to play the game, don't.*

The game sends you text alerts whenever you stop playing. If you block them, they will start again from a different number. If you die thirteen times on level 13, the game won't let you play anymore, but the text alerts will continue. First the game will tell you, "Ur pathetic." Then you'll get images of a skull.

If you keep seeing the skull, you will die in real life.

Maybe it's the power of suggestion and conditioning—a devilish psychology experiment. Maybe it's a curse. It doesn't really matter.

This game killed its first tester. It will kill you.

Don't look for this game. Don't play this game. I am posting this as a public-service announcement.

My vision starts to blur as I skim the rest. People have posted stories about how somebody—their boyfriend's friend's niece, their sister's ex, their cousin's in-law's brother—found the Glare and started playing and then died under mysterious circumstances. Drownings, falls, car accidents. One person has posted a supposed text alert from the Glare, but it's too blurry to identify.

The article says "L13Survivor" has posted again over the years, repeating their warnings. Skeptics think the anonymous poster made up the entire story "for the lulz," but no one has ever unmasked them, "and so the legend lives on to tempt intrepid explorers of the internet's dark places."

"You knew all this," I repeat, straightening and looking down on Mireya, my nails pricking my palms. "And you still let me play."

Her eyes turn hooded, defensive. "Look, when I first tried your link, I'd never heard of the Glare. Rory's the one who knew about the urban legend—when I told him I was playing this weird game, he practically came over and grabbed it off my hard drive.

He said nobody's proven the Glare even exists. You can't search the Dark Web, and no one's ever posted a verified link."

"Nobody *should* post a link. You see what it says, right?" *Don't. You will die.* How can someone ignore a warning like that?

Mireya sets her jaw. "Hedda, come on. I know you're a noob, but this is obviously a hoax. Rory thinks somebody coded our game to feed the legend of the Glare—that's why it's so simple, like a mock-up. Or maybe the Glare is real, but the 'cursed level thirteen' part is a legend. I mean, obviously, right? How can a game kill people?"

"I don't know!" Anger boils up in me, but she looks so sure that I shove it back down. *Control yourself.* "My mom thinks screens can kind of...possess you."

"Like the devil? Seriously?" Mireya turns to the keyboard and types madly, search results flashing on the screen. "Check out some of these other stories, okay? The Glare isn't the first 'deadly game' meme."

She gives me the desk chair, and I read while she sits hunched in a straight chair beside me, chewing her bottom lip, eyes fixed on the screen.

I read about the 1980s arcade game that supposedly gave kids seizures and memory loss, and the demonic Dark Web game that supposedly brought swarms of flies to your window, and another with images so horrifying it drove people literally insane. None of them ever proven to exist, just campfire tales fabricated by kids eager for clicks. Or that's the majority opinion.

I want to imagine glittering strings of text zipping back and forth across the globe as thousands of people debate the Glare and conclude it isn't real. Except it *is* real, because I've played it, and I've died thirteen times on level 13, and *who knows?*

"Isn't it wild?" Mireya says. "All these urban legends, and the Glare could be real. This is, like, historic. We could be the first people to post an authentic link to it."

"Don't." The word is a creature forcing its way out of my throat. "Don't post anything, please."

I stop, because she's staring too hard at me.

"You don't seriously believe these unsourced stories from random people? Ellis could just be trying to get a rise out of you. You saw how tanked he was. And Emily—her asshole boyfriend probably sent her that skull. I don't know what made her jump, but I can tell you it wasn't a game."

"You should have told me." She's as stubborn as Mom, not even listening to me. "Even if it's a hoax, I need to know this stuff. I need to have *control*."

But I was the one who gave up control, wasn't I? Why'd I keep playing night after night? The Glare went round and round like a carousel, like a roller coaster. The highs were always giddy, and the lows were cold sludge in my gut, and every time I told myself I was going to stop, I got one of those texts, and a calm voice in my head said, *You were doing so well, just try the next level,* and so I tried until I died for the last time.

Sweat trickles down my neck, though the room isn't hot. I rise and go to the window, press my face to the screen, and breathe in earth, grass, car exhaust.

I still want to play. I remember wanting to be inside that tower more than anything. Mowing down Randoms. Running and not making it. Dying over and over.

114

I can control myself. I can, I can.

A touch on my arm, and I whip around to see Mireya looking frazzled. "Ellis shouldn't have freaked you out that way," she says. "Even if it's all true about what happened when you were kids, you're not kids anymore."

I close my eyes and see the desert, vast and tawny on the horizon. Penning me in, keeping me safe. "Still, you should've told me."

"You could've googled it yourself. It's not like I stopped you!"

Those iron bands grip my chest again. I haven't felt angry like this since my last night with Mom. "Did you want to see what the Glare would do to me? You keep saying I'm weird, brainwashed or whatever—was this your idea of shock treatment?"

Mireya backs away from me. "You have gaps in your memory— that's not normal. I'm trying to *help* you."

"No, you think I'm a freak. You watched me play that game to see what would happen, and now maybe you want to see me come apart like Emily."

Her face reddens. "Don't you dare compare yourself to Emily. What happened to her has nothing to do with a stupid game."

"I don't know why she ran off that cliff!" My cheeks are burning, too, as I push my way past her to the door. I need to get out of here before I say something even more horrible. "I got a skull text last night, okay, Mireya? That's what I was going to tell you on the way to the beach, but then I was scared you'd laugh at me. I got one, too."

. . .

I don't cry till I get home to my safe, well-lighted kitchen. Even then, it's not crying so much as tremors that grip my shoulders in waves, squeezing stray tears from my eyes. My hands shake so hard I spill Erika's fancy pomegranate juice on the floor, so I stop trying to pretend everything's fine and lean back against the counter and let it wash over me.

Mireya's right—I shouldn't compare myself to Emily. Mireya would never knowingly hurt me, but I keep remembering what Mom used to say about how normal kids would roll their eyes and treat me like a freak show. Mireya was barely even interested in hanging out with me till she found out I had missing memories.

What if I'm just a specimen to her? What if she *did* send me that ugly image, just to mess with me, and I accidentally deleted it? The tiles blur as I remember the warm thrill that snuck up my spine every time she texted or messaged me and I realized I had someone to tell things to. A friend.

As if it remembers, too, my phone buzzes inside my hoodie. The message is from her, but I don't even read it, just click over to the two texts from last night. I scroll up and down, up and down, faster and faster, willing the image I remember to pop back into existence, because it *was* there. *Ur pathetic,* my phone keeps telling me, and scarlet juice is pooling on the dingy pink tiles, and all this has happened before. I remember this.

I close my eyes, my whole head buzzing now, as memories swarm through my mind. I'm in a bright kitchen—this kitchen, but with the countertop closer to eye level. A distant grandfather clock tick-tocks, tick-tocks.

On the counter sits eyeless Raggedy Ann, one of her Mary

Janes resting on a tablet. On the tablet's screen is a picture—a skull. In my hand is a knife.

Blood drips off my left forearm onto the floor, two currents of blood flowing into a single river. It trickles in the cracks between the dingy pink tiles that Mommy wants to replace with new travertine. I feel no pain, just icy tingling, as the clock ticks off seconds of the night.

And I feel something else—pride, because I've finally figured it out. Once I finish writing the words on my skin, once I release the Glare inside, I will be really, truly alive, and they'll never come after me again. No more taunting pictures that disappear before I can ever show them to anybody. No more phantoms looming and disappearing on my bedroom wall. No more *Ur pathetic*. No more *them*.

They won't get me, because I'm real and they are *not real*.

White flashes across the doorway. I try to ignore it, raising the knife in my shaking fingers.

"Hedda!" Mom's voice, scared.

But it's not Mom, because it has no mouth or eyes or nose, only glowing white blankness. Its wrist stretches like elastic until its fingers clamp me, cold and slippery as fog, and I scream and scream, because I'm dying again—

And I'm back in the present, on the floor leaning against the cabinets, knees to my chest, staring at the doorway to the living room. There's nothing there but shadows, an oblong of carpet, the faint hump of the couch. No sounds—no keening, no rustling. Nothing.

Nothing, but tears roll down my cheeks.

I sit there for a while, shuddering and gazing into the dark, and then I raise my left forearm and look at the old scars there. Mom's told me dozens of times how, right after we moved to the ranch, I fell out of a cottonwood and cut my arm on a barbed wire fence. But do I actually remember the accident, or only the story?

As always, when I look at the scars I see faint outlines of letters. *N t rea*. And now I know what they're meant to say: *Not real*. Someone was using a knife to write there.

14

"I know now, Mom," I say. "I know what you meant when you said the Glare knocked me off-kilter."

Mom says, "Your dad told you."

I expected her to be angry, like she'll be when she gets my letter. Furious at me for disobeying her rules and discovering the truth. But instead she sounds resigned, possibly even relieved. Like she's been dreading this moment so long she just wants it to be over.

"No! Dad didn't tell me anything. I figured things out and I remembered."

I've taken the landline out on the deck, where I can see the blue haze of the bay. The warm, golden sunlight makes everything that happened last night seem impossible—Emily's legs flailing in the air, Ellis vomiting, Mireya backing away as I practically yelled at her. She texted me last night saying, *I'm sorry*, and eventually I texted back, *Me too, just need to sleep*, but I don't know if things can be the same between us.

Far away in Australia, Mom is adjusting to the new reality. Knowing, as I do, that we can never go back. "Oh, Hedda," she says.

"You should've told me." That seems to be my refrain now. "It's not normal for six-year-olds to hurt themselves like that."

Her breath comes faster, sharper, serving as confirmation, or close to it. The scars on my left forearm glisten in the California sun.

She says, "The moment I came into the kitchen and found you—doing *that*—is something I still have nightmares about. As a parent, it doesn't get worse. I think we've both spent the last ten years healing."

How could I heal from something I didn't know about, something she hid from me? "You should have told me about the game, too," I say, zeroing in on what I need to know.

"The game?"

"The Dark Web game called the Glare. The skull texts."

"Oh, those creepy texts you were getting on your tablet." Her voice tightens at the memory. "It was those two little friends who wouldn't stop tormenting you with nasty posts. After I talked to their parents, I thought things were over."

"Mireya and Lily didn't do that." The timeline is starting to come clear. "After I had a fight with them, after what happened to Caroline, I started playing the Glare. It wasn't just screens in general affecting me, Mom; it was *that* game. Did Caroline give it to me? Do you know?"

She makes a dismissive sound. "Hedda, there was no *one* game. You played anything you could get your hands on, but Caroline was a bad influence, yes. I'll never forget the night I came home after midnight and found her in your dad's study glued to some game on the big monitor, so zoned out she barely looked up when I spoke to her. Then I went upstairs and found you wide awake and playing a game on your tablet! I was only starting to understand the effects of the Glare, but that was the last time Caroline Westover ever sat for you."

I try to rein in my impatience. "Please don't say 'the Glare' when you're talking about the whole internet."

"But that was *your* word for it, Hedda, always. The Glare."

"I was a little kid!" I wonder if screens could affect me in a way they don't affect other people, making my brain go haywire like a bad smoke detector reacting to innocent grains of dust. But it wasn't just me. "I know how you feel about screens, Mom. And you're right—they're powerful. I can barely get Dad away from his phone long enough to notice I exist. But 'screens' didn't make Caroline hurt herself—or me. I think the Glare did."

I try to explain the legend of the Glare, pretending to know about it solely from my own memories and Mireya's googling. But when I get into the stuff about Randoms and dying thirteen times, she cuts me off: "Does it matter? Video games *all* reprogram you to crave them. Your friends' bullying isolated you, so you turned where you'd always turned—to a screen."

I stare out at the bay, fists clenching. *Please, Mom. Listen for once.*

But she goes right on: "It got to the point where just hearing a phone or tablet buzz would turn you into a nervous wreck.

You'd ask me to come look at another 'mean picture,' and there'd be nothing there—or only that skull."

Nothing there. She thinks it was just me, but it wasn't; it can't be. "How do you explain what happened to Caroline, though? She was sixteen, not six."

"Video game psychosis. Ask your dad—it's a real thing. Caroline's little brother used to come over and fill your ears with scary stories about her, which didn't help with your anxiety. You haven't been talking to him again, have you?"

Warm blood floods my face. "What happened to me wasn't Ellis's fault. He said *I* showed him the Glare."

"I don't know whose fault it was. I just know you spun a paranoid delusion, because that's what the Glare does—what screen culture does. It makes us scared, all the time."

She clears her throat, as if running out of steam now that I've stopped arguing with her. "I'm glad we're talking about this. All these years I've been afraid to tell you, worried about how you'd react—and yes, I know that makes me a coward. But will you promise me not to get too close to that Westover boy? I'm not saying he's a bad kid, but what happened with his sister threw him way off-kilter."

And there it is again. We're just *off-kilter*, all of us, from too many screens too young, and if she ever knew more about the Glare, she clearly doesn't now.

"I promise to avoid Ellis Westover," I say in a flat voice. If Mom were really listening to me, she could tell I'm lying.

. . .

"Dad!" I dash down the stairs as he opens the door, headed to the office on a Sunday afternoon. "Can you wait just a second?"

His shoulders hunch as if he's afraid I'll confront him again. "I've signed your forms, hon. Erika's got them."

"I know! Thank you." I feel almost guilty now. "I'm really excited about school tomorrow. I just wanted to ask you one thing. How well do you remember Caroline Westover?"

He blinks. "Your mom's intern."

"Intern?"

"She was your babysitter, too, of course." His head bobs toward the Westovers' house. "The girl who—"

"I know what she did! But I thought she was only the babysitter. She worked at your company?"

Dad rolls his shoulders. "At a company where your mom was moonlighting, actually. Sinnestauschen Labs. We were both working multiple jobs while we got our start-up off the ground."

"What did Caroline do there?" It's not like Mom to omit a detail, even a trivial one.

"From what Jane said, she was mainly a tester, but with a talent for design. After she hurt herself, your mom decided she suffered from video-game-related psychosis. That's when Jane started going to meetings of a screen-free group in the South Bay. It didn't take her long to decide you were in danger, too."

My throat tightens. "Did you believe that?" If he knows what I did to myself, then he must have worried about me.

But Dad only sighs and says, "You know your mom and I have different views on this. Why were you wondering about Caroline?"

"No reason. Just that I saw her brother yesterday." I want to ask him more about Caroline, but a voice deep inside me whispers, *Don't let him know you played the Glare. Don't let anyone know. It's our secret.* So instead I pat his arm awkwardly—he's wearing a T-shirt, no meetings today—and say, "Thanks again."

Going back upstairs, thinking about school, I skip every other step, and when I arrive at the top, my phone buzzes.

Seeing Mireya's name light up on the screen, I can't be mad anymore. I fit again, a piece of the world connecting to other people. The echoing emptiness retreats.

Hey, like I said, I'm sorry. Can I still drive you to school tomorrow?

I send her the most sheepish emoji I can find. *I'm the one who should be apologizing. How's Emily?*

Still in the ICU, but stable. Rory & Anil are coming over, you should too. See you on my porch round 10?

15

All the lights at Mireya's house are out, but someone's moving on the porch. As I cross the street, weed wafts through the air along with a deep male chuckle. Mireya calls, "Hedda?"

"Hedda!" It's Rory, sounding so friendly my heart leaps again. *Someone's happy to see me.*

They're huddled up there in the dark: Mireya and Rory in the porch swing with his head on her shoulder, and their friend Anil perched on the brick railing with a joint in one hand. "Hey," he says, offering it, his teeth flashing in a shy smile. "Join the party."

"No thanks." Their postures are tense and intimate at once, like they're waiting for something. I squat with my back against a pillar, feeling guilty for everything I said to Mireya last night. I still wish she'd told me about the Glare, but it's not her fault I can't dismiss the idea of an evil game as easily as she can.

"How's Emily doing?" I ask.

Rory and Mireya look at Anil, who says, "She had bleeding in her brain today—from the concussion. They're doing surgery to stop it."

"I'm so sorry." Is that the right thing to say? I want to ask if Emily was playing the Glare, but it's not the right time, and anyway, Mireya swore only Rory was. I can't start doubting her again when we're just making up.

"So, tomorrow, Hedda," Mireya says. "You gonna come experience the glory of San Rafael High with the rest of us normies?"

I nod, trying to look more casual than I feel. "Can't wait."

She plucks the joint from Rory's fingers. "Don't expect to have your mind blown or anything. School is bullshit."

"What's the big deal about school?" Anil asks.

"Her mom homeschooled her so she wouldn't use computers. Some technophobic weirdness." Mireya flicks something off Rory's forehead. "But now we're corrupting her."

An electronic burble slices the air, and all three of them go stock-still like they've seen a ghost. Anil fumbles in his jacket, pulls out his phone, and starts tapping it. After a moment, his shoulders go slack. "It's okay. Just my mom bugging me about driving my little sister to swim practice."

Mireya exhales audibly. "When did you last hear from Chey?"

"Around four, when they were prepping Emily. I don't know when it's supposed to be over." Anil pulls his knees up, trembling. Mireya stands up and starts rubbing his shoulders.

Rory inhales, the joint glowing. "It doesn't feel real," he says to me. "I mean, when it happened, I thought it was just like Ellis clowning around on the cliff. Like, she'd land on her feet and we'd laugh."

"I know." I press my back to the brick pillar like it's stopping me from falling off a cliff of my own. Ellis seemed so sure the skull text made Emily jump. But why would it affect her that way when I'm fine?

A pale figure emerges from the dark, jogging toward us on the sidewalk, the streetlight revealing coppery hair. *Speak of the devil.*

Ellis lopes up two porch steps and stops a few yards from us. "Hey." For an instant his eyes lock on mine. "Any news?"

"She's still in surgery." Rory holds out the joint toward him, a half-hearted motion.

"No thanks, dude. I'm training."

"Yeah?" Anil asks. "When's the meet?"

"Next week."

You were right, I could say to Ellis if we were alone. But I can tell from the others' postures, from the tone of Anil's voice, that they don't like him. Mom warned me away from him, too.

"Better get to it." Ellis jogs back down the steps. "See you guys tomorrow?"

"See you!" Mireya calls as he runs down the street, a tart note to her voice.

When he's out of earshot, Rory says, "Guess he's got a special training regimen. You see how wrecked he was last night?"

The others giggle. "He's been acting weird," Mireya says. "Laid some shit on Hedda about stuff from the past."

"Past?" Anil grimaces. "I thought Westover drowned at the bottom of a bottle of Jack and was reborn as a jock asshole."

"What did he do that's so bad?" I know why Mom hates Ellis—she wants to blame him for my off-kilterness—but they must have better reasons.

They share glances. "Ancient history," Mireya says. "We used to all hang out, but we were kind of dweebs—"

"*Are* kind of dweebs," Rory corrects.

"Right, and so was Ellis, but then he got shiny new friends, and he ditched us the night of Anil's fourteenth birthday party, and after that he ghosted us like we were the problem."

"That's the worst." Like I know anything about having friends beyond the fact that I don't want Mireya to hate me. Next time we're alone, I'll apologize for everything I said last night in depth, but for now I get up. "I should go."

"Already?" Rory sounds disappointed.

"I didn't get much sleep last night. You'll tell me if anything happens?"

"Absolutely," Mireya says. "Be here at seven thirty for your ride."

. . .

I don't know what to wear to a real high school. Erika's promised to take me shopping, but we haven't had a chance yet, so I try on outfit after outfit that stinks to me of ranch dust even though everything's been meticulously laundered.

Finally, frustrated, I sit down and search on the laptop for "what teenage girls wear to school this year." That leads to a lot of clothes I can't buy because I don't have a credit card and couldn't get in time for school tomorrow anyway, and next thing I know, I'm searching "Caroline Westover."

Articles scroll down the screen. Most are the kind with lots of pop-up ads and headlines that practically say, *Come look at the freak show!*

Caroline Westover, 16, injected Drano into both eyes with an eye dropper. Her affluent parents, who were attending a wine tasting in Napa Valley, had left her six-year-old brother in her care.

A neighbor, who spoke on condition of anonymity, said he heard Caroline repeating the words, "I can still see." In fact, according to Dr. Elias Sorkin of Marin General Hospital, the teen had virtually no vision following the accident, but he had confidence cataract operations would eventually restore some of her sight.

I click and click. Sixteen-year-old Caroline had springy copper curls, blue eyes like Ellis's, and a radiant, teasing smile. In one photo, she swans for the camera, showing off a white leather fringed purse.

An online rumor that Caroline participated in a "wannabe blind" community has not been substantiated. She has been admitted to a psychiatric ward, hospital officials said.

None of the stories mentions anything about a video game. Only this:

Staff at Sinnestauschen Labs, where Caroline interned two months before the incident, called her a talented aspiring game designer. Jane Vikdal, her former supervisor, said she trusted Caroline with testing experimental software.

Mom must have felt responsible for Caroline. I'm not surprised she didn't tell me about the internship, but I'm still disappointed. I'm tempted to call her right now and ask what "experimental software" means, but she'd probably just mutter something about getting unstuck from reality, assuming she hasn't already received my letter and hit the roof.

Instead, I search Sinnestauschen Labs. It still exists, "exploring the exciting nexus of entertainment and advertising, with a special emphasis on strategies for approaching the burgeoning gamer demographic."

Mom described her job a little differently, I remember: It was all about creating new ways to addict people. If Sinnestauschen was making addictive games, Caroline could have been testing them—games not available to the public. *This game killed its first tester,* the post from L13Survivor said.

But how would L13Survivor know that?

Maybe they're still out there. Why not ask *them* about Caroline?

I search through the pages Mireya showed me. L13Survivor posted most recently on r/weirdgames last year, offering the usual warning about the Glare: *This game will kill you.*

How can a game kill people? someone replied. *Are you saying it makes them kill themselves? Even if I thought the Glare existed, your little creepypasta would be impossible to prove.*

I don't care whether you believe me, L13Survivor shot back.

To which someone else replied, *this is ridikulus.*

I make an account and post my own reply to the thread:

I believe you. I might be a survivor, too, but I need proof. Can

you tell me if the Glare is connected to the case of Caroline Westover?
Was her mind deceived?

One of the many probably useless things I learned as part of my homeschooling curriculum was German. "Sinnestauschen" means "mind deception." If L13Survivor ever worked at Sinnestauschen Labs, they probably know that, too.

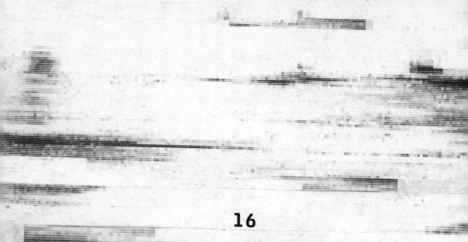

16

On the threshold of the school, I almost turn back. I can hear the tumult inside, like rising floodwaters, and I'm not ready, but Mireya takes my arm and says, "It's okay."

Inside, people are at high tide. They roar. They thunder. They stream past me, jostling me from all directions, while my eyes tear and I cling to Mireya like she's my life raft.

This is like the airport all over again, and though my own phone nestles in my pocket now, I'll never be ready. I see girls using phones as mirrors to fix their hair. Girls texting and talking at the same time, splitting their attention between two conversations. (How do you *do* that?) Too many people packed together under low corkboard ceilings, too many fluorescent lights and narrow windows, too many clothing and hair and piercing styles to keep track of.

All the curious glances make me feel like I'm dodging Randoms. Only now there's no gun or tower on my side, just Mireya's confidence and my own determined attempts to smile and be normal.

"Doing all right?" Mireya asks as we sit down in English class. She wears a full-skirted dress with a pattern of green onions.

"Sure." I stayed up too late checking for responses on the forum, but so far, nothing. Mireya must see the dark circles under my eyes. "What about you?" She told me on the way here that Emily's surgery was a success, but she's still in the ICU.

"Been better." Mireya twirls a pen. "Look, I've been thinking about some of the stuff you said on Saturday."

I shake my head, cutting her off. Somehow it's easier to have this conversation with other conversations buzzing around us, distractions waiting to happen. "I shouldn't have said those things. I was just freaked out."

"Of course! And I should have told you about the urban legend. I just want you to know I don't think you're a freak, Hedda. You grew up differently, so you react to things differently. I get that."

The room quiets, the teacher fiddling with something on her desk. Mireya's eyes are steady on mine, holding the connection. "When you said the game wouldn't let you play anymore, I should've asked if you got a skull. I should've explained everything. But I wussed out."

Warmth rises from my chest to my cheeks. "It's not your fault. I—"

I can't go on because Glare is exploding in my eyes, blinding me, swarming and buzzing and hissing. A big, blank screen has lit up at the front of the room—so big, too big. This is worse than the plane—why didn't someone warn me?

Then I blink and…it's just a screen like any other screen, nothing that can hurt me. A blankness for images to appear on. A tool.

"It's called a SMART Board." Mireya's hand finds mine across the aisle, squeezes it. "I'll show you how to use it. You okay?"

I squeeze back, embarrassed by my brief slip, hoping she didn't see how close I came, for a fraction of an instant, to my old fears. "I'm fine."

. . .

Fighting my way toward the cafeteria, I spot a flash of copper, head and shoulders riding above the crowd, backpack slumped to the elbows. Ellis stops at a locker, and I halt beside him, gathering my courage. "Hey."

"Hey, Heady Hedda!" He gives me an easy grin, the one I remember from the barbecue, as if the darker conversation after the beach party never happened. "What're you doing here?"

"I'm a junior, too!" I practically yell it, like a total goober.

Ellis keeps grinning, showing off his white teeth. "Yeah? Cool. Just don't eat the vegan protein loaf in the cafeteria. Somebody found a whole fingernail in it."

"I'm sorry about Saturday night." This is not the way I wanted to say it, but I can't keep putting it off. I inch toward him, lowering my voice. "I searched the Glare like you said to. I know about the legend now. Your sister—"

But his blue eyes are roaming away, lighting on a boy sporting a fade and an athletic jacket. "Hey, Jackson! You gonna pay up?"

I don't move while they exchange incomprehensible words—threats? encouragements?—and bump fists. This doesn't feel right. He doesn't want to talk about Caroline, or not at school. Maybe he doesn't want to talk to me, period.

Jackson drifts back into the stream. Ellis's eyes return to me, and I try to sound breezy as I say, "Anyway, I just wanted to say hi. I should go before Mireya thinks I'm lost."

His gaze feels too intense, like fire, so I turn on the last word and start walking, even as he calls, "Hey, Hedda!"

I can't tell if he's calling me back or dismissing me as I force my legs to move on down the hall, trying to ignore the empty feeling that seeps into me even here, where it's impossible to be alone. If Ellis wants to talk after all, I guess he can just climb my porch roof again.

Reaching the roaring, booming cafeteria, I teeter on the threshold, a weak swimmer in the shallows. *You don't belong here. They'll laugh,* says Mom's voice in my head, but I tighten my jaw and head toward Mireya, who's waving me over.

She sits with some of the people from the beach party—Lily, Lily's girlfriend, Anil, and Cheyenne, the girl who was talking with Emily about mochi right before it happened. Her stick-straight, corn-silk hair brings it all back. I dive into the seat Mireya offers me.

Cheyenne clears her throat, and I realize she was in the middle of telling a story. "Her parents were freaking," she goes on. "They hate him in the first place, and him coming high as a kite to her hospital room? It's disgusting."

135

"Liam's such a douche," Lily says. "Bet the cops are putting him under a microscope."

"He's gotta be the one who gave Emily the stuff," Anil suggests.

Lily shoots a wary glance at Cheyenne. "He could even have dosed her on purpose."

"You guys are so unbelievably suburban," says a boy with a buzz cut and a neck tattoo.

Cheyenne glares at him. "And why is that, Alton?"

"You just assume she was on something. According to Caleigh's cousin, the cop, there were no substances in Emily's system."

"Sober people don't jump off cliffs." Lily's girlfriend's voice squeaks a little. "And who texted her the creepy skull? Do they even know?"

The skull. It's like having my midnight fears thrust into the fluorescent glow of the cafeteria. "Is Emily a gamer?" I blurt out.

Mireya gives me a warning look, but it's too late. Cheyenne's blue death glare has redirected itself to me.

"Who are *you*?" she asks. "Do you even know her?"

Heat spreads on my face. "No. But I mean, that text. That . . . skull." I look to Mireya for support, but she's staring down at her bag lunch. "It's from a game."

Cheyenne thrusts her chair back. "My friend just got out of surgery, and you're asking me about her *hobbies*." She spits out the word. "And the rest of you—you're gossiping about this like it's a Very Special Episode. Like it's not even real." Tears gleam in her eyes as she grabs her tray. "Well, she is. So fucking spare me your amateur detective work."

My lunch turns to a stone in my stomach as she stalks off, leaving everybody looking at me. I've said the exact wrong thing again, and she's right—I have no place here.

Mireya coughs nervously. "Sorry about that, Hedda. She's super on edge."

"They're best friends," Lily says, not looking at me. "I can't even imagine how Chey must feel right now."

The rest of lunch takes place in near-silence, everyone busy on their phones. Mireya says she needs to redo her lipstick and runs off to the restroom, leaving me puzzling over the proper distribution of lunch waste into trash, compost, and recycling bins.

"Hey," someone says.

It's Anil, with his wrestler's chest and movie-star eyelashes. I flinch, but his smile is still shy, not mean or mocking, as he says, "Sorry about what went down back there."

Cheeks burning, I unzip my backpack and pretend to do an inventory of the contents. "My fault. I was totally inappropriate." *Weird. A freak.*

"About that, though." Anil follows me out into the hall, his paces a little shorter than mine. "How'd you know to ask about games? Are you playing the Glare?"

I stop short, letting people and noise stream around us. "*You* know about that?"

"I got it from Rory. Did you?"

Words jam themselves up in my throat. I don't want him to know it came originally from me, don't want anyone to know who doesn't already. "So, you're playing it. And Emily—"

Anil makes a quick check of the area, then leans in. "Emily and me—well, I had a crush on her for a while. Her parents are

137

super strict, made her study all the time, so I'd bring her games to help her de-stress. Her folks thought they were addictive, so she used to joke and say I was her pusher."

He looks almost proud, as if Emily's gaming habits were an intimate secret between them. "So, yeah, I gave her the Glare. I thought she'd get a kick out of the whole 'death game' thing. I didn't think she'd actually play it, because it asks for your phone number, and Emily's fanatical about privacy. But that text...you have to play to a high level to get the skull, right?"

The colors of the crowded hallway run together, voices turning to sharp-edged shrieks and liquid burbles. I see the whole chain now: I stole the address of the Glare from Caroline and gave it to Mireya, who gave it to Rory, who gave it to Anil, who gave it to Emily.

But if the Glare really does hurt people, why was Emily affected first? Was she the first to hit level 13? I assumed I was, since Mireya's pretty much lost interest in the game, but maybe not.

Even if Emily did get a skull first, I haven't been affected yet. Did Emily get an awful picture that disappeared, the way I did?

I remember how naive Mireya thought I was for believing the L13Survivor posts, and my throat tightens as I ask, "Have you? Gotten the skull?"

A game is a game. A myth is a myth. Technology gives us what we bring to it.

As Anil starts to answer, commotion jars me out of the haze. A chilly voice says, "Would you kindly move it?"

It's Cheyenne, walking with her eyes on her phone. Guiltily, we both step clear of her—me backing into the lockers, while Anil darts down a side corridor. "Gotta go. See you, Hedda!"

"Wait!" But when he pauses, looking back, the words die in my throat. If I tell him to stop playing, he'll think what Cheyenne does: that there's something wrong with me.

I duck my head and turn away. "See you later."

17

"How's the homework going?" Erika asks, pausing in the middle of prepping food for the grill. "Manageable?"

I mutter, "A salmon-pink cardigan sweater is stalking me."

She stares, so I explain: It started last night with my search for school clothes. Stumbling into a fashion blog, I clicked on a pair of shiny riding boots, which took me to a sweater sale, which took me to the cardigan with its pretty pearl buttons. Now, wherever I go, it seems to be waiting for me. I keep clicking away, and sometimes I think I've shaken it, but it always pops up again.

"It sounds stupid, I know." I have no words for the unease I felt creeping over my scalp when I was at the laptop: a feeling of being known, described, watched.

"It's not stupid." Erika opens a plastic container of pearl

onions, already peeled. "Hedda, I think you're having a bit of culture shock. What happened at that party Saturday didn't help."

"I guess not." Shock? I feel like I've wolfed down an enormous meal without digesting it, words still inadequate to express the strange, sudden girth of my new life.

"Do you want to talk about it?"

"There's not much to say. I didn't even know her." I told Erika about Emily when I got home, because I trusted her not to freak out or forbid me to leave the house or anything Mom might have done, and she didn't. "Thanks for not telling Dad. So, how do I get rid of the sweater?"

As I thread three skewers with beef and onions and pepper chunks, Erika explains how advertisements track you like you're leaving a trail of breadcrumbs in the online forest, only the breadcrumbs are called "cookies." "They want to squirm into your consciousness until you finally break down and buy something. And once you do that, it won't be over—they'll keep trying to entice you back. When you click that buy button, it gives you a little burst of endorphins—a high, just like when you beat a level in a game or get a good response to a post. The marketers will keep dangling rewards in front of you till you come back for more of the good feeling. That's how they hook you."

Just like when you beat a level in a game. I think of the Glare's texts with safe trees in them—enticing me back—and then the skull. Mom was right about one thing—that game hooked me. I still want the routine of running to the tower and fueling up my gun, the certainty of aiming for the next level. I want those rune trees on my phone. I even miss the Randoms. The terror of death by Random should have kept me from playing, but instead it made me want to beat the game, to feel that rush over and over.

By the time Erika's explained how to make the sweater vanish, I barely care anymore. I prick the skin of a green pepper chunk over and over, watching the juice bleed out.

"I don't know if Mom's ever going to forgive me," I say. "For where I was today. For everything I've done."

Worry flits across Erika's face. "I'm sorry. Maybe this was all a bad idea—"

"No. It had to happen sooner or later."

Erika lines up a chicken breast and plucks a knife from the butcher's block. Plunges the blade into petal-pink flesh. "My mom wanted me to live at home for college," she says. "She was terrified that if I didn't, I'd move in with a boy. But I couldn't stay in that house one more year with her always watching me."

"What did you do?"

"I ended up working myself through school and moving in with *three* boys—as platonic roommates."

I imagine Mom's face if she ever saw me with a cell phone, or playing the Glare. "Did you ever regret it?"

"Never. It took a while for Mom to deal with me being me, but we're okay now."

"But how did you *show* her? I mean, that living with boys wouldn't hurt you?"

Erika sections the chicken breast into neat cubes. "I don't think it's a question of showing or proving. Best-case scenario, you can meet each other halfway, and then you both just agree to...love each other anyway."

I remember how I felt after the chess game with Dad, like

I was threading a needle. With Erika, it's different. I don't have to convince her of anything; I can let myself breathe, here in the safe warmth of the kitchen where copper-bottomed skillets glint on the walls.

It's a relief after the chaos of school, all those strangers looking at me. Mireya says not to mind about Cheyenne. I didn't tell her I was right about Emily and the game, though, because she might think I'm getting weird again.

"Thanks," I say.

"For what?"

"For being here."

A sly smile curves Erika's lips. "If you really want to thank me, go play a game with Clint while I get some e-mails done. I think he'd like to teach you."

Clint's educational game turns out to be surprisingly exciting. He shows me how to use his console, and twenty minutes later, he's yelling, "Eat the pomegranate. The pomegranate!" while I work the controller, dodging a hideous violet *Staphylococcus*. Just in time, I reach the pomegranate and mash the button to ingest its vitamin C.

Too late—an orange bacterium with magenta cilia corners me where the maze dead-ends. My character dies loathsomely, drowned in cytoplasm.

I flop back on Clint's beanbag chair, fighting an intense, unexpected feeling that I can only describe as missing an inanimate object and an imaginary world. *I want the Glare back. I wasn't finished with it.* "You said this game was easy."

For the first time since I've known him, my brother looks like he's suppressing a grin. "Restart. You'll get better."

I'm already hitting the restart button, the urge to beat the level itching at me like an old war wound. I know this feeling—the dry eyes, the shoulders achy from hunching, the absolute concentration.

Bacteria aren't Randoms, and this silly maze that's supposed to represent the human digestive system isn't my forest or my tower, but it'll have to do. The maze pops up again, and I'm off—dashing, flitting, hitting the button till it rattles. No matter how much I nourish my little avatar, I feel empty.

When I die again, inches from a broccoli floret, Clint asks, "Want to do multiplayer?"

We play as a team for a while, his avatar running out ahead and clearing a path for mine until we start working like a single unit rather than two separate ones. "You're good," Clint says in his matter-of-fact way.

"Thanks." *But not good enough to beat level 13.* I recline in the beanbag again, starting to feel tired of the game and its good-nutrition preaching, and examine the stuffed animals lined up on Clint's bookshelf. "Why's there a blindfold on your panda?"

"What? Oh, him." Clint hops up on the bed and tugs the red bandanna off the bear's button eyes, looking sheepish. "He shouldn't have that."

"But why?"

"I was watching a *Goosebumps* movie a *long* time ago—years, I think—and Po doesn't like to be scared." He fixes me hard in the eye. "I mean, I know he's not real now, obviously. But back then I wanted to make sure he wouldn't see."

. . .

L13Survivor hasn't responded to my message. A few anonymous people are jeering at me for believing the Glare legend, calling me stupid and gullible. No one has anything to say about Caroline.

I've studied enough of these forums now to know that the more L13Survivor warns people to avoid the Glare, the more they'll beg and bully, demanding a link. It's forbidden fruit, and everybody wants a taste. But maybe that's only because they're like Mireya, not believing.

Something clanks downstairs. An AC duct hums, vibration rising from the soles of my feet.

My phone buzzes, and the room goes still, sound sucked from the world till I can hear blood pumping in my ears. *I'm connected. Not alone.* It's obviously Mireya, it's always her, but...

But L13Survivor says the skulls keep coming until you hurt yourself or someone else. As I remember that skull on my screen, the clouds forming gaping eyes and fleshless cheeks, something white flits in the corner of my vision. *Just the curtains.*

I get up to check for a breeze outside, but the air is stiflingly still. On the porch roof, a pale pool of moonlight flickers against dark shingles. No Ellis tonight.

I drop the curtain, balling my fists. If I ask Rory and Anil to stop playing the Glare, will they laugh at me the way Mireya did? Will they want the forbidden fruit even more?

I died thirteen times on level 13, and I'm fine.

I plop down on the bed, scoop up Raggedy Ann, and examine the snipped fabric where her eyes should be. Clint blindfolded his panda to keep it from seeing what he was afraid to see. I close my eyes and try to imagine myself six years old, sitting in that desk chair and playing a game I wasn't supposed to play, full of scary monsters that ambushed and throttled and suffocated me.

I lie in bed, Ann tight to my chest. The computer screen is dark, but the darkness is full of... things. Every time I drift toward sleep, I almost hear something, and then I open my eyes and almost see something. I can close my eyes, but Ann has no eyelids, so she has to see it all.

Is that a real memory, or just imagination? I'm shuddering, hugging the doll so hard she seems to have become part of my body. The phone buzzes again.

Adrenaline surges through me, warm and angry. *Not again.* I drop Ann and go grab the phone.

There's a text from Mireya, just checking in, and a new e-mail alert. Reminding myself to figure out how to turn off all these notifications I thought I wanted, I click to a message from someone named Clelia Rosenbaum.

The subject line is "Sinnestäuschen." And for a moment I seem to be falling, the wind whistling and keening in my ears.

The ground hardens under my feet again, and the glowing letters resolve themselves into words.

I saw your forum post. I know about the lab and Caroline, yeah. If you're playing, STOP.

*S*omewhere, *in a room ironically illuminated by a red lava lamp, a boy has died thirteen times on level 13.*

So that's all there is to it. I'm dead. *Feeling satisfied and let down at once, he takes a screenshot of the "death message," e-mails it to a friend (with strict instructions not to post it anywhere; he promised), clicks to another window, and waits.*

He knows what to expect. First the skull, then the text that says simply, Ur pathetic. *He has screenshots of both texts Emily got, thanks to her friend Cheyenne, so he can compare them. Maybe Emily really was playing the game, though Mireya swears she didn't give it to her.*

He doesn't want to believe the Glare made Emily jump off a cliff. But if there's even a sliver of truth to the legend, if he can document it, he'll become a legend himself. He needs to know, and he's not afraid.

His phone vibrates at last, and here's the skull, right on schedule. His heart skips a beat, then subsides. He writes down the time so he can figure out how many seconds it took.

He's read all about game-induced hallucinations, ranging from ghostly menus to Tetris blocks floating in midair. The brain is good at fooling itself. But those flimsy apparitions never killed anyone.

His phone vibrates a second time.

He reaches for it, knowing exactly what to expect, and sees—no, that's not possible. The leering Joker avatar is so painfully familiar it makes his throat close.

SirGanksalot hasn't contacted him for nearly three years, not since that disastrous failed raid when they had a blowup and Ganksalot turned into a troll and called him words he doesn't like to remember. His face used to burn whenever he thought about it, and he deleted his account and never played that game again.

But there it is, the hated avatar, right beside the exact words the boy was expecting: Ur pathetic. *Restricted number.*

Why's Ganksalot after him now? Does he know about the Glare? Is he using it to take some kind of nasty little revenge?

The phone goes dark, and the boy stands up, his heart zooming from zero to sixty. There's a staticky rush in his ears, like a dead radio station or a high wind in dry leaves. It grows louder as he sees a luminous flicker just inside the closet.

He's in there, something inside him says, though that makes no sense. SirGanksalot could live anywhere, be anybody. There's no reason to think he's become a psycho stalker.

The boy yanks back the folding doors, tosses aside the piles of fallen clothes. Nothing. Well, of course nothing. That second text, though.

When he picks up the phone again to check, he finds only the skull followed by the words Ur pathetic. *His enemy's avatar is gone like it never existed, but he knows he saw it. It wasn't his imagination.*

Somewhere in the distance, he hears keening.

18

All the screens are starting to bother me.

Nearly every teacher uses a SMART Board, and for some classes we use laptops and tablets, and between classes it's phones, phones, all the time. My eyes itch from staring into the bluish light, and when I refocus on real things, my vision blurs.

Right now I'm focusing on a girl in a cheerleader uniform who glances back and forth, from her phone to Ellis Westover, as he talks between bites of fries. He's got that lazy grin I remember from the barbecue, like nothing he's saying is serious. She has full lips and a waterfall of auburn hair, and when she reaches out and rubs the scruff of Ellis's neck almost absentmindedly, I tense.

Anil is staring at them, too. "Shit, did Westover bag Jerusha Pierce?"

Mireya bonks him on the head with *Hard Times*. "Sexist language. Maybe she bagged him!"

"I'm sorry, I'm just in awe that that dude ever hung out with us."

"His loss," Mireya says, while Lily offers, "I have it on good authority that guys aren't Jerusha's thing."

On the way out of the cafeteria, Ellis and the cheerleader drift apart, and he heads to his locker. I walk past him with my head down, wishing Mireya weren't off doing her post-lunch makeup routine.

A tap on my shoulder makes me swing around—and there he is, his face sober and focused now, no trace of the grin, an oxford shirt hanging out of his jeans. "Hey! You ran away yesterday like somebody was after you."

Blood rushes to my cheeks. "You seemed busy."

"You said something about Caroline." His voice lowers on her name, and it's like we're back on my porch, alone in the dark. "Did you remember something more about her and the game?"

He edges back to his locker, where we're out of the crowd, and I follow like he's pulling me on a string. I can't help it—I need to talk about this without getting one of Mireya's lectures on my internet naivete. "No memories. But...I've heard that Emily actually was playing."

I'm half-afraid Ellis will try to make me rat out Anil, but he just says, "Figured. You and Mireya, you've stopped, right?"

I nod. "It won't let me play anymore, remember? But I've only had the one skull text, and nothing's happened to me."

"Good." He says it the way someone might say "yet." "Could anybody else be playing?"

Anil. Rory. I know Rory the best, but I can already tell he won't listen to me; he's playing *because* of the legend. Maybe they both are. How do you fight that? "I don't think so," I say guiltily. "But listen, I've been doing some research. Did you know your sister used to be my mom's intern?"

Ellis shakes his head. "I knew she had some internship, but not where."

"A place called Sinnestauschen Labs." I explain about my forum inquiry, then take out my phone and show him Clelia Rosenbaum's e-mail.

Ellis's brow corrugates as he reads. "Who do you think that is—this Clelia person?"

"No idea."

His expression continues to darken as I explain what Sinnestauschen does and how Caroline tested software there. "Maybe the Glare is something the lab invented, a game designed to addict people, and Caroline was the first to test it." It's making more and more sense in my head: If a game made Caroline hurt herself, wouldn't she want to warn other people? But anonymously, so they wouldn't think she was crazy and lock her up again. "Maybe your sister *is* L13Survivor."

Ellis shoves books in his pack. "She can't be—I've seen those forum posts. They started when Caroline was locked in the psych ward without internet access."

"Okay, so maybe it's not her. But when we were six, I got the Glare address from Caroline—you said that yourself. Which means that, if she's out there somewhere, she could be—"

"She's out there." He clips the words too sharply. "She might even be reading that forum."

"You think?" I'm surprised he isn't resisting my theory anymore. "Do you know if she left stuff in her room like, I don't know, files? Notes?"

"She wiped her devices before she . . . got hurt, and all she left were paper diaries and scrapbooks. I read them—standard teenage girl stuff. Nothing about 'Whoops, I tested a killer game and accidentally gave it to a kid.'"

"I'm not trying to blame your sister, Ellis. I know you don't want to talk about her."

"When did I ever say that?" The late bell rings, and Ellis hoists his pack onto one shoulder. "She's not L13Survivor, Hedda. But I don't think L13Survivor sent you that message."

"Who did, then?"

Ellis leans down, his face abruptly inches from mine, so I can see his now-faint freckles.

"Clelia Rosenbaum was a lady who used to clean our house when I was little," he says. "She was at least seventy. Caroline loved her. She always said if she became a spy and needed an alias, she'd use Clelia's name."

. . .

Caroline read my forum post. Caroline sent me a message warning me away from the Glare. I'm still trying to absorb it as the last bell rings and I follow Mireya down the corridor, dodging groups of kids who are wearing face paint and chanting about beating some rival team.

She was always just the faceless heroine of a gruesome cautionary tale—"the babysitter." Now she's real. I need to write her back, but there are too many questions to ask. What if I scare her away?

Lily nearly barrels into us, phone in hand, her hoodie half on and her backpack unzipped. Mireya grabs her by the shoulders to stop her forward momentum. "Look where you're going, girl!"

Then she must see, as I do, how wide and scared Lily's eyes are, because she asks, "Emily?"

Lily's gaze darts to me, then back to Mireya. She looks like she ran all the way to us, her small frame straining with the effort of each breath, and now words burst from her:

"Her dad—he had his phone in the hospital room. He got a text, and Emily went berserk. She grabbed the phone and smashed it, like to *bits* smashed it, and then she got out of bed and tried to crawl out of the ward dragging her broken leg, screaming and crying the whole time. It took three nurses to get her down and give her a shot, and now she's in restraints."

Lily stops for breath with a gulp, leaning back into the arm Mireya's wrapped around her shoulders. Her eyes glisten with tears, and I feel mine filling, too.

"Shit," Mireya says. "I thought they said she'd be okay."

"Me too." Lily sniffles and rubs her eyes. "Cheyenne thinks it was her dirtbag boyfriend's fault for trying to visit her. He wasn't in the room, but the whole time she was yelling at him to leave her alone, to stop texting her. And she was *scared*, Chey says. Like an ax murderer was after her."

19

"I love it," Erika says as I twist in the mirror, savoring the strange feeling of a filmy skirt against my legs. "That color brings out the pink in your cheeks."

She's right; I look more like the girls at school now. Like I actually care. I have a sudden urge to blow-dry my hair into sleekness and put on lipstick like Mireya. "It's not something I could ever wear on the ranch, though."

"So maybe it can be your going-to-town dress."

No one wears dresses in our town, Mom reproaches in my head, but I ignore her. I follow Erika to the register, where it turns out she was right: Buying things gives me a little high. Even when I'm not paying. The glint of the track lighting and the rustle of the shiny bag are almost enough to make me forget the terror in Lily's eyes earlier this afternoon.

But not quite.

I want to say I'll get a job and pay Erika back, or something like that, but I'm starting to understand that sometimes you just have to say thank you and let it be, so that's what I do.

We go to the food court and have fancy coffees with whipped cream, just the way I imagined when I was on the plane. Then Erika goes to pick up a leather jacket she had cleaned, leaving me in charge of Clint, who's been practically sleeping upright through the clothes shopping.

When he realizes we're alone, he wakes up with a vengeance. "Come on!" he yells, running down the high-ceilinged corridor.

"Wait!" I dump my cup in the trash and dash after him.

The corridor jolts me from light into greenish shadow and back. Each store beckons distractingly with its own perfume and music, its own seductive twilight, as I zigzag between groups of ladies with shopping bags.

"Slow down!" I yell, keeping my eye on Clint's green hoodie. I'm winded by the time I catch up with him, in front of a store with cardboard cutouts and giant screens in the window. One screen shows a disembodied hand shooting a machine gun, sending groups of Nazi soldiers flying in clouds of dirt and blood.

A shiver slides down my spine. "You know I don't have any money to buy you games, right?"

Clint doesn't spare a glance for me, his eyes glued to the moving images. "I'd never buy anything at a *store*. I just want to see the demo on a bigger screen."

Cotton-candy hair catches my eye. It's Rory—only a few yards from us, wearing a Sbarro uniform and holding his phone up to his face tilted lengthwise, the way you do to take a picture.

"I need to say hi to a friend, okay?" I squeeze my brother's shoulder.

"Your boyfriend?"

"No!" Rory's still peering intently through the camera—facing me, but not aiming at me. I make my way over to him, trying to think of a way to ask him to stop playing the Glare without sounding like a bossy weirdo.

Rory's lips move. As I approach, he lowers the phone screen, but only a few inches. "Hey!"

"Hey." I take a deep breath. "I guess you heard about Emily."

His shoulders tighten, and his eyes flicker behind his glasses as if he's monitoring something over my shoulder. "Yeah. At least she's got good supervision, there in the hospital. They won't let her hurt herself again."

"Right." Rory's still looking at me sidelong through the camera, and it makes me uneasy. I want to ask him to put it down. "Are you, uh, making a video?"

"Nah." Rory gives a little start. "Shit! There it is again."

He begins to walk briskly. Clint is still hovering by the game store window, so I snag him by his hood, ignoring his protests, and drag him along with us.

I have an odd feeling Rory shouldn't be alone. "What are you looking at?"

"You wouldn't believe it, Hedda."

I glance where he's aiming the phone and see only sad potted palms, storefronts, and middle-aged women toting crinkly bags. "Rory, I need to ask you about something. Are you still playing the Glare?"

"Ha, no. Take a look. If you *can* see it—you probably can't."

He holds out the phone to me and laughs, sounding nervous and giddy at once. "This is a trip!"

I peer over Rory's shoulder, keeping my hold on Clint. The jewel-bright screen shows the exact same corridor, only smaller and farther away. "What am I looking for?"

His shoulder jerks, and he backs into me, stabbing the screen. "Right there. He was *just* there. Did you see?"

"What? I mean, who?"

Rory begins to walk again. "Halfway up that potted palm, and then gone. He does that. Teases me."

"Rory." I stare at the potted palm, wondering if this is some kind of joke. "I don't see anything. Who's 'he'?"

We're almost at an exit, the glass wall flooded with sunlight. Rory squints through it. He goes rigid, breath coming fast. "I think he's outside now. Shit! I can't lose him."

"Lose who?" Still hauling Clint, I follow Rory out through the sliding doors.

"He's playing a game," Clint says, as if this should be boringly obvious.

"But I don't *see* anything."

I dodge around Rory to look through the camera again, almost expecting to see a skull. There's nothing in the viewfinder but sunlight, asphalt, parked cars, bottlebrush trees.

He's playing a prank on me. Unless—

"Hedda," Rory says, "Mireya said you made it to level thirteen. You should know what I'm talking about."

No. Goose pimples break out all over me, and I tug Clint closer. "Level thirteen? But you shouldn't. I mean, did you? Did you get a skull?"

"Don't worry, I won't post the link." Rory gazes off into the parking lot. "I think I understand how it works now. Why Emily reacted that way. It's some kind of hypnotic game transfer phenomenon, but it plays like the most amazing mixed-reality experience I've ever had."

"I don't understand. What do you think Emily saw?"

"Something she didn't want to see. It doesn't really matter what." For the first time this afternoon, Rory turns to meet my gaze. His pupils are blown, and his whole face looks younger somehow. "You know that feeling when every alert you get on your phone makes you want to die? So you turn it off, but then you just want to die more, so you turn it on again?"

"I don't know." Then I remember how I felt when my phone buzzed twice last night with alerts and I was almost too scared to check it. "Maybe."

"I think that's what happens when the Randoms perma-kill you." Rory's voice has a dreamy note now. "It tells you *Ur pathetic,* and you go to the epic fail circle of hell, where you relive your worst online fail, over and over."

Clint squirms. My eyes scour the parking lot—still nothing there, or nothing that could possibly make sense of what Rory's saying.

Then I remember the image of me with horns—the image that vanished, or never existed at all. Is that my worst fail? "But what are you *seeing*? Is it even real?"

"To you it is." A strange expression passes over Rory's face, like he's seeing something grotesque and wonderful at once, and he bends and whispers in my ear, "Just don't freak out. I think that's the key. If you run from what you see, it'll come after you. You have to face it head-on."

Then he straightens, brandishing the phone. "Over there. Gotta go!"

He steps off the curb into the path of a cream-colored Lexus. I yell, "Stop!"

The Lexus squeals to a halt with an aggrieved honk. Rory canters obliviously off across the parking lot, weaving among the cars.

I start to follow, but Clint squirms free and heads back through the cloudy reflections on the glass doors. Just inside, Erika stands looking baffled, with the jacket draped over one arm and the other lugging bags. "Where were you?"

"Just talking to a friend."

I watch Rory make his way across the lot. He keeps pausing to peer through the viewfinder, and twice he ducks as if hiding from an invisible observer.

If you run from what you see, it'll come after you. I saw something terrifying in the living room doorway when I was a child. I felt fingers close around my wrist on the plane. I saw a photo that wasn't there. But Rory's talk about a new circle of hell only half makes sense to me.

"He's playing a game," Clint says authoritatively. "He said level thirteen."

"His screen didn't show anything." I scrutinize my brother. "Did *you* see something?"

Clint clings to his mother's hand and doesn't answer.

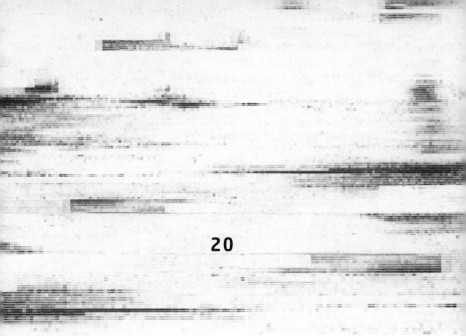

20

"What's 'mixed reality'?" I ask Dad.

"Who told you about that?"

"A friend."

"A cute friend?" Erika shoots me a shy smile. She sits touching elbows with Dad, wearing a flowered sundress, both of them relaxed in a way I haven't seen before.

To celebrate the first week of school, Dad left work early so we could all go to a movie. "They're running it on thirty-five and not digital, so your mom won't mind," he told me with a wink, then explained about the different kinds of projection.

We walked under trees strung with lights to the downtown theater, where we watched a black-and-white movie about a haunted house. I kept having to close my eyes and remind myself it wasn't real. Scary books I can deal with, but seeing a ghost float through a hallway or hearing it rap on a wall made me jump every time.

Now, sitting on the outdoor terrace of the ice cream shop, I still feel woozy from my jangled nerves, like one of the surfers at Stinson Beach after a wipeout.

"In mixed reality, real and digital objects interact," Dad says. "Very hot field in the gaming and simulations industry. So, for instance, if you were looking through your phone, and you saw a sparkly purple goblin sitting right there"—he indicates the nearest table—"it would be mixed reality. Either that, or you've gone batshit."

I wince. Someone called Emily that.

Erika nuzzles against Dad and reprimands him for his language. Deprived of his phone and tablet for the evening, Clint is busy ramming a tray of sugar packets against a saltshaker and making *boom smash* noises.

"Mike," Erika asks, "have you called Marnie Golden yet? The Realtor?"

They start talking about some property that Erika wants Dad to sell so they can have more "liquidity." I half listen, watching Clint shoot a finger gun across the terrace.

"I'm zapping the purple goblin," he tells me.

I point my own finger gun. "Bam bam! You're dead."

Clint giggles. "I'm beating level thirteen."

Did he pick that up from Rory? "There's no level thirteen," I say sharply.

Clint drops his eyes, and I feel a pang of guilt.

Erika complains that the property up north is going to waste, but Dad assures her they won't need extra cash once he signs the contracts on his latest project. "Don't worry, I can feed the college funds and still cover the day-to-day."

My head jerks up. Funds plural? Is he planning to send me to college for real?

Erika pats my hand. "Are you okay, Hedda? You jumped about a dozen times during the movie."

My face goes hot, because no one else seemed scared, not even Clint. But I know the experience will stay with me, disturbing my sleep, if I don't talk about it. "It was just... once you were inside that house, it felt like there was no outside. It was like being in hell. Where would anyone get an idea like that? Why would they put it up on a screen for everybody to see?"

"I wonder that myself," Erika says, while Dad says, "To exorcise inner demons."

"What does that mean?" I think of my Glare dreams. Maybe Dad would understand, since he used to have nightmares, too.

But his eyes have that glazed look they always get when he stops listening to me. "Like you said, when you're stuck inside a nightmare, you forget there's an outside. Maybe when you put your nightmare outside you, when you turn it into a book or movie, it loses the power to hurt you."

"That movie wasn't scary. It was a million years old," Clint announces with the assurance of a professional critic. "But I liked the part where the giant hand came out of the closet and grabbed the professor."

"Like this?" Dad pretends to give Clint a lethal handshake. Clint spread-eagles and fakes a backward plunge off his chair. An ache hatches in my chest as I try to imagine Dad ever being that relaxed with me.

But when he releases Clint, he turns to me, his eyes going wistful. "Remember our Sunday-afternoon double features, Hedda? Every week while your mom went to yoga, we fired up my old DVDs."

"You forced your childhood favorites on her?" Erika teases.

"I had to make sure my daughter grew up with good taste." Dad's looking at me like his head is full of fond memories of us making popcorn and watching screens.

Mine isn't, but I say, "I remember."

"My proudest moment as a parent—well, one of them—was when your mom and I were having a stupid argument, and you quoted the classic line from *WarGames*: 'The only winning move is not to play.'"

Not to play. I should have followed my own advice. I wonder if Rory's still off chasing invisible things in his viewfinder, maybe still in that same parking lot, and hairs prickle on the back of my neck.

Dad keeps on gazing at me like he's seeing a different version of me—young, impressionable, eager to love all the things he loves. A version I could still be.

"And you were right," he says. "We wasted so much time playing games we couldn't win that we—I—lost track of the things that mattered."

. . .

While Erika takes Clint up to bed, I find Dad in the kitchen. He's making coffee, which means he's headed back to the office, though it's nearly ten.

I fiddle with a small brush he's left on the table, its soft bristles bleeding dirt-like grounds. "Dad, I'm still wondering about Caroline Westover. Why did Mom think she had video game psychosis?"

Dad removes a steaming kettle from the burner and places it on a pad. "Confirmation bias. Once Jane started thinking technology was dangerous, she saw evidence of it everywhere."

"But Caroline *was* an aspiring game designer, right?" I paint my wrist with the brush, the dark grounds outlining fine hairs. "The newspaper articles said she was testing software. Was it a game?"

Dad trickles hot water into a plastic cylinder, careful as someone doing a chemistry experiment. "At the time, Sinnestauschen was working on native advertising that could be embedded in free games. I only know what your mother told me, but apparently Caroline had an idea—a game that would condition players to associate particular images with good feelings and then use text messages to bring those associations into their daily lives."

My skin starts to crawl. "What kind of images?"

"Well, like product logos. For her prototype, she used random images—Norse runes, I think. But the theory was that, if you could get players to associate a company's logo with safety and winning, they'd be more likely to respond to that company's ads."

Runes carved on trees, marking them as safe. "How'd the game work? Do you know?"

"It was supposed to be a first-person survival horror game. According to Jane, the idea was to evoke fear, our most primal reaction, so players would feel an equally powerful need for safety.

Fear puts people in a suggestible state"—he chuckles—"as all politicians know."

Power of suggestion. "You mean, like, the game would hypnotize the players?"

"Now you're back to your mom's mind-control theory. Nothing that radical is possible, believe me. But you can nudge people in one direction or another."

Dad presses the plunger on top of the cylinder, holding it down, and the hot liquid inside seethes and hisses into his cup. The sound seeps into me, becoming a rushing in treetops, a slither in dry leaves.

Could Caroline have put her own nightmares into the Glare? Did she free herself that way?

"Did Caroline ever actually make this game?" I ask.

Dad holds the cylinder over the trash and gives it a sharp tap. A disc of wet grounds tumbles out. "No idea. Maybe your mother knows, but I have a feeling she wouldn't want you even knowing enough to ask these questions. Is there a reason you keep wondering about Caroline?"

If I tell him I played the Glare again, he'll tell Mom. I tug my sleeves down, covering the scars. "Just curious, I guess."

. . .

My fingers are poised over the keyboard. There are so many things I want to know, to ask. *Are you Caroline? Did you create the Glare? Did my mom know about what you were doing, and what it did to you, and take me away so that would never happen to me? If*

166

I can't trust what I think I see with my own eyes, any more than you could, what do I do?

In the end I don't write anything. But before I go to bed, I hide my phone in the closet where it can vibrate all it wants, and I won't hear.

. . .

I stand in a green forest dotted with red, the square black tower rising above me.

The sky is gray. Wind thrashes the trees, a storm rising, and I run for the tower. Where's Ellis? He needs me; he always does, and maybe I need him, too.

My shoes dig into the forest floor, soggy with fallen leaves. Despite the roar of the treetops, I can hear things moving in there—slithering, sliding.

A boy rockets toward me, legs a blur. Not Ellis, but Rory. "They're coming!" he cries.

"What? I don't see anything!" Now the eerie keening rises above the wind, coming from all sides at once. "Find a safe tree, quick!"

The forest floor begins to swell around Rory, like giant worms are burrowing in the dead leaves. He staggers to a stop as the furrow grows—circling him, penning him in. He tries to take a step, and—

A cry. A flash of white. The wind sends leaves swirling high in the air.

Fighting the storm, I run toward Rory, twigs and needles

167

stinging my face. As I reach the spot where he should be, the wind falls. The forest goes silent as a church.

My blood pumps like thunder.

I find a great ocher pile of leaves and pine needles, and in the center, a pale living hand. It flaps desperately, fingers scrabbling for purchase on the forest floor.

I kneel and tear at the pile of leaves, scooping them up in mucky armfuls to free him, but the keening slices through my eardrums. My whole body freezes, my breath dying in my throat.

And I wake gulping great mouthfuls of air, staring into the darkness.

21

The physics teacher drones at the bottom of the small amphi-theater, bending to scribble on the SMART Board, challeng-ing us to produce a convincing proof the Earth isn't flat. I want to pay attention, but her monotone voice blurs the sentences into a featureless mass, and every few seconds she blinks like clockwork: phrase phrase phrase *blink*. Phrase phrase phrase *blink*.

My eyelids slip shut—then snap open as people behind us rustle and giggle. Mireya gives me a nudge with a quick glance over her shoulder.

I turn as discreetly as I can and see Ellis lounging in the back row. He's mouthing the teacher's words a millisecond after her, doing a spot-on imitation of her lecturing-blinking routine. People around him are cracking up. When a girl whinnies with laughter, the teacher wheels to look straight at Ellis, whose face is now innocently blank.

Mireya shakes her head and mouths, *He's a dick*, but she's smiling, too. I face front and fold my arms on the desk, trying to ignore the warmth in my cheeks. How can a boy who refuses to take anything seriously insist we're all in danger from a game?

The teacher's making good points, regardless of her poor presentation style. She's saying we shouldn't take anything on faith, which makes me think of Rory staring into that phone.

What did he see?

The Earth is round. Games are games. And the forbidden fruit keeps passing from person to person. I haven't told Ellis yet that Rory and Anil played it as well as Emily, or about Rory's strange behavior, or that they all played it because of me. I've been looking out for Rory today, but I haven't seen him.

The phone buzzes in my backpack, vibrating against my calf.

I go taut, heat prickling behind my temples. Mireya's sitting right beside me, and Erika hardly ever texts me. I'll have to wait until the end of the period to check it. Twenty-seven minutes of trying to focus on angles and vectors and satellite footage and—

Something white moves at the edge of the SMART Board.

I blink to clear my eyes. The white thing detaches itself from the glowing background, long and fluid as a snake—no, as an arm.

It's my imagination. A trick of the light showing me a disembodied human arm with a flicker of rapid movement at the end—five radiant outlines, like fingers. But it's not going away.

I stop breathing as the fingers lick at the edge of the screen. They flinch, a tiny under-the-skin shiver that makes me think of a nervous cat, and then the whole armlike shape floats away from the board, into midair. Its whiteness is flecked with seething blue like the board itself, yet somehow it's solid and three-dimensional against the drab classroom.

Does anyone else see this? No. The teacher keeps talking about confirmation bias. Isn't that what Dad told me Mom's problem was? Once you start looking for something, you find it everywhere, whether it's evidence of the evil of video games or—whatever this is. Rory planted the idea in my head, and now I'm seeing things, too.

The rustling in the back of the room has died down, except for the occasional hiccup of stifled laughter. I inch away as the pale arm floats upward, still connected to the SMART Board where a shoulder should be. It seems close and far at once, its half-thereness confusing, and its ghostly fingers extend as if in benediction. Toward me.

Tiny hairs go erect on the nape of my neck.

In front of me, a boy raises his hand and says something about sending a spaceship into orbit. Behind me, a girl giggles.

My senses are going weird again, voices slowing to a demonic drone. The room telescopes, so I'm not sure if the spectral hand is wavering twenty feet from my face or two.

It's not real. Forget about Rory. As a child, I saw things like this and lost touch with reality, and I hurt myself and was banished from the Glare forever. But I can control myself now, and that's why I'm here, I can, I can—

I'm standing up right in the center of the amphitheater—sounds deafening, colors blinding, blood thudding painfully in my temples. My throat is tense with expelled words, but I don't know what I said.

Mireya's instantly on her feet, a protective arm around me. "What happened?"

She's looking at me. They're all looking at me. My eyes sweep the room, my cheeks flooding with blood.

"Are you all right?" the teacher asks, her blinks coming faster now. "Are you all right, uh...?"

"Hedda," Mireya says at the same time that a pair of long, blue-jeaned legs slide over the empty desk beside me, and a pair of Converse slap the floor.

It's Ellis, holding out a bottle of water. He doesn't seem winded from clambering over the desks. "Are you okay, Hedda?"

"Fine." Not thirsty, I gulp the water anyway, trying to think of an excuse. "I had a leg cramp. I'm so sorry."

The teacher sighs long-sufferingly. "Mr. Westover, please return to your seat. I don't think your medical services are required. No, not *on* the desks this time."

As Mireya and I sit down, and Ellis trudges into the aisle and back to his seat, people recoil and titter. People turn to look. I smell Sharpie ink and disinfectant and somebody's mint gum.

When I turn to face the front, the arm is still there.

It's retreated to the edge of the glowing board, no longer showing me its palm, but I see the shifting and pulsing of its strange, flexible, shiny skin.

I barely breathe, but I don't look away. What did Rory say about facing it head-on? *Is* this what Rory saw? Maybe we're not just confirming each other's bias, after all.

Minutes crawl. Bit by bit, the roundness of the Earth is proved. I remember Mom telling me the Glare would get inside my brain and reprogram me, and I remember the goats butting against my hand, and I smell the mud of our creek bed, and I watch the second hand move until, at last, the bell rings and the room explodes with commotion.

Mireya waits, with none of her usual impatience, as I stand up—carefully, no sudden moves, because *it* is still there. "What did I say?" I ask.

"What?" She turns to scowl at Ellis, who's come to hover on my other side. "Show's over, Westover. No need for a white knight."

Ellis ignores her, perched on the desk. "When you stood up? It wasn't that loud, but I think you said—"

"'Go away,'" Mireya finishes. "Which is probably what you should do, Ellis, because ever since you started feeding Hedda that bullshit about a killer game, she's been on edge. She was raised to be scared of screens. You should know better."

I try to protest, but right now I'm grateful for Mireya's firm hand guiding me past the SMART Board (*don't look again*) and out into the hall. As we head for fifth period, Mireya says, "Just ignore him. He's got some kind of weirdness about you."

"I'm the weird one. I think I was half-asleep and dreaming back there." I tug myself gently from her grip as we pass the restroom. "I'm going to wash the sweat off my face, okay?"

"I'll go with you."

So it's not until I'm alone in the stall that I have a chance to pull out my phone and see the new skull text staring back at me.

22

Once when I was eleven, a rattler got inside the house and Mom had to shoot it. For months afterward, my gaze licked the edges of each room, checking for fluid flickers of scales. The fear was worse than the reality, and it only retreated after Mom showed me how to load and shoot the rifle myself.

I can't shoot at every white thing I've seen in my peripheral vision since leaving physics class. So far, no ghostly arms. Everything has been 110 percent normal.

But I can't go back to the time before I saw it. I can't go back to the place where I felt safe. If I tell Mireya, she'll think I'm ready to be committed. If I tell Ellis, he'll think I'm on the brink of doing something like Caroline did. Rory's most likely to understand and not freak out, but he's not answering my texts.

I remind myself I belong in school—a real, enrolled student.

If I can't stay on-kilter, I'll have no future. But if I try to focus on the homework we got today, I'll end up staring at the wall waiting for white shapes to emerge. I need to *do* something.

Ellis has sent me a short e-mail: *Hope you're really ok. If I'm scaring you like Mireya said, just tell me and I'll back off. But I searched Clelia Rosenbaum. Check it out.*

A bunch of links follow. The top search result is a newspaper obituary: Clelia Rosenbaum died nearly two years ago in Richmond, California, at the age of seventy-two, survived by her three daughters and five grandchildren.

But there's a second Clelia Rosenbaum. According to a site called People Lightning Check, she lives in Bolinas, California, twenty-six years old.

That's less than an hour away, Ellis finishes. *Gonna do some more digging and get her street address.* He doesn't need to tell me that Caroline would be twenty-six now.

My phone buzzes, and though I know it's probably Rory, my first thought is *Please just stop. Please.*

It's not a skull text, just one from a number I don't recognize. *Thought u should see this.* And a link to something called Dish. I click automatically and read:

Did anyone see the freaky new girl in physics 1 today? She stood up in the middle of class and said go away and stared at us like she was tripping balls. My sources say she was raised in a cult and drank goat's blood.

The poster is anonymous, but the thread is called "San Rafael HS." I slam the phone down, my thudding pulse bringing heat to my cheeks. Again I have the itchy, unsavory sense of being watched by the dark screen.

Three days at school, and already people think I'm a freak. "Tripping," like Emily. A cult girl from the desert. Anyone from physics could have made that posting, but who alerted me to it? Someone I know? Lily, Anil, Cheyenne, or someone closer to me? There are all kinds of ways to call and text anonymously, according to the research I've been doing on the skull texts.

This must be how it felt when I was six and Lily and Mireya posted those mocking pics of me. I remember the disappearing image, and what Rory said about the "epic fail circle of hell" starts to make a little more sense. Maybe the skull texts inspire us to relive those bad moments, whatever they were for us, germinating phantoms that bloom in our heads.

Ur pathetic.

Except what I got just now was a real text from a real person—not from a restricted number, not vanishing from my phone. I need to talk to Mireya before these dark thoughts stick to me; I need the reassurance of her confident voice. But her feed says she's spending the evening in the city with her boyfriend—*night on the town!*

I message Rory again: *Sorry to keep bugging you, but I'm kind of spooked now.*

No reply.

Night creeps in earlier now it's nearly Labor Day. I tug back a curtain to survey the street, trying to shake off the sensation of something filthy sticking to me, leaching into my skin. *Freaky. Cult.*

Fog has drifted in from the bay, haloing each lamppost and porch light. Our neighbors watch a game on their giant-screen

TV, curtains wide open. Their tabby cat's sinuous shadow hugs a fence.

My phone sits on my desk, a wafer-thin rectangle of concentrated fear and power, bad and good news, danger and safety. Silent.

. . .

I pad downstairs and find Dad in his study, the door open for once.

He turns to look at me, his face washed sapphire by the giant screen. "Hedda, it's after midnight."

"I can't sleep."

I almost expect him to read the look on my face, call up Mom on the spot, and arrange to have me sent back to the desert—or to an institution somewhere. *Freak.*

But he only says, "I just heard about that poor Emily Stoller— Erika says she's a friend of a friend of yours. What a nightmare for the parents. Did you know she won a regional youth violin competition?"

"It sounds like she got through surgery okay." If I tell him Emily had another freak-out, he'll probably lament she's missing violin practice. Because that's who Dad is, I'm realizing: a person who values other people for their measurable achievements, not for the intangible whatever that makes them who they are.

No wonder he doesn't have time for me—but in a way, knowing him better is a relief. Given my current lack of achievements, I can stop worrying about his opinion.

"Dad, I've been thinking about Caroline Westover again.

Was there any warning before she…you know? I mean, did she seem strange?" I remember Mom's story about finding Caroline and me awake at midnight, both mesmerized by screens. Caroline was in here—was she looking at this computer?

Right now, Dad's screen is covered with a dense fretwork of code, like hieroglyphics. "I'm not sure, honestly," he says. "Jane usually handled things—paying Caroline for babysitting jobs, I mean. She was doing a lot of night work at Sinnestauschen, while I was at my company, so we came home at different times. And as your mother loves to remind me, I'm not the world's most observant person."

"Were Mom and Caroline…friends?" The newspaper article made Mom sound like Caroline's mentor. But when she talked to me about "the babysitter," it was always in a distant, disapproving way, without using details or even a name. As if she'd censored that part of her life out of existence.

Dad swings his chair toward me. The dark room and the screen glow turn his expression into a play of light: concerned, perturbed, calm. "Well, I know Jane thought Caroline was bright, and she encouraged her to develop that game concept of hers. Has Caroline's brother been asking you about this?"

"No!" People need to stop blaming Ellis for whatever's wrong with me. It comes in a rush: "Dad, I think Caroline did create that game. I think she posted it on the Dark Web, and I stole the link from her. And I think I played it."

Dad has gone very still. "Where's this coming from?"

"I've been remembering things." I wonder if he's even noticed Erika's old laptop in my room. Probably not, though it's right out on the desk. "Being in my room, talking to Ellis and Mireya—it brought things back."

The light on his screen seethes, and I brace myself, but nothing emerges from it. *There is no arm.*

"Jane thought you were being bullied," Dad says. "And now you're saying you actually remember playing a...game?"

"I don't *exactly* remember," I admit. "It's all pretty vague. But you said Caroline wanted to use fear to control people."

"To suggest things to them."

"So the game would have to be scary, right? And it would send messages to people. How? Does someone have to control it?"

Dad clears his throat. "Well, I can't speak for this particular game—assuming it existed—but no, the controller would be AI. Players would probably connect to a central game server, which would obtain access to their phone numbers or social media accounts, and that server would monitor their gameplay and send out the—but I'm just confusing you."

I fold my scarred arm tight to my chest, making a mental note to ask Ellis or Mireya what a server is. "I'm not as clueless as you think." My mouth is open, ready to spill everything, when I realize I might be getting Erika in trouble.

She shouldn't be punished for my choices. And despite my dread of another skull text, the thought of Dad taking my phone away makes my stomach twist. I need to stay connected, need to know what people are saying about me.

Dad rocks gently in his chair. "I still don't quite understand. What makes you think you were playing Caroline's game—if it even existed?"

My nails dig into my palm, my breath going shallow, but we can't just never talk about it. I pull up my sleeve and thrust the scars in front of him, turning them to catch the screen's light. "Remember how I got these?"

"Hedda." His face has gone wobbly, helpless.

"Mom told me I fell in barbed wire, but on Saturday night, I remembered what really happened."

He looks away. "I always told Jane she should tell you. She was afraid to."

"I know. She admitted it. Now I want to know what *you* remember."

Dad's voice is studiously neutral. "I was on a business trip that night. Jane said she came into the kitchen and found your arm covered in blood. You screamed and thrashed as if she were attacking you. At first, the ER doctors thought she might really have hurt you, but the wound pattern indicated self-infliction."

I let out my breath.

"Jane absolutely refused to try medication and therapy," he goes on. "It wasn't the first time you'd acted out, and she was convinced it was all because we'd allowed you—*I'd* allowed you—to have so many devices so young. She wanted to bring you to the ranch and start over, and I . . . well, we had some lively discussions about it, but in the end, I respected her choices."

Standard Dad-speak translated: Mom's unruly emotions bugged him, inconvenienced him, scared him. "If you thought something was wrong with me, and I needed medication, why'd you let her have me? Didn't you care?" The last part comes out more pleading than I meant it to. *Tell me you cared.*

Dad wraps his arms tight around himself. "Of course I cared.

But your mother made me feel like you'd be better off without me. And…it sounds like maybe now you're agreeing with her, Hedda. Are you saying this game could've made you hurt yourself?"

When he wants to, he knows how to get right to the point. But I'm not ready to tell him I think I was hallucinating Randoms that night, so I say, "It scared me—the game. I know that. But I'm *not* agreeing with Mom. I don't think running away was the answer. We were all alone on the ranch, and I can't live my whole life that way, but now it's like I don't fit in anywhere. I want to belong at school, but…"

I expect him to ask what's been happening at school, but he only nods as if he's not surprised. "I had the same problem when I was your age. A terminal lack of belonging. My dad thought computers were for sissies—not that he could have afforded one anyway—so I learned to code in the school lab with a bunch of other misfits. My dad and granddad were constantly on my case. 'Go outside, Mike! Nail a board, chop some wood, shoot something! Make yourself useful for once!'"

My gaze flits up to the family photos—my grandparents, with their hard eyes. The sliced-up image of the boy with a fishing pole.

"Is that you?" I ask, pointing at it. And when he nods, "Why did you cut it up?"

Dad gazes up at the photo. The shadows press on it, enfolding his child self.

"I'm not sure," he says. "But you remember what I said about my grandpa Frank: He was a dark man. Sometimes we think that by cutting the worst things out of our lives, just severing them, we can get past them. It's a sort of magical thinking."

Is he talking about himself now, or Mom? She mentored and

181

encouraged Caroline and then scissored the memories out of her life, turning her into a cardboard cautionary tale to scare me. And even me—my brain censored those memories of the Glare.

Dad's still talking: "But it's not that easy to leave our old selves behind. When I finally escaped and went to Berkeley on scholarship, people laughed at my polyester button-up shirts and my hick accent, and I was an outcast all over again."

I press my lips together. So maybe he does understand. "You're not an outcast now."

"It took a while. Sometimes you have to turn your back on the old demons and rise above the bullshit, Hedda. Don't let anyone make you question yourself."

No wonder he hardly ever talks about his family, keeping them penned in those photos on his desk. But if Dad thinks Mom and the desert and my old life are my demons, he's wrong. There's so much more.

He darkens the screen, then stands and walks past me to turn on the hall light. "Come on. We both need our sleep."

Freak. Cult, say the voices in my head.

"Just tell me one thing. Did you see me write on these walls?"

He looks ready to object, so I add, "I know it happened."

Dad's shoulders go limp. He points to a strip of wall behind the door, just above the baseboard.

I drop to my knees. Beneath a thin layer of smooth white paint, dark streaks rise like veins under skin—crudely formed letters. A pulse thumps in my temple as I read:

Not real not real not real

"Hedda." Dad raises me gently to my feet, and I realize in a dim way that my forehead has been resting against the wall.

"That isn't you anymore," he says as he walks me out into the light. "Whatever happened back then, focus on what happens next. Look forward. That's the key."

I go without protest, because my brain is working—not forward, but back. Remembering.

23

I n my room, by the light of the desk lamp, I kneel and run my
fingers along the edge of the baseboard molding. Where it isn't
flush to the wall, I explore the cracks with a fingernail.

Kneeling by the baseboard in Dad's study reminded
me—*There are cracks. You can hide things.* Long ago, that's what
I did.

Under the desk, I find what I'm looking for: sharp edges of
stiff paper. I tug the pieces out, five in all, and assemble them
on the desk.

I'm looking at an old photograph cut with scissors. In the
foreground stands a rustic cabin; in the background, the square-
edged black tower. It's the real thing, absolutely recognizable. My
whole body tingles as I tape the pieces back together.

When I turn the photo over, I find the Dark Web address I

know far too well, this time written in a neat, fluid hand. Not a child's writing.

This is what I stole from Caroline. I remember the guilt I felt hiding the mutilated photo behind the baseboard, eager to be rid of the evidence but even more eager to play the Glare.

The tower is real, and if Caroline based the Glare on a real place she knew as a kid, maybe Ellis knows where it is, too. Maybe she's there now. I grab my phone to text Ellis, but before I can touch it, it lights up and buzzes in my hand.

The skull again, the damn skull.

Next thing I know, the phone is lying on the bed—did I drop it? I'm shaking so hard everything blurs, feeling my head spin. Hearing the distant creaking rustle I heard on my first night here, like the wind in the treetops. And somewhere behind and beyond it, a high, silvery sound—a keening.

My eyes zip around the room. With the keening comes a scraping or slithering, like something struggling out of the underbrush.

From down the hall, where Clint is sleeping.

Maybe this is real, after all. Maybe someone's gotten into the house. I look around for something heavy. No baseball bat or trophies, but my utility knife from the ranch sits on the bookcase. I grab it, along with my phone, and tiptoe to my door.

Light spills into the hallway, the ceiling vanishing in shadows. The stairs are a pool of blackness, and I don't hear the keening now.

Sliding my back along the wall, I reach the bathroom I share with Clint. Flick on the light, pull back the shower curtain.

Behind me.

185

It's the slightest whoosh, like a snake deep in a pile of dry leaves. I return to the hall, where Clint's door stands closed, and press my ear to it.

Sssshhh. Something slithering, sliding.

I knock lightly, so he's only likely to hear if he's already awake. Listen again.

Silence now, but I'm sure the noise came from inside. Using my knife hand, I turn the knob and inch the door open. It doesn't creak like my own.

A ruddy night-light shaped like a rocket illuminates the room at floor level. I make out stretches of rug and hardwood, then the edge of the comforter, also decorated with rockets. The curtained window glows spectrally above. The bed is a dark hump, my brother a smaller dark hump in it.

The closet door hangs open, blocked by a heap of clothes. I'm headed there when the dry-leaf rustle comes again. Then the keening, gentle and soft like a single cricket.

In the bed. As if Clint is sleeping on the forest floor and not on rocket-patterned sheets.

The sounds are so subtle. Not nearly loud enough to carry all the way to my room.

My brother lies on his left side, face to the wall, his shoulder and ribs gently pulsing with his breath. The trilling keening doesn't stop, so close, in the bed, and now I think I understand what Rory was doing at the mall.

Something *is* here, and I need to see it. Something is making its presence known.

I transfer the knife to my trembling left hand and use my right to wake my phone. *Don't look at the skull.*

Stepping back, I open the camera and frame the bed in the viewfinder. The screen is black at first, the glowing yellow box trying to find something bright enough to focus on. And then I see.

On top of my brother, its head turned away from me, crouches a glowing bluish-white person no bigger than Clint himself.

No, not a person—a Random. Its right arm is too long, longer than a human arm, and it's wrapped around Clint's neck like a scarf.

Randoms aren't real. They're game monsters. Rough drafts. But I know what I'm seeing. Everything starts undulating again, and it's all I can do to keep hold of the phone. My breath catches as the Random turns its face to me—or the place where its face should be. It has no eyes, nose, or mouth, just flat, hideous Glare.

What are you? Why are you here? Are you real?

As if in answer to my silent questions, something swells within the Glare, an outline like the plaster cast of a human face—alive and struggling, trapped inside the light. The jaws open in a gleeful grimace, mocking and cruel. Milky, pupil-less eyes widen. Hair streams out behind.

A little girl. Just like *me* as I imagine myself, daring Ellis to play the Glare.

It's not me. It's real, and it's going to hurt Clint. The phone thuds from my trembling hand to the floor, but I still have the knife, and I switch it to my right hand, my grip tightening as I dive for the bed. No way to see it now, but I know exactly where it is, and this is no harder than killing a snake. *Now*, before that impossible arm tightens—

My eyes close and my ears rush, the windy sound caught

inside my head. The keening is an orchestra. I stab and stab and stab into something soft.

Too soft. Not struggling.

Control yourself.

I let the knife go. My body is swollen tight with ferocity; it whooshes out like air from a balloon as I open my eyes and look down. What did I just do?

My fingers clutch a large stuffed toy, black and white, with round ears and a potbelly—Po the panda. The knife is embedded in his chest, stuffing escaping from four or five stab wounds.

I'm inches from the dark hump of Clint's body.

Oh God, please. Oh God, no. My throat tightens on my breath, strangling it, as I bend over him. The keening and rustling are gone, but the pounding in my head is deafening, and he's so still. Is his chest rising and falling, or is it my own trembling that makes everything seem to pulse again?

Just as I'm ready to scream, Clint's mouth opens in a faint sigh. He turns over on his stomach and burrows deeper into the blankets.

Asleep. Breathing. Like none of it ever happened.

Weak as if I've been pulled from the churning ocean, I sink to the floor and crouch there. Feel the knife hilt in my hand, the stabbing motion. How close was I to hurting him? How close, because I thought I heard and saw—what?

And I realize it doesn't matter if the Randoms are real. All that matters is that they're real to me.

What did I almost do? What will I do next time?

A boy lies awake in the darkness. When his phone buzzes, he doesn't bother to open his eyes.

They're coming more often now. Catching him off guard. At first he was fascinated, almost tickled by every manifestation, but that was before he realized they could touch him.

He tried turning off his phone for a while, but when he turned it back on, there were two skull texts waiting, and that's when he first felt a cold, long-fingered hand wrap around his ankle. He was in Starbucks, because he'd felt safer in public. Not anymore.

Facing them head-on works as long as there's a slight time gap between the text and the vision. But it can still surprise him. So he's working on a new strategy: close his eyes and pretend it's not happening. Because he can't freak out now, absolutely not, not when he's finally figured it out.

Amazing how real it feels. He's sure that if he opens his eyes he'll see that leering Joker avatar inches from his face, gazing down at him. Though he knows it's just his brain filling in the details of his personal worst fail, he is not going to look. NOT.

Something brushes his hand. He goes rigid as it explores his knuckles—cold, sinuous, chalk-dry.

Tears trickle down his cheeks. He thinks about how tomorrow, when he posts about this, he will be internet famous. Everyone will want to interview him. He just has to get one person's permission first, because without her, he would never have known.

He won't tell them about this part. The keening in his ears, the cold, glowing flesh against his. And now a weight settling on his chest, making itself comfortable. The part he's still not 100 percent sure isn't real.

24

Very late or very early, in the dark, the phone buzzes from the nightstand where I've hidden it in a tissue box. I ignore it and roll over—onto Po the panda. What's he doing here?

I fall asleep wondering—and then sit up with a jerk to find the curtains silver blue with morning. I snuck Po into my room so I could mend his wounds before Clint noticed anything wrong, but I couldn't find sewing supplies. I searched my whole room for them. I need to ask Erika. I need—

It's not quite time for the alarm to go off, but I need to know if I missed any more skulls. I pull the phone from the box and unlock it, shoving night-wild hair out of my face. The house is quiet.

Last night comes back in more detail. Oh God, if I was

hallucinating—is this what happened to Caroline? Did she see Randoms threatening her family members?

It's okay, I tell myself, trying to be firm and soothing like Mireya. Whatever was here last night isn't here now.

A new text came in at 4:11 this morning. It's from Rory: *We need to talk, now. Coming over.*

Coming over? How does he know where I live? And if he was coming over two hours ago, where is he?

Maybe he's been following the clues to Caroline, too, and we can pool our data. Rory's logical that way—he barely even seemed scared, and right now I'd be happy to listen to his wild theories. I shove Po under the blankets, then rise and open the curtains. Sedge-green cottonwoods shiver against the sky, which is coral over the eastern roofs.

The street is lined with the familiar Priuses and Avalons and Tauruses—starter cars bought for teenagers by generous parents, parked outside because the family garage is full. With one exception: a dusty little maroon hatchback I've never seen before. Could that be Rory double-checking the address, or working up the courage to come knock on our door? Why hasn't he texted again?

I tug on jeans and a hoodie and glide down the stairs. Outside, the blue day is veined with saffron, the sun's first rays so bright they seem solid. Morning air presses against me, inside me, sharp with a hint of brine.

From the porch, I can't see the driver's seat of the hatchback, but it feels unoccupied. Could Rory be wandering around with his phone the way he did at the mall, searching behind the blue bins and bougainvillea for things I can't see?

If you run from what you see, it'll come after you.

Across the street, a door clicks open. A man's voice calls, "C'mon, Lex Luthor! Hey, Lexy, big fellow!"

The big tabby cat races across the street and through the open door, ready for breakfast. It's only a few strides down the sidewalk to the hatchback, but now I feel stupid. Rory probably meant he was coming over later, after school. No one comes to discuss theories about an urban legend at six in the morning.

The neighborhood is waking up: A garage door growls open. NPR bleeds through a sunroom window. I'm about to turn tail and go home, to a hot shower and breakfast, when I see something smudged on the driver's-side window of the hatchback, dark against the sallow reflections of morning.

A red handprint.

A woman's voice cries in the distance, "Don't forget your lunch!" A car rumbles past as I stare at the handprint on the window, and the world goes blurry and slow around my heartbeat.

I don't tell my legs to walk over, but they do it anyway. I don't tell my eyes to look. The trees, the sky, the street lose their colors. Only the interior of the hatchback's cab remains in focus. Only the body slumped over the steering wheel.

It is a *body*, not a person. His back isn't swelling gently with each exhale. I can't see his face, only the cotton-candy hair.

Below it, his damp T-shirt is the same maroon as the car and the handprint, except for the left sleeve, which is snow white.

The maroon is blood. Blood coats the fine hairs on his neck.

My heartbeat slows and my body shifts into some new mode, as if I'm breathing underwater.

Rory's left arm is caught under his body, while the right arm trails to the side. Blood has gushed down his neck and puddled in the ridges of the passenger seat, thick and gummy. It's caked under the fingernails of his pale hand, splayed on the vinyl beside a phone and a chef's knife.

The hand in the pile of leaves.

The knife's wide blade is cloudy with blood. A duller-red welt circles Rory's right wrist—as if he was bound, or as if something coiled itself around him.

Just as my head begins to spin, nausea weakening my legs, the glint of sun on the knife jars me back to reality. I stagger away from the car, reaching for my phone, but it's not there.

What was I doing with a phone? Why didn't I stay in the desert?

Why is it taking so long to walk back to the house? Why is that passing driver staring at me? Maybe my own skin is coated in drying blood. Last night I almost killed Clint because I acted on the evidence of my eyes and ears.

I blink the stickiness out of my eyes. I can't wait to get inside and sluice it off my back and scrub it from under my fingernails.

Blood trickling between the kitchen tiles. Blood on my arm. Blood on the sand where Emily lies flailing, and *freak, freak, freak*. This is what happens when we play and lose, when our mistakes and old fears come back to haunt us, and nothing about it is random.

25

"May I see that text again?" Detective Lu asks.

I expected the police station to be noisy, but everyone speaks in undertones, barely audible over the purr of air-conditioning. It's me who's disrupting their morning—shivering in my T-shirt, clinging tight to the vinyl chair, unable to lose that sensation of blood congealing on my skin.

A shower wasn't enough.

The detective has a neat, functional bowl cut and an air of competence. I want her to lay everything out in a flow chart and explain it in her calm, even voice, even if the conclusion is that *I* killed Rory.

When I'm not worrying about Clint noticing Po is gone, I keep imagining how I might have done it.

Gravel pattering on my window in the predawn dark. Rory

down below. Me sneaking outside to talk in his car, carrying a knife—none of which I remember, but what does that prove?

On my way back inside to tell Erika and call the police, I checked the butcher's block in our kitchen. All the knives were in their proper slots.

Detective Lu puts down my phone, and I see she was reading the text from Rory, the one I've already shown her. "Do you have any idea what he might have wanted to talk to you about?"

It's the second time she's asked. The first time was about five minutes ago, when Erika was still in the cubicle with us. That time, I said I wasn't sure, I barely knew Rory, but I'd seen him acting weird at the mall a few days ago.

Then I asked Erika if she could get the hoodie I'd left in the car, because the AC here is making me shiver and because I wanted to talk to Detective Lu alone.

"I think Rory wanted to talk about this." I grab the phone, pull up the skull text from last night—trying not to flinch—and slide it to her.

What happened to Caroline is happening to me. The knowledge is like the mysterious threats in a dream, a writhing snakes' nest or a ruined house about to collapse on my head—I can't explain it, describe it, or prove it, but there it is.

Even Mireya won't believe me.

Still I make a half-hearted try. "Can you trace the number? I'm almost sure Rory has texts like this on his phone, too."

Detective Lu examines my phone. Her expression doesn't change—friendly but inquisitive. "Is this some kind of prank, sending this picture back and forth?"

I wrap my arms around myself, trying not to see blood on the knife, blood on the vinyl seat. "It's not a prank. It's part of a game called the Glare. If you look up the report on Emily Stoller, you'll see the same skull. It's the alert she got right before she ran off the cliff."

Not alerts, I realize—triggers. If the rune-tree texts make us think happy thoughts and send us back to the Glare, the skulls send us to our darkest places, where we're the prey. The danger is inside our heads—inside *my* head. Hardwired in us.

"Emily Stoller." The detective frowns. "That was out of our jurisdiction, but she told medical personnel she thought someone was chasing her, if I remember correctly."

"The Glare! They were both playing a game called the Glare that came from the Dark Web. The last time I saw Rory, at the mall, I think he was looking for, uh, the monsters in the game. He was seeing them inside his phone. Just look up 'Glare' and 'skull text'—please."

Meme, Mireya whispers in my head. *Legend. Tall tale. No one will believe you.*

After a brief hesitation, Detective Lu hits a few keys on her computer, but her eyes keep flitting back to me. "You recently arrived from Arizona, correct? Your stepmom told us you had an unconventional upbringing."

"It was actually my fault," I say in a rush, because I can feel her reaching for the easy explanation—that someone as sheltered as me will believe anything. *Cult. Freak.* "I found the game. I gave it to my friend, who gave it to Rory. He should never have been playing it. I didn't think it could hurt anyone; I don't know if a game *can* hurt anyone, but people keep getting hurt, and—"

I stop, because she's looking straight at me, and her eyes are filmy with something familiar. It's the look Erika gave me when I told her about my cardigan sweater stalker—one part amusement, two parts pity.

The detective takes a long chug from the coffee cup on her desk. "This stuff may all be new to you, Hedda, but it's not unusual these days for kids to walk around looking for monsters inside their phones. My twelve-year-old almost got run over on her way to a PokéStop."

"This was different." Clint has explained to me all about Pokémon Go. "I saw Rory's screen, and there was *nothing* on it."

The detective props her chin on her fists. "Did Rory seem depressed to you that day at the mall? Nervous?"

"Definitely nervous—and excited. You'll look at all his texts, right?"

She nods. "Do you think it's possible he texted you and then drove over to your house because he had a crush on you?"

The detective's turning this into a story that makes sense to her, a story without the game in it. A story where I might well be the main suspect.

I shake my head too hard. "We barely knew each other. Have you seen that welt on his wrist? It looked...weird. Like something had hold of him."

"I promise you, the medical examiner will deliver a comprehensive report." Detective Lu tilts her head, examining me intently now. "What are you thinking could have had hold of Rory?"

She's trying to trap me. To tug on a thread that might lead to a tearful confession.

I force myself to look directly into her pleasant eyes. "I don't know."

. . .

"I'll grab my backpack. I can be at school in time for third period."

"Hedda." Bolting the door behind us, Erika looks almost as drained as I do. "You can't go to school after this."

"But Mireya's expecting me! I was supposed to meet her, and when I texted her, I probably didn't make much sense. I made her late...."

I follow Erika into the kitchen, a desperate energy making me light-headed. I need to see Mireya, to talk to Ellis. I need *Rory*. Friends, classes, homework, the promise of a new life—it can't end now, just as it's starting. "What about Clint? Where is he?"

"He went to school with Conor's mom. I'm going to tell him later." Erika touches my shoulder. "He's fine. Sit down."

He's not fine. He's probably already missing Po. I've ruined everything, but I can't go back to the desert. *Never. Never.* But Rory will never go home or to the mall or to college or anywhere, and now I'm babbling: "I'm fine! I mean, I'm not fine, but I'm not going off-kilter. There are people I need to see at school—Rory's friends. I need to talk to them. I need to tell them everything so they don't just hear the rumors. So they *know*."

Anil. I need to be sure he's stopped playing.

I grab for my phone, but just as I touch it, it buzzes, making me go stock-still. It's a text from an unfamiliar number—the same as last night? no idea—and it says: *Did u do it, freak?*

No!!! Who are you? But I'm shaking so hard the message comes out as a jumble, and I end up deleting it.

Who would send that? The same person who passed on the gossip yesterday? Does everyone at that school hate me now, after only three days?

I don't protest when Erika steers me into a chair and puts water on for tea. I just ask, "Do you have a sewing kit? Please?"

She doesn't ask me why, but while the tea's brewing, she goes and gets one. We sit and drink the tea together, and the whole time she murmurs reassuringly about how I can return to school tomorrow, how I've just had a terrible shock, how she's asked Dad to come home—

"I don't want to see him! He'll blame me for everything, and he'll make me go back and live with Mom because he doesn't think I belong here."

The childish outburst hangs in the air. I want to reach out and stuff it back inside, because last night Dad almost seemed to understand. And what does it matter whether he thinks I belong here when *I* know that a single skull text could put me on the path to hurting myself or someone else?

I'll stop using my phone. Turn it back to silent, maybe even hide it.

Erika just clasps my hand. "It sounds like *you* think you belong here," she says. "I think so, too. Doesn't that count for something?"

. . .

Alone in my room, I take out my phone, my throat closing. I haven't heard any new alerts, but—

No new texts accusing me of killing Rory. No e-mails directing me to new posts about what a freak I am. *Safe.*

As I switch the phone to Do Not Disturb mode, a cool wave of relief washes over me, though soon dread creeps back on spindly insect legs. *This morning was real. But last night?*

My hands need to be busy, so I thread a needle and start sewing up Po's stab wounds, restuffing him as I go. On the ranch, we'd spend rainy evenings mending, and each stitch helps me breathe a little easier. Clint may still notice, but it's the least I can do.

As I work, I keep trying to remember Rory alive—sitting cross-legged in the sand, calling to me from Mireya's porch, running out in front of the Lexus. But there aren't enough memories to draw on. And so I always end up seeing the interior of that car, the blood congealing in plastic grooves.

When I've reduced Po's wounds to puckered scars, I tuck him back in Clint's messy bed, then return to my room. I don't have Anil's phone number, so I message one of his social feeds from the laptop: *If you haven't already, please stop playing the Glare. It hurt Rory. Please believe me. We can talk tomorrow.*

Then, though it's probably pointless, I write back to Clelia Rosenbaum: *The game is hurting people again, and it's my fault. Do you have the server? Can you stop the texts?*

. . .

"Nobody thinks you did it, Hedda," Mireya says. "You barely knew each other. You're being paranoid."

Her eyes are red-rimmed. The floral comforter is balled in one corner of the unmade bed. Her voice has a new quality: leaden, as if every word is a wasted effort.

"*Somebody* thinks I did." But I've already told her about the text, and I don't want to keep harping on it and make this about me.

"Trolls trying to stir shit up. Tragedies bring out the worst in people."

"I tried to tell the detective about the Glare. I probably shouldn't have, but—"

Mireya stops me with a slash of her hand. "Caleigh's mom heard from Leah's mom that Rory's mom recognized the knife. Because it came from her own kitchen."

"What does that mean?"

"I've been looking it up." She doesn't look at me as she speaks. "Self-stabbing is a rare method of suicide, most common in people who've been diagnosed with psychosis."

"Rory didn't seem suicidal." I remember how excited he seemed at the mall, how eager to explain.

Mireya's eyelids are drooping as if she's struggling to see through a fog. "Not everybody does."

Don't give up. Not now. I need you. I sink down opposite her on the bed. "Mireya. We need to find a way to make people stop playing the Glare."

"I told you not to obsess about that."

"It's not just me! Rory was playing, and so was Emily. Anil told me. He gave it to her."

I relate what Anil said, then my encounter with Rory at the mall. "That was Tuesday, and he mentioned level thirteen, and he looked so weird—like he was seeing something that made him happy and scared at once."

"Hedda, you barely even know Rory. Knew him."

She keeps saying that and she's right, but she hasn't seen what I have. I reach for my phone. "I know what happens after level thirteen. I'm still getting the texts. I got one last night."

I half expect Mireya to refuse to look, but she examines the skull and says in her foggy voice, "Just like Emily's. Have you gotten any since...?"

She doesn't need to finish. What I saw in the hatchback has divided my life into before and after, just like Mom when she took me away to the desert. "None since last night. But—"

"Hedda." Mireya drops the phone and raises her eyes to me. "Texts don't make people hurt themselves unless there's already something going on. Emily's boyfriend was a jerk who was practically stalking her. And Rory...well, you didn't know him, but he took meds for depression. He had bad periods when he'd talk about hurting himself. Maybe when he texted you and came over, it was because he liked you. Maybe he felt rejected when you didn't text back."

"At four in the morning?" I slide off the bed and pace the desert-rose carpet. "No, Mireya."

"Sometimes a person seems fine right before..."

"You think he stabbed himself in front of my house because I didn't answer a text?"

"He wasn't being rational, obviously. But he was already being weird at the mall, and this seems likelier to me than a deadly game."

"It's not 'deadly' necessarily. It could just...trigger things. Throw people off-kilter."

In a rush, I tell her everything I've learned—about Caroline being Mom's intern, about her wanting to design a game that would provoke conditioned responses, about the message I received from someone who could be her. I leave out my own reactions to the skull texts, because I don't trust Mireya not to call up Dad and Erika and tell them I need help before I end up like Rory.

She might even be right.

"Dad says the alerts come from a server, which means some-body's running it," I finish.

"Well, obviously." Mireya rises and grabs her tablet, looking slightly more awake. "Whoever it is, they're using a proxy server to hide their location—that's the point of being on the Dark Web."

"If it really is Caroline, and she really is in Bolinas, we could go there. We could turn the server off."

Mireya flicks something on her tablet. "Then what? Rory comes back to life?"

Before I can answer, she flips the tablet to show me a screen full of jumbled letters, numbers, and symbols. "Last night, he sent me a file of code. I don't know why or what it is. Does that sound like a stable person to you?"

"I guess not." Trying to convince her is a losing battle, but I can keep warning her. "You aren't still playing the Glare, are you?"

This time Mireya doesn't answer right away. Her eyes rove around the room as if she's checking for something, which makes me start doing it, too. We're both so still now, the clock ticking in the hallway sounds like thunder.

"I know you could last longer than me on level thirteen," I say. "But don't try, okay? And please, ask Anil to stop, too."

Mireya's eyes flash, her old spirit coming back. "*You're* the one who played to the end, Hedda. But believe me, right now, playing a game is the last thing I feel like doing."

26

The new e-mail is from Clelia Rosenbaum.

In my last message, I asked if she was the one running the server, if she could stop the skulls. She's written back: *Not me. Never been me. If you're who I think you are, the place in the picture is my best guess. If you're getting the skulls, stay away from phones—all of them.*

. . .

I'm on the dark sidewalk, halfway to Ellis's house, when I nearly walk straight into him.

"Hey!" He grasps me by the elbows. "Were you coming to see me?"

I came to tell him about Clelia's message, bringing along

the taped-together photograph I found behind my baseboard last night (*years ago*). But now there's a lump in my throat, and I just nod.

"Same here. I found the address of 'Clelia' in Bolinas. We could drive out there Saturday morning."

Then he looks where I'm looking, because we're next to the spot where the hatchback stood all afternoon, surrounded by police tape, before finally being towed away. I keep seeing this morning in a flash and blur—Rory parallel parking in the predawn darkness; the cat dashing across the street; me stepping outside under the coral sky.

Ellis's hands rise tentatively up my bare arms, rub them in small circles. "I wasn't sure if I should bother you, but you didn't answer my texts. I'm so fucking sorry about Rory."

"I put the phone on Do Not Disturb." I clear my throat and swallow, hard. "Do you have something to drink?"

We end up in a pool of blackness on my deck, outside the range of the motion-detecting floodlight. Ellis hands me a flask, and a stink unfurls from it, pungent as gasoline. I force a swig down my throat, choke, and raise it again.

Strong fingers cover mine, stopping me. Ellis is a sliver of white T-shirt and a ghost of hair as he says, "Seriously, go slow with that."

"I need it." I've never really drunk alcohol before, and the burn of whiskey in my throat is melting into a warmth behind my breastbone. I close my eyes, the dark behind my lids vibrating in time with the insects in the grass. "Ellis, this is all my fault."

"How?" Surprise puts an unlikely squeak in his voice.

Sitting beside him, precariously balanced on the deck railing,

I can smell his sweat, feel the curve of his shoulder close in the dark. He's not slurring his words, not the bad kind of drunk he was the night of the beach party, not yet.

But I know he's not as strong as he wants people to think. He may scale the porch roof, risk his neck on a cliff, and court detention at school, but his face falls apart when he talks about his sister, or about the Glare.

I raise the flask again. "One more." Ellis doesn't stop me, just reaches for it when I'm done and takes a swig himself.

"It's my fault because I'm the one who found the game—again." My mouth tastes bitter, but the words feel weightless now. "I gave it to Mireya, and we both played it, and somehow other people ended up with it—Anil. Emily. Rory."

"Are you saying...?"

"Rory died thirteen times on level thirteen."

"Shit," Ellis whispers. He cradles the flask in both hands as I tell him everything—almost.

He nods and begins contributing details of his own. "You hear keening. You hear rustling. You see things that look sort of human, but—"

"They're made of light, and they don't have faces. Randoms." Cold moves down my spine as if saying the word might summon them. I haven't told him about cutting myself as a child, seeing my own apparition in a Random, or stabbing Clint's panda, and I don't plan to. "Do you remember all that from playing the game? Or have you seen them, too?"

"In real life? No. I didn't play to level thirteen. I was too chicken, remember?"

He believes me. It makes me want to hug him, and to cover up the impulse, I say, "I thought you were a daredevil."

"On my feed, sure. It's easy to do stupid shit when you're trashed and still be a freaking coward inside."

"I don't think you're a coward."

His head swivels to me, and though I can't see his face, the scrutiny burns. "I am. When I told you I didn't find anything in Caroline's room, that wasn't the absolute truth. After what happened with Emily, I checked again, and I found this in an old notebook."

He passes me a scrap of paper, illuminating it with his phone. I see a pencil drawing that looks at first glance like a rough rendering of a man's face. But when I examine it closer—

The sight of the familiar skull grips my body like a chilly wind. I teeter on the deck railing and leap down into the wet grass. There I sit, hugging my knees, smelling moist dirt and manzanita, my nerves singing a high, sustained note that echoes in the rush of my blood.

Caroline drew the skull. I should be grateful for more proof that she designed the Glare, but I only feel cold.

I want to be the girl I was when I was six—cocky and carefree, Heady Hedda riding the Dark Web like a pirate on the high seas, never suspecting that all her clever toys could be taken away. Who would I be if I'd never stolen the Glare from Caroline? Would Rory still be alive?

When Ellis's shadow falls across me, I say again, "It's all my fault."

Six-year-old Hedda engineered her own downfall. She was too good at getting what she wanted, and what she wanted was for her mom and dad to think she was brilliant. She wanted their attention. She wanted to play Caroline's special, secret game and win.

It didn't turn out that way. And then, when I found the Glare again, I had to try and beat it a second time like I hadn't learned a thing. Only this time I pulled more people in with me.

Ellis's hand brushes my shoulder, warm and tentative. "It's *not* your fault. Even if the Glare actually does kill people, you couldn't have known."

"I dared you to play it. Mireya and Lily were right—I was a horrible, selfish person. I hurt you."

"Are you going to blame yourself for my general shittiness since you left? Because, no thanks, I don't need you taking responsibility for me. And I doubt Rory would want you to take responsibility for him, either."

"Stop it." My voice is choked up. "He's—"

"I know. Believe me, I'm not comparing us. But, Hedda, you were *six*."

I lean back against his hand, feeling the pulse of his breath. "Your life isn't shitty. When I met you at the barbecue, you seemed so sure of yourself, like you owned the world."

Ellis makes a dry sound, not quite a laugh. "I don't own even this moment. But if I can do one thing, I want to find my sister. I want to know what happened to her—or what she did."

I take out the photo with the game's address and the tower image. "I think she's running the game server. We need to turn it off. Check your mail—I forwarded you a new message from Clelia."

Ellis pulls out his phone, and the darkness goes taut between us as he reads the thread. "If this is Caroline, she says she's *not* running it. You think this is the picture she meant? This place with the black tower?"

I turn the image over. "Does this look like her handwriting?"

Ellis peers at it. "Yeah. This is what you stole from her?"

"Must be. Do you recognize the place in the picture?"

For an instant, I allow myself to hope the black tower is adjacent to some Westover wilderness cottage or summer getaway, but he shakes his head. "I'll try a reverse-image search, but we need to go to Bolinas. If she's there, she'll explain."

Or she won't want to explain, and she'll be running the game server, and she'll be violent with a shaky grasp on reality. Remembering what Dad said after the horror movie, I wonder again if running the Glare could be Caroline's way of trying to control the thing that scares her—the screens she never managed to stop seeing. But I keep my thoughts to myself.

"I'm not saying we'd rush in and hug it out," Ellis says, as if sensing my misgivings. "She disappeared for a reason. Maybe it's better if I go alone—"

"No," I say just as his phone vibrates on the grass between us.

I don't decide to pick it up. All I know is suddenly I'm holding it, and then I'm hurling it across the lawn.

The phone lands under a Japanese maple and buzzes again, its glow turning the darkness oily with menace. It's barely audible now, yet I can almost hear the keening. That sensation of being watched crawls over my skin.

Ellis stares at me. "The fuck? You know I'm not getting skulls."

Don't look for flashes of white. "I know, it's just...I can't explain. The noise." *Conditioned response.* "I'm sorry. I hope it's okay."

Ellis goes and retrieves the phone. It illuminates his face briefly before blinking into darkness. "It's fine. I'm turning vibration off."

Stay away from phones, all of them. If anyone understands the danger, it's Caroline. But why would she help me avoid it?

*I*n a room lit by a vanilla-scented candle that is being used to muffle the stink from a foot-high bong, a boy dies for the thirteenth time.

He wasn't going to bother finishing the game, but today in fifth period he got a text with a picture of a safety rune. Right after that, he heard the first whispers about Rory.

He didn't remember the text till he was home again, sitting at the computer, taking hits and staring at an inbox full of old messages from his dead friend.

His vision blurring with tears, he clicked randomly on a window he hadn't bothered to close. Next thing he knew, he was dodging and weaving through the game forest, shooting Randoms with Glare-bolts.

He got a bunch more messages while he was playing, probably about Rory, but he ignored them. The game was a good distraction, *but now it's over. Like everyone else, he has not survived level 13. He is doomed.*

So what? Everyone dies in the end.

Rory told him not to post the link, but maybe he will, just for fun. Just to see what happens. Wondering if there even is a level 14, he leans back in his chair, gazing at a crack in the plaster ceiling. His phone buzzes.

He doesn't need to look; it'll be the skull. Ha-ha. Terrifying.

He closes his eyes. What kind of crazy sick fuck would kill Rory? And that poor weird new girl, having to find him. Seeing all that blood.

The phone buzzes a second time. This time he looks, and what he sees makes him sit upright with a jolt.

The first text is the stupid skull, yeah. But the second text says, Ur pathetic.

There's an image attached—a screenshot of the chat he had with Emily back when he sent her the Glare. Hey, Rory gave me this, thought you might get a kick out of it. There's a meme that says it can literally kill you, haha. No one ever gets to level 14.

His eyes sting at the sight of his own words, and his gut twists. Obviously the game didn't make her jump off the cliff, but still, what was he thinking? How could he send a friend something like that and think it was funny?

And who's sending him the screenshot, calling him pathetic? Emily's in a psych ward now. Did she show someone their chat? How many people know what a callous ass he is? He reaches for the phone again, then glances up as he hears something rustle above him, like a mouse or bird trapped in the vents.

The crack in the plaster widens. Dust rains gently on his head. The hell?

Down the hall, multiple voices sing a single high-pitched note—keening, just like in the game.

Shit. This is weed, not 'shrooms. Maybe his brain is serving up hallucinations so he doesn't have to think about Rory anymore. Thanks, brain. He watches with mild interest as a bluish-white finger pokes its way through the now-inch-wide crack above his head.

Time to go downstairs for a snack. He's just upset, that's all. Riddled with grief and survivor's guilt. Not right in his head.

Sure enough, when he returns, the crack is back to its normal size. The finger is gone.

27

Morning light is a cool green haze through the cottonwoods. I lurk behind a row of arborvitae until Mireya's mom comes down the front steps of the duplex, then intercept her at the door of her Chevy Tahoe. "Hey, Ms. Rios! Is Mireya coming to school?"

Anil hasn't messaged me back, and I need to make sure he's not playing. I must not be hiding my nerves well, or my sleeplessness, because Mireya's mom nearly drops her key fob. "Hedda! No, she's not feeling well. She has a cold, and she's upset about Rory, so I told her to take today off."

"My phone's broken." Too late, I realize how pathetic I sound.

I ended up turning my phone completely off, and even that way, I didn't sleep well. I kept sitting bolt upright, thinking I'd heard the vibration.

"I don't think she's awake yet—she took some NyQuil. Want me to ask her to e-mail you when I check on her?"

"That would be great." Ellis and I will drive out to Bolinas today after school, and someone should know where we're going. Maybe I can even persuade Mireya to come along.

I want to find the black tower, too, to see it for myself, but that's not what matters now. *The server could be there. Take out the server.*

I'm heading back to Ellis's house, hoping to catch a ride with him, when the Tesla pulls up beside me. Erika sticks her head out the driver's window, hair in a messy knot, her expression grimmer than I've ever seen it before. "Where are you going? You just disappeared!"

"I was going to school with Mireya, but she's sick." Clint's playing his game in the back, and I slide in next to him. Ever since that awful night in his room, I haven't known how to look at him, though if he's noticed the rush surgery I did on his panda, he hasn't said so. "Will you take me?"

"Of course! I said I'd drive you." Erika's voice shakes as she pulls out. "You were out late last night, and you didn't come to breakfast. After yesterday, I need to know where you are."

"I was just in the backyard. I'm fine!"

Clint looks up as my voice rises in volume. Though his expression doesn't change, I can tell the argument bothers him.

Not him, I'll never hurt him. Just thinking about it is like turning over an innocent-looking desert rock and finding a welter of slithering, seething things. I want to be the one who protects and reassures him—his big sister.

I lower my voice. "I just wanted to check in with Mireya about something. I didn't mean to scare you."

Erika sighs. "Good. I'm picking you up at the end of the day."

I sit in silence while she drops off Clint at his school, then say, "Some friends and I were talking about going to the beach this afternoon." Maybe I can prevent a second fight after school.

"The beach, really? I was hoping to get your dad to come home for dinner. You two should talk after everything that's—"

"We're having a bonfire for Rory, and I don't need to talk to Dad." My voice pitches upward again, blood rushing to my temples. It doesn't feel right lying to her, but I wish she'd stop trying to pretend Dad is one of those dads in books who sit down and have serious little talks that make you feel older and wiser. When Dad and I talk, it always seems to end with him telling me a long story about himself. "He's not going to make me feel better about what happened yesterday. He's always away, and I get that he's had a lot of problems in his own life, but he doesn't *notice* things. He's almost as bad as Mom, and *she's* in deep denial about the person she used to be."

Just thinking about returning to the desert, to the prison of ignorance Mom built for me, makes me shudder with rage. Stealing the Glare was my fault, but Dad should never have let Mom take me away, and Mom should have warned me. Wasn't that her job? She mentored Caroline; she knew what really happened better than anyone.

"*You*," I say, "are the only adult who's really listened to me since I got here. So please listen now. I need to go with my friends tonight."

"Hedda." Erika lets out a long breath. "We'll discuss that after school. But you and Mike need to talk, too. I'm glad you trust me, but I can't always be the go-between."

"Fine." I try to focus on the sunlight and the alleys rioting with bougainvillea. "I'll talk with him."

But not until after we've been to Bolinas. If I tell Dad everything now, he'll cock his head to one side and decide I'm just as delusional as Mom, only he won't even *tell* me, just start speaking in a new, velvet-edged voice, the way you talk to small children and crazy people.

I need proof. I need Caroline.

. . .

Is that Anil over by the vending machines, behind the big boy with the dreadlocks?

He's headed for the recycling station, or maybe toward the exit. This is the first I've seen of him all day, and I leave my seat and sprint across the cafeteria, determined not to let him escape.

I weave sideways to dodge a group of athletes and crash into someone smaller on the other side, sending us both sprawling to the hard tiles. "What?" she grunts.

It's Cheyenne, with her silky hair and eyeliner that makes her look like a cheetah. She brushes herself off, scowling at me. "What's your problem?"

What *is* my problem? The adrenaline's bleeding away, leaving me cold all over. My left hip aches, and from my new vantage, I can see the boy at the recycling station isn't Anil after all.

I remember standing in the desert and reaching out my imaginary antennae and finding nothing. Having friends feels like the biggest gift I've ever received, and the heaviest responsibility.

But *are* these my friends? If even Mireya won't listen to me, why should they?

I follow Cheyenne back to her table. She carries a cup of green tea like she's serving the queen of England, her head high and her bangs sharp as sword grass.

"I need to find Anil," I tell her, my eyes sweeping up and down the table full of Mireya's friends. "I thought he had lunch this period."

"I don't know. He's probably home because of Rory." Cheyenne sits down with a hard grate of her chair. "I kind of thought you would be, too, after what happened."

Could she have sent me the text asking if I did it? Girls' nervous laughter sounds in the background, crackly as tinsel, then goes silent. I meet Lily Chen's eyes, and she drops them immediately. It could have been her, too. Could have been any of them.

"None of you know where Anil is?"

Some shake their heads. Most don't look at me at all. Only Cheyenne stares me in the eyes, her own blue and frigid. "Shall I give him a message from you?"

"I already messaged him!" There's nothing more I can do here, but more words leap from my mouth: "Listen, when you visit Emily, don't bring your phone. Keep phones away from her!"

Cheyenne's lips seem about to release words, then clamp again.

"Whether it's real or not, it can hurt you. It can make you hurt other people, or yourself. You need to..."

Ignore it? When I think of the Random sitting on Clint's chest, the glowing arm wrapped around his neck, I fall backward into a narrow cavity in my mind that smells of rotting leaves. Falling and falling, never hitting bottom.

It's a relief to come back to the fluorescent-lit cafeteria—though, if you could flay someone with a glance, Cheyenne would be doing it to me now.

"I don't know what really happened between you and Rory," she says, flinching a little on his name, "but I wish you would just stay the fuck away from all of us. Everything was fine until you came."

28

Fifth period's over, and a happy hum of voices carries me down the hall. People who didn't know Rory are singing, laughing, reviewing weekend plans. Every now and then a stranger gives me a rapid sidelong look, and I wonder if they know I found Rory, if they think I could have hurt him, if they sent the text. But they always glance away again.

I'm almost to the library when I spot Anil walking toward me, tugging off his headphones. *Finally!* I step into his path, half expecting him to dodge me, but he stops like it's the most natural thing in the world.

He wears a bright red-and-black-checked shirt, like a lumberjack only more stylish, and he looks a little sad and distant, but not unfriendly, as he asks, "How're you holding up?"

I should be asking you that. "Okay." Then I blurt out, "I've been looking for you all day."

"Yeah? I cut some classes and tried to go see Emily earlier, but they wouldn't let me in. Relatives only. I'm kind of in maintenance mode right now."

"I'm sorry to bug you." I clasp my hands, hard. "And I know this is going to sound weird. But...you did stop playing the Glare, right?"

I'm expecting a reaction like Mireya's, or even Cheyenne's. But Anil only twirls the headphones around a finger, his eyes going hollow. "Oh. Yeah. About that."

A stale cavity grows in my stomach. "Did you get to level thirteen?"

"Last night. Kinda just happened."

My heart sinks, and I know it shows on my face, but he's so weirdly casual that I can't tell whether he understands why. "You got the skull? Anil, have you seen anything yet?"

Anil pulls a notebook from his pack, followed by a small, sharp-edged steel ruler with a pocket clip at one end. He shoots me a grin, but his dark eyes are damp, his long lashes glistening. "What should I see? Ghosts coming to take me to the underworld?"

Behind us, a phone buzzes. We both go still at the same instant, Anil's hand freezing in midair.

The smile melts off his face, leaving blankness—and then a look of intense concentration. His eyes seem to be tracking the progress of something behind me. "Emily?" he says.

Before I can turn and look, motion flickers above my head.

Keening.

One of the corkboard ceiling tiles has come loose, leaving a dark crack. Something glimmers up there—and my nerves go taut, each breath an ocean in my ears.

My phone is off. This shouldn't be happening. Clelia said—
She said I should stay away from *all* phones.

A blue-white arm unfurls itself and creeps along the ceiling. Its skin is depthless, luminous.

"Shit. Shit!" Anil staggers away from me, his backpack and notebook thudding to the floor. His arms twist and contort, his hands grasping at nothing.

"It's not on you!" Then I realize he's looking in the wrong direction—not up, but out into the crowd.

Into the crowd, where no one has a face.

They're still laughing and talking and high-fiving. But their heads are white, filmy, featureless, as if they've been swaddled in glowing spider silk. Smooth indentations where eyes should be. Struggling holes for mouths.

They're all Randoms, and the keening is getting louder, soaring above their talking, and there's no air to breathe. I need my gun to shoot them, I need the black tower. I need to get past them any way I can, or else they'll—

A scream rises in my throat, but I choke it down and blink hard instead—darkness, light. Remembering the mistake I made in Clint's bedroom, I force myself to visualize the dirt where things grow. I feel it between my fingers—my connection to the earth. When I was six, I tried to make that connection with a knife, but I don't need to bleed to know I'm real.

On my second blink, everyone is back to normal. Eyes, noses, mouths. Opaque, non-glowing skin.

Except Anil.

He's his human self, but his eyes are white and wild, his mouth drawn tight with terror. As he turns to bolt, I know he's still seeing what I was an instant ago.

A whole school of Randoms.

"Wait!" I shout.

People scatter as Anil barrels down the hall, his limbs flailing. He runs from an echoing hallway full of eyeless monsters that will strangle him with their long arms, tear him limb from limb. And there are no safe trees, no black tower for him to run to.

When we die in the game, it comes to us.

I dash after him, my vision narrowing to his red-and-black shirt, heart pounding and adrenaline singing. *Not you, too. Cheyenne's right, this is all my fault—*

The crowd closes in Anil's wake, and I lose sight of him behind the enormous shoulders of a boy in a varsity jacket. "Anil! Please!"

The press of people drowns my yell; I'm trapped in a dream where the air thickens to molasses. Down the hallway, someone yelps. Voices rise in annoyance, others shrilling with alarm.

"What's he on?"

"Is there a gun?"

Then everyone's pressing and surging, curiosity turning to panic, people craning their necks to see what or whom Anil is running from. I'm one of the few people looking toward him, not after him, and I'm just in time to see his mad sprint for the glass door at the corridor's far end.

A burly man in a navy-blue suit—a teacher?—darts out of nowhere and seizes Anil by his collar, stopping him short. Anil kicks fiercely, but the teacher is stronger and trawls him in. Anil whirls to face him and slams something into his eye.

It glints. The sharp-edged silver ruler, buried almost to the clip end. Anil pulls it out again.

Behind me, somebody screams.

Fifty feet away, it looks like a choreographed dance, a stage illusion. But the teacher staggers backward, hands to his face. I recoil, too, my head light with the sensation of falling, nausea blurring my vision.

Light pours through the glass door. Anil is gone.

The girl who screamed earlier has started ranting in a raw-edged voice: something about *Did you see it?* Or maybe it's a different girl. Half the people in the corridor are yelling hysterically, and the other half are telling them to shut up; this isn't a drill. All down the corridor, people pour into open classrooms, making beelines for the nearest door. The only ones not moving are the ones watching as the teacher sinks to his knees.

There's no blood on his cheek. Shouldn't there be blood?

My paralysis leaves me, and I hurry toward the door where Anil disappeared, clammy sweat beading on my palms and neck, my breath coming fast and shallow. I'm the only one who knows what Anil saw, why he hurt that man, and I need to stop him, need to make him understand (*not real, not real*).

When I'm fifteen feet away, someone bursts from the door of the nearest classroom, fighting the tide. Copper hair—Ellis.

He's headed outdoors, too, taking the hallway in a few bounding strides. I'm about to call out his name when fingers close on my arm, and I turn to find a teacher with dangly earrings and a grim expression.

When I turn back, Ellis is already dodging the knot of people gathered around the fallen teacher. Arms reach out to stop him, but he yanks free, snaps the glass door, and disappears.

Is he going to try to calm Anil? What if Anil uses the ruler again?

I drag the teacher toward the door, trying to see outside, but she pulls me just as hard. "Take cover," she says, bundling me toward an open classroom. "This isn't a drill."

. . .

My phone is silent. My phone is off. It doesn't matter.

Maybe Anil's phone was off, too.

A dozen people huddle with me behind a teacher's desk, barely moving. Two boys whisper back and forth until everyone else shushes them. Someone breathes with a sharp little whimper on each exhale.

I can't stop myself from running scenarios in my head. Ellis grabbing Anil's arm, yanking him around, and Anil driving the steel ruler into his eye. Or his chest. Ellis collapsing to his knees, blood trickling down his cheek. Anil running straight into a line of cops, falling in a volley of bullets and a spray of blood.

But we haven't heard any shooting. Why didn't I warn Ellis? Why didn't I yell?

People keep whispering about a gun, but there doesn't need to be a gun. Phones pulse in backpacks like bombs ticking off seconds. On the way here, I almost tossed my own in the trash, but the momentum of the crowd carried me on.

Somehow that sound set us both off. If this is another level of the game, I don't understand the rules.

Please let Ellis know what to do. Please let him not have risked his life for nothing.

Leaves shiver on the windowpane; the teacher didn't get the blind all the way closed. I try not to check the ceiling for dark cracks, the corners for flickers.

I keep seeing the blankness on Anil's face when he heard that buzz, like a phone's screen before a new app comes up. Everything wiped clean—did I look that way, too?

My left leg is practically numb, when a skinny, intent-faced boy with a phone whispers to his neighbor, "Gomez's outside. Says they got a body bag."

For who? Tears prickle in my sinuses, but the awareness of the boy's phone keeps me centered. It's pulsing. Ticking. Any moment it could buzz, and I could hear.

People are stirring and fidgeting. The news their phones are feeding them seems to have made fears of a shooter recede, while mine keep mounting.

"Westover's still out there trying to be a big hero," mutters the skinny boy.

"Mr. Nedrick's the hero," a girl says.

"Nedrick's not dead. They took him to the hospital." The boy's eyes flick to me, then away. "Gomez says it's the kid who stabbed Nedrick, the one in the plaid shirt. The bag's for him."

I feel my hands come together on my chest. Guilty relief that it's not Ellis, followed by a sick, sinking sensation. *But he was just here.* Somewhere close by, a tiny black hole has opened, sucking us toward it.

"Anil? He's dead?" And then, though it shouldn't matter, "But how?"

"Drugs, probably," another boy grunts.

The skinny boy ignores him. "Embolism or something? They say he got outside and just keeled over like he couldn't run anymore."

*S*omewhere, in a room where sunlight glows through closed petal-pink curtains, a girl loses a game that she was going to win. Was supposed to win.

She's been preparing for level 13 for days, analyzing the game mechanics, looking for what less patient players miss. She knows that if you touch your Glare-gun to the message carved on the big oak, you receive a 30 percent strength boost for twenty seconds. She knows all the safe trees, and the patterns of the Randoms—how they don't generally attack and give you a kill shot until they've buzzed you four or five times with their ambiguous slithers and flickers.

But sometimes they break pattern and attack with no warning. That's what happened this time.

The screen informs her she is dead for the last time. She takes a screenshot.

And she waits.

And waits. She goes downstairs to get a snack, taking her phone.

She needs to show Hedda that the Glare didn't kill Rory. Some people need a reason for everything. They don't want to believe that bad things just happen.

Like her dad leaving a week after her grandma died. For months afterward, she saw everything through a haze of grief. The world felt like a giant game skewed against her, and she wondered what she'd done wrong. But gradually things returned to normal. She and her mom ordered pizza and laughed at dumb movies. Life went on.

Rory was a person—goofy laugh, nervous hands, mercurial hair, beating heart. When she was twelve and her cat died, he put together a video called "Fluffer's Greatest Hits" that made her laugh and cry. She doesn't know what happened in that car at dawn, but Rory was not code, not rewritable. He was real.

Her phone buzzes while she's returning the juice to the fridge.

So this is it. Moment of truth. She has to admit, she's curious.

As she picks up her phone, something moves on top of her mom's china hutch, ten feet away—but no, it's a shadow.

First comes the skull text, then one that just says, Ur pathetic. No image.

She goes upstairs, whistling, past the family photos in the hallway. She uses the bathroom, then examines herself in the vanity.

Her breath dies in her throat. The phone slips from her grasp.

Her heartbeat is loud and distant at the same time, like the pounding of a hammer next door. She can't move, only stare at the face that used to be hers.

It has no visible mouth, eyes, or nose, yet something bulges inside it—the outlines of a firm chin and stubborn forehead. Beneath the rubbery bluish-white coating that covers every inch of her, human lips open in a silent scream.

Not her lips. This isn't her face. It's Hedda's.

Horns jut from the hairline now, growing inches before her eyes. The forehead swells like a balloon. It's the monstrous image of Hedda that she and Lily posted long ago, only now it's inside her, and she can't get it out.

She presses her fingertips to the hideous face, and they begin to tingle: cold, cold, cold. She bangs her forehead—its forehead—against the glass, once, twice, three times. Until she feels dizzy and sick. Until blood starts trickling into her—its—eyes.

Her legs carry her back down the hallway, but her core has gone cold, too. The keening rises around her. The faces in all the photos are gone, replaced by featureless white heads.

She did something wrong, something terrible, and now the Randoms are coming for her. There are no real people left in the world. They're all Randoms, every one.

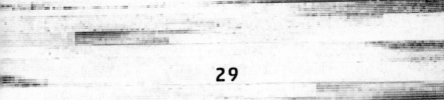

29

"You knew," Lily says, turning her car out of the school driveway. "How'd you know? Why were you looking for him?"

"It's hard to explain. Just something he said a few days ago." I keep staring at my sneaker; the lace is untied, but somehow I can't bend and tie it. One stray movement could be like hitting a domino and toppling the whole chain. "I just need to see Mireya."

Lily frowns, but maybe the world feels as fragile to her right now as it does to me, because she doesn't press the point.

We had to wait to leave till the PA system reassured us there was no active shooter on campus, only a "stabbing suspect" who had been apprehended. People around me sobbed, while rumors flew: Anil had an undiagnosed heart condition—no, an undiagnosed psychosis. He died from shock. He died from pure fright.

Dead is dead.

I looked everywhere for Ellis until I heard someone say he was in the office being grilled about his act of would-be heroism. Then I got away from school as quickly as I could, pausing only to turn on my phone and text Erika, *I'm okay, catching a ride, be there soon*, then turn it off. I begged a ride from Lily, who seemed too numb to say no.

By the time we reach Mireya's duplex, chalky clouds have covered the sky, and fog hangs low over the brown hills. "You okay?" Lily asks, pulling up. Without Cheyenne around, she seems almost friendly.

"Yeah. Thank you. Do you want to come in?" *Please say no.*

She shakes her head. "Better get home before my mom freaks out."

I wait for her to pull away, then hit the doorbell, my heart slamming my ribs. Does Mireya know yet? I need her now—her steadiness, her rational explanations. I need to tell her what *I* saw happen before she reads too many online rumors. She needs to know shutting down the server will stop this.

But will it? Based on what I saw today, the signals that trigger us don't have to be skulls anymore.

Silence. I hit the doorbell again, then knock in case it's broken. Mireya's mom must be at work, but Mireya's car is here. The curtains are drawn.

I pull out my phone to text her—oh, right.

Living without the Glare is slow and hard—I should know. But if other people's alerts and ringtones can trigger us, then living *in* the Glare is impossible.

Did Mom guess that? Or did she do the right thing accidentally?

I go around back and toss a few pieces of decorative gravel at Mireya's window. A neighbor's dog starts barking. Returning to the front, I trip on my shoelace, then bend and knot it tightly. *Feet on the ground.*

On the front porch, I search for a spare key. It's not under the mat, or in the planter with the geraniums, or in the mailbox, or on the sill of the little sunken window by the door.

The window's granite frame continues all the way around. To reach the top, I climb onto the porch railing and stand on tiptoe, holding the door frame for support.

The key falls from the ledge with a glitter and a tinkle. One scramble in the grass later, I'm opening the door and stepping inside.

The house is silent, sun seeping greenish through curtains and shades.

"Mireya?"

If she were here, she'd have answered the door. But some undefinable quality of the air, like water seething before it boils, makes me think I'm not alone.

"Mireya? It's Hedda. I'm coming up." My heart begins to thud as I reach the stairs. "Mireya, did you hear about Anil?"

No answer.

When I reach the upstairs hall, the sizzle of my nerves makes it hard to listen for external sounds. Maybe her boyfriend picked her up and took her into the city. She's not here, and I'm being an idiot, and I'll return the key and go home.

A Frida Kahlo print hangs on her closed door, along with a

withered corsage tacked up in a loop of silky ribbon. My knock echoes everywhere, like rain pattering on the roof. It's too late to turn back.

I turn the knob and step inside onto something that splinters with a foreboding crunch.

A tablet, tossed on the floor. The screen is cracked in a spiderweb pattern as if someone hit it with a hammer.

Light bleeds blearily through the curtains, illuminating posters of all-girl rock bands and cartoon boys with enormous eyes. The bed is unmade, empty. And the desk—

Bare. The giant monitor lies on the floor beside the keyboard—its screen shattered. On the daisy-printed bedspread, I find a small heap of glass and plastic that was probably once a phone.

Behind me, something slides. Something crinkles.

There's nothing back there but a closet. My nerves go electric, blood rushing in my temples and roaring in my ears. I have to force myself to take small, jerky steps toward the half-open door, fighting for control, as if I'm a puppet with something larger than me holding the strings.

The closet door is the kind that slides in a groove. I push.

After Rory, after Anil, I know I can't be prepared for what I'll see. The door makes a grating sound.

When I see her—way at the back, hugging her knees—I almost sob with relief. Her hair covers her face, and her shoulders shake, but she's *fine*. Breathing. I extend an unsteady hand toward her. "Mireya?"

Her hair parts, revealing dark blood caked on her forehead, trickles of it extending all the way to her chin.

My hands go to my own face as if to hold it together. Again I sense something like a tiny, distant explosion. "What did you—"

Her eyes pop open, white all around the iris, staring at me. Her lips pull back to bare her teeth. Her hand creeps along the closet floor, knuckles pale on the handle of a claw hammer.

"Out." Her voice is a growl, barely human.

I inch backward, knowing somehow that she won't hesitate to spring at me and use that hammer the way she did on the machines. "Whatever you saw, it's gone now," I whisper. "It's not real."

"*You're* not real." The hand not clutching the hammer points at me, the index finger trembling so violently it blurs.

"You're not!" Her voice trails into an animal cry of pain. "You're one of them. Get out! Get out! Get out!"

She staggers to her feet and comes for me. I make a grab for the hammer, but she swings it into my hip.

Pain shoots through me, sending acid into my throat, and I stumble backward as she dashes into the hall, slamming the door behind her.

By the time I've reached the landing, limping, she's down the stairs. The front door hangs open, revealing only pearly sunlight—she's gone. I hear the chime of a car lock, then the thrum of a motor.

She won't stop until she's as far from me as possible, hunkered down somewhere she feels safe. Somewhere with no phones, no devices, no Glare. No signals to warn or activate her. No one like me who's walking around when they're supposed to be dead—just like her.

She died in the Glare, and now she understands what I did

and how much is my fault. Maybe the Randoms who torment her look like me. Air lurches into my lungs as if I've been holding my breath all this time, and I slam the door and run out and down the sidewalk like I could catch her, crying her name, my heart beating a new pattern: *stop this, stop it, make it stop.*

30

"**E**rika!" I burst into a house where everything is bizarrely the same—naked sunlight glazing the windows in back, cool green filtering through the ones in front.

But the big TV is playing footage of my school surrounded by police cars, and Erika leaps up from the couch with a yelp. "I called you so many times. Is your phone off?"

"You got my text, right? I'm fine." I dump books out of my backpack, trying to decide what to bring. "I need to go out for a few hours to look for Mireya." The lie comes effortlessly. "She was upset about Anil, and she took off—I couldn't stop her. Ellis is going to drive."

That part isn't a lie. Ellis has been watching for my return since he got home. I told him about Mireya, and we made our new plan in ten seconds flat, in the shrubbery.

"Could you do me a huge favor?" I ask now. "Call Mireya's mom and tell her? She...hurt herself. I'm kind of freaked out about her." That part isn't a lie, either.

Erika already has her phone in her hand. "We'll take you. I was so worried about you."

"No, it might take a while!" I'm already halfway up the stairs. Passing Clint's door, I spy him reading an actual book. Good.

If people keep sharing the Glare, how long will it take to filter down to the lower grades? The thought makes me go cold as I stuff a hoodie, my utility knife, and my useless phone in the pack, imagining the sheer futility of trying to persuade Clint not to play a game that everyone describes as grown-up and dangerous.

I always wanted the forbidden, too.

I pack the taped-together photo of the place with the tower. Eyeless Raggedy Ann sits with her head drooping, looking miserable. I think of Erika coming in and seeing her, and my hand shoots out and packs her, too. *We need to stick together.*

Erika intercepts me in the downstairs hallway. "How long are you going to be gone? I keep calling your father, but he's not picking up."

"As long as it takes to find her. Please don't worry—you'll call her mom, right?" I slide past her and open the door. "Ask her to turn off her phone around Mireya. I'll explain later."

Behind me, she keeps begging for explanations, but by the time she reaches the top of the porch steps, I've taken them in two bounds and have hurled myself into the passenger seat of Ellis's car.

"Go," I say.

. . .

The sun's still well above the horizon as we head for the coastal highway, the strip malls and condo developments giving way to fields and trees.

"I can't believe you did that," I say. "Ran out after him. It was brave."

"It was pointless," Ellis says. He hasn't looked at me once since we left our street behind, just listened while I told him what I saw in Mireya's house. "People started pouring into the classroom, saying Anil had stabbed a teacher in the eye, and I just—I thought I could help. It seemed so unreal."

It's real. I watch the sun cut tangerine strips on the crowns of the oaks, feel the thrum of his Prius under me, don't say anything.

"Anil was my best friend after you left," Ellis says after a moment. "Fourth, fifth, sixth grade, we rode our dirt bikes all over Gerstle Park. He could always make me laugh. Last time I really talked to him was at Mireya's fourteenth birthday party, and I left early to go to a rager I thought would be more fun."

"Anil said you were reborn from the bottom of a bottle of Jack."

He stares straight ahead at the road. "He had a good way of putting things. I was sick of being the poor kid who was traumatized by his sister going batshit, so I became an asshole."

"You're not an asshole. You ran after Anil when nobody else did."

"And I really helped." His knuckles whiten on the wheel. "Sorry, Hedda. Here I am making this all about me again."

I remember the letter I wrote to Mom—a necessary letter,

241

maybe, but also a desperate challenge to her. I remember forcing Dad to look at my scars. "I've done some of that, too. I should have warned Anil better, sooner."

"You did everything you could. I should've talked to Anil and Mireya, too, but that past shit got in the way."

A blinding blue haze peeks over the horizon—the ocean. He steers us toward it.

"You'll see Mireya again," I say. "If you want to apologize to her for stuff that's way in the past—well, she'll probably tell you to get a grip, but then she'll accept your apology."

He laughs half-heartedly. "Hope so."

She should be here with us. She would tell Ellis to stop "wallowing" and get with the program. She would tell me it doesn't matter whose fault it is; the Glare is not going to take us down. For Anil, for Rory, for all those future people who might play it, we'll stop this.

But when I close my eyes, I see her hunched in the closet with the hammer, blood on her face.

"I sure as hell hope so," Ellis repeats. "I guess it's just—well, when people die, they take a piece of you. When I got to Anil outside the school, he was curled up on the ground. All the tension was gone, like he was a bag of groceries someone dropped, and I knew he was dead before I saw his face. It was just so surreal—everybody running around inside, terrified of him, and there he was. I *wanted* him to jump up and attack me."

Images of those moments in the hallway flood back, and I bite down on the inside of my cheek. "Ellis, when we were first triggered, when the first Random came, Anil said Emily's name. I think he was seeing her. They . . . look like people sometimes."

He looks at me sharply. "You didn't mention that before."

I didn't want to tell him that the Random I saw was myself. "When he was running around the mall, Rory kept saying 'he' like he was seeing a specific person. And he said getting the skulls makes us relive our greatest online fails."

"Why would Emily be Anil's greatest fail?"

I think of how I felt seeing the Random that looked like child me. I hated myself for having been that girl, for forcing Ellis to play the game. And then I remember what Anil told me outside the cafeteria, leaning in close so his friends wouldn't hear.

"Anil liked Emily, and I think she didn't like him back, at least not that way. Then he gave her the Glare, and she jumped off that cliff. So to him, even if he didn't mean to hurt her, that might seem like the worst thing he ever did online."

Maybe the Randoms aren't just faceless people who come after us, like whoever called me a freak and whoever asked if I killed Rory. Maybe sometimes they *are* us.

"The same thing could've happened to Caroline," I say. "Even if she created the Glare, it could have latched on to her memories, her fears."

Ellis is nodding. "One time when we had dinner together, after Caroline got out, my mom was bitching about online blow-back she got for something, and Caroline said, 'Randoms can only hurt you if you let them.' The way she said it made us all shut up. Like she wanted it to be true."

I want it to be true, too. But Rory believed in facing the Randoms head-on, and he's dead. "If that's what's happening," I say, "why hasn't it been as bad with me? I mean—well, you saw what happened in physics. And there've been other things." *I could have killed Clint.* "But with the others, it got bad faster. Anil said he got to level thirteen just last night."

Ellis drives with his left hand, the right resting flat on the seat between us. "Maybe it's like a virus—some people get really sick right away, and others hold out. Maybe all those years out in the desert gave you a stronger immune system."

I don't want Mom to be right, but it's true that remembering the smell of earth helped me in the school hallway. "You said the desert missed me. At the beach party."

Ellis blushes. "I was drunk."

I cover his fingers lightly with mine, and we stay quiet like that for a while.

31

Bolinas is a secret.

"There's no sign to tell you where to turn," Ellis explains as we speed along Highway 1. "A couple of my surfer friends brought me once."

We've been soaring along the edges of cliffs, the ocean winking on our left. Now we shoot into a tunnel of foliage that filters the sun: pampas grass, tangled vines, eucalyptus.

Light glints on a nearby lagoon. The beige bluffs echo it, and the whole landscape is dreamlike, veiled in gold.

This isn't the kind of place you go to find someone who created a killer game. It's the kind of place you go to spread a blanket and doze until your skin has soaked up the day's warmth, and the reflection of sunset in your companion's bruise-blue eyes makes you want to touch his cheek. *Stop it right now,* I tell myself. No distractions.

"We need a plan," I say. "If Caroline is Clelia, she mentioned knowing who I am. Maybe she remembers me stealing her game. How much else does she know?"

Ellis scratches under the neck of his oversized T-shirt. "If she's running the server, she could know which IP addresses are downloading the game. The server gets people's phone numbers, too—that's probably automated."

So whoever's running the server could be killing people without really thinking about it. "Do you think your sister wants to hurt anyone?"

Ellis's lips tighten beneath his aviator shades. "Look, as far as we know, she's never hurt anybody but herself."

"So, Caroline creates the Glare, and she tests it on herself, and she's the first victim of the Glare. But once she knows how it affects people, why does she set up the server?"

"*Keep* up the server. When you were six and getting those skull texts, she was in the psych ward, which means either that server worked without her for years, or someone's helping her."

"Maybe." My voice comes out sharper than I intend. "In which case, she'll have to tell us who's helping her and where they are."

"Or maybe the person running the server stole it from her, just like you stole the address."

He brakes as we reach a ramshackle main drag: no stoplight, one gas station, two surf shops. Some buildings are nautical white, others naturally weathered; everything's tangled in vines and hazed with diffuse light.

"Look, I know you're thinking maybe I can't be objective, because it's my sister. And you're right that I don't feel ready for this. When Caroline went away, when my parents wouldn't talk about her, I stopped being a brother. And now...I'm not sure I'm ready to see her. I'm not sure who I'll be."

"Let me do the talking, then." The past few hours have stuck to me, a gritty residue under my clothes. My hip throbs where Mireya whacked it, and a certainty thumps under my breastbone: Caroline may be a victim, too, but if she's running the Glare, she has to be stopped.

"Okay," Ellis says. "But, Hedda?"

"What?"

His throat works. "You need to be careful. Anil was so scared the moment...the moment before. You didn't see his face."

The street dead-ends in a blaze of ocean and sky. Ellis consults a crumpled map in his lap, and I realize he'd normally be using his phone.

Mom would be so proud—now I'm keeping my new friends away from their devices, too. In her confused way, she intuited what I needed, but she understood so little.

Ellis backtracks, muttering to himself, until he finds a winding residential street that leads toward the coast. We're back in the country now, and it's rich-people country, despite the scraggly junipers and hedgerows overgrown with wildflowers. The tall gates and long drives, the distant glitters of giant windows, tell me the ocean can't be far.

Caroline can't afford this address. She should be skulking in a basement, her face washed in computer light. The closer we come, the less stable this travel-magazine landscape feels, as if we might slide off its edge into a nightmare.

Red-speckled trees. Lurid light of a storm. Square black tower.

I run my fingertips over the scars on my forearm. "If Caroline created the Glare, why couldn't she win it?"

"Maybe there's no way to win. No level fourteen."

We're skimming the edge of a tall bluff covered with silver grass as smooth as sand. A fortress of a house rears its head there, all wine-red wood and glass.

"If there's no way to win, it's not a game," I say—then remember Dad's movie quote. *The only winning move is not to play.*

Ellis guides the Prius to the road's shoulder. "Here we are."

We step out into a stiff breeze, chilly for late summer. Ellis pulls on a hooded Andean sweater.

"That's 35," he says, gesturing at the mansion that looms at the end of the gray spit of driveway. "Clelia lives in 35-B, which I'm guessing means a carriage house or guesthouse or stable."

Fenceless, the estate would look abandoned if it weren't for the neatly mowed paths. I scan the landscape, half expecting to see the black tower. "Across the road—there's buildings back there." Shingled rooftops protrude from a belt of evergreens.

"Good call," Ellis says.

A dirt road winds among wind-frazzled juniper and rows of Lombardy poplars. We pass a kitchen garden, a cluster of berry bushes, and a luxurious henhouse full of Rhode Island Reds. They're making an eternal fuss, the way hens do. I'm tempted to pause, but my nerves pull me after Ellis, who's veered off the road.

He's heading for the pines that hide the rooftops. My heart starts to natter like the hens as we wend our way among rough trunks. There's something weird about this place, something wrong. The light is still golden, gloriously unreal, but no insects keen in the grass. The carpet of needles muffles our footsteps. Above our heads, boughs swish in the breeze.

Ellis stops. "Here."

Where the pines end, a cabin rises from the silver grass. Weathered by decades of winds, it's neat and compact, with five steps up to a door. The porch railing is made of driftwood, the uneven pieces jagged as human bones.

Dangling from a nail above the doorbell, a brass plaque announces in dainty script *35-B*.

As we climb the steps, I feel like I'm stepping too fast off an up escalator. *No turning back*. I touch my tongue to my front teeth, forcing my throat to relax. The heavily curtained window offers no clues.

"Ready?" Ellis has removed the sunglasses, and his freckles stand out in stark relief.

I nod, and he moves his finger to the doorbell. The chime echoes faintly inside, but nothing stirs. He tries it again. Knocks— then draws in his breath. "Hey, I think it's open."

My breath catches. "Knock again."

This time, when nothing happens, he doesn't ask my permission to turn the knob and push the door open.

"Ellis—" I break off, realizing the cabin's empty.

The place is like a studio apartment: kitchenette on one end, bed on the other, desk in the middle. On either end, the curtains have been thrown wide open, and watery light bounces off dark paneling, coffee mugs, and dozens of sheets of paper taped to the windowless back wall.

Before I can stop myself, I've crossed the rag rug for a closer look. Because, yes, I would recognize that particular shape anywhere.

The black tower.

Ellis bangs open a door, closet or bathroom. "Nobody's here."

"Look." My voice sounds oddly reverent in the half-light.

Together we look. The sheets of paper are photocopies of old photographs, all seemingly depicting the same place.

A thick inland forest, mostly pine and spruce. A square black tower with bricked-up archways at the bottom. A more rudimentary log cabin than this one. Some photos show the cabin in the foreground and the tower in the distance, as if the two perch on neighboring hilltops.

In the deep silence, Ellis's breath comes quick like mine. "It's a real place."

Some of the pictures aren't photos, but cartoonlike still images from the Glare. Here's the real tower, and here's the game version of the tower, a little taller and more massive. Here's the cabin in a hilltop grove, and here's the game version of the same grove—but the cabin has been erased. Here's a maple, and here's a maple with a rune glimmering on its trunk.

Ellis jams his hands in his pockets, as if he's bracing himself. "You're right. She built the game."

Find the server. I tear my eyes away from the pictures. "Ellis... shouldn't there be computers?"

The desk holds a pile of paperback fantasy novels, some notebooks, and—I see as I draw closer—a mug with black residue at the bottom. Dust comes away when I run my finger over the maple veneer, until it reaches a clean rectangle. "Is that big enough for a server?"

Ellis bends to peer at the dustless place. "Looks like a laptop."

Behind us, a whoosh and scrape. I wheel, tottering back a step.

"Can I help you?"

A woman stands on the doorstep, over sixty, with a mop of steel-gray hair, strong features, and twilight-blue eyes. She wears jeans and a hoodie and holds a broom in one hand, a dust rag in the other.

Ellis speaks first, too fast: "We're family of Clelia Rosenbaum—well, I am. We didn't mean to barge in, but the door was open."

The woman's head juts to the side, reminding me of a hawk getting a bead on its prey. "Did the sheriff's department call you?"

We exchange glances, and fear slithers inside my chest. Has Clelia done something wrong? If we ask, then it'll be clear the sheriff didn't summon us.

"I'm her brother," Ellis says. He crosses the room, face solemn, and pulls something out of his wallet. "This is the last picture I have of her."

The woman leans her broom against the door and examines the photo. "Huh. I'm so sorry." She looks up at him, her eyes liquid. "So very sorry. Are your parents coming, too?"

Ellis stares at her, his brows drawing down hard, as we both process her tone. "They . . . yeah. They're making arrangements."

I take hold of his arm, suddenly feeling formal as if we're at a funeral. "They didn't tell us much of anything."

"Come around back," the woman says. "Let's talk in the garden. It always calms me down."

"The garden" is a small oval of paving stones surrounded by herbs. I smell lavender, thyme, basil, rosemary, marjoram, sage—a winter's worth of hearty stews.

Our host sits on a low stone bench, then rises and signals Ellis to sit instead. "Where are my manners? The smells are soothing, aren't they? Bargain aromatherapy is how I think of it."

I sit down stiffly beside Ellis, who stares straight ahead. "Very soothing."

The woman turns away. When she pivots back to us, tears flow down her cheeks, but her voice is steady as a radio announcer's. "Please excuse me, but it was very sudden, and I wasn't expecting anyone to show up today. The sheriff told me it might take weeks to locate her family. I'm the one who found Clelia, you see, just this morning. On the beach. The paramedics say she was dead on impact."

32

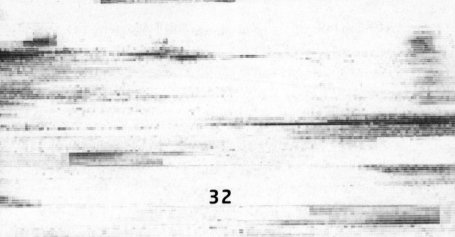

The woman's name is Lazuli Leverett ("Marjorie by birth. Changed it in the Summer of Love and couldn't be bothered to change it back"). She is sole owner of the estate ("since the divorce") and insists on serving us tea on the terrace of the main house.

The tea reminds me of sitting in the kitchen with Erika, and I know I should call her. But I'll probably be home all too soon.

"I wish we could have met under better circumstances," Lazuli says, plunking gummy mugs before us. "The whole time I knew Clelia, I never saw her have visitors. But I could tell she wasn't alone in the world."

Below us, across an enormous yellowed lawn, the ocean thunders against the cliffs. The sun inclines west, drawing out Ellis's freckles and the pink line of his lips, showing me the ghost of the shy boy he once was.

A glossiness comes and goes in his eyes, but he hasn't cried, and he hasn't spoken any more than necessary, letting me handle the small talk. He said he didn't feel like a brother because Caroline had erased herself from his life, and I have a feeling he's wishing he hadn't expressed it that way.

But it's not his fault. Dead is dead.

Lazuli is talking to fill the spaces, telling us how she first met "Clelia" working at a farm stand on Olema Bolinas Road. They compared theories of the afterlife and hit it off, and Lazuli offered Clelia a caretaker position, watching over the estate while the Leveretts traveled the world.

Clelia/Caroline moved into the tidy cabin behind the pines and thrived there, doing her job with immaculate efficiency—until last night or this morning. No one knows yet exactly when it happened.

"She said she was estranged from her family, and she wasn't forthcoming about her personal life." Lazuli props her sneakered feet on a redwood table, her gaze discreetly not resting on Ellis. "My ex and I didn't ask questions—we appreciated Clelia's hermit tendencies. Too many of our caretakers invited their friends up for wild parties while we were in Europe or India."

"Her name wasn't Clelia," Ellis says sharply. He rotates his cup between his palms. "It was Caroline Westover."

Lazuli Leverett inclines her head. "I'm sorry. We never knew. She asked us to pay her under the table, so I wasn't surprised when the sheriff said her ID was a fake. But I didn't expect them to find her family so soon."

"The sheriff must be very efficient," I lie, my mind working.

Lazuli has made it clear, in a polite and roundabout way, that Caroline jumped or slipped or fell off the cliff below the house. Whichever it is, all those photos on Caroline's wall mean something.

Maybe she's covering up for someone else. Maybe she didn't want to face the consequences. But then why e-mail me at all?

"I wish I could simply give you her things," Lazuli is saying, "but the sheriff's office is in charge. They'll need some kind of documentation."

"My parents will handle all that." There's a set to Ellis's jaw like something's stuck in his throat, twisting his face in two directions. Like he's still not sure he's not dreaming all this. "There was a space on her desk. Did they already take her computers?"

"Just the one laptop, I believe. Clelia—Caroline—didn't use computers any more than she had to. She refused to keep a cell phone, said she'd come out here to escape all that."

My eyes lock on Ellis's.

Why would Caroline fear the Glare's alerts if she was running the server? *Where is it?*

There's a question I have to ask, though I wish I didn't have to do it in front of Ellis, and I know I won't get a straight answer. "Ms. Leverett...well, I mean, I know the sheriff is doing an inquest, but what do *you* think? How did she seem?"

Lazuli gazes at me, calm as granite. "I think these cliffs can be treacherous in the dark. I don't choose to speculate further."

"But did she—I mean, do you think—"

"Can we see where it happened?" Ellis asks.

. . .

A path winds along the edge of the cliff through a scrim of stunted juniper. The fall is maybe sixty feet, the beach below all gray pebbles, waves foaming hungrily ten feet from the base.

"Here in this inlet," Lazuli says. "After midnight, the sheriff thinks. Toward high tide, but apparently not high enough, because I found her when I came out for my usual walk in the morning."

Waves leap silver in the inlet, crashing against a rocky protrusion. The juniper grow sparse here, making it an easy place to jump—or to push someone. Where an oval of yellow caution tape pens in a scuffle of footprints, I recognize the crisscrossed soles of Converse sneakers.

"They took lots of photos there," Lazuli says, following my eyes. "Those are her Chucks, but the rest—who can tell?"

Ellis takes a step beyond me, to the edge, and raises his head to the fuzzy blue horizon. "It happened on impact, they said?"

"Yes. I wish I could say she looked peaceful when I found her, but…well, who would look peaceful, really?" Lazuli clears her throat, clearly doubting her qualifications as a grief counselor. "Anyway, you're welcome to stay as long as you like."

After she leaves, Ellis stands looking out to where the sun, bloated and scarlet, has just touched the ocean. He doesn't speak.

I sit down cross-legged and trace circles in the dirt outside the yellow tape. Inside it, around the juniper's gnarled trunk, it's too sandy and dry for firm impressions; I see one deep heel print, larger than the Chucks, but nothing else.

I imagine Caroline standing here last night in the dark,

listening to high tide crunch on the pebbled shore. Was she alone? Did someone surprise her? Did Lazuli make the larger print weeks or months earlier on one of her morning constitutionals?

From this angle, the sun sets Ellis's face on fire. Until his shoulders quiver, I don't realize he's crying.

I go to him and touch his shoulder, warmth seeping through the thin T-shirt. He says, "This sucks," his voice fractured like the pebbles on the beach.

"I know."

He leans slightly into me, rubbing his face with both hands. "I keep thinking of that day when you were writing on the wall with the Sharpie. I felt so lost. You were my only real friend, and I couldn't help you, and I couldn't help Anil today. And now my sister's gone, *really* gone, and I keep thinking about that server, and I think it hurt her, too, Hedda. I think she was a victim."

I slip my arm tentatively around him until our fingers clasp, the sea breeze shearing past us as the sun sinks. "I think so, too." I want to believe it.

His silhouette is black and solid against the pool of flame on the horizon, and the closeness of his shoulder blades and hips to my body is palpable. "We need to find Mireya. No, first we need to go back to that cabin and look for clues—anything."

"Your parents should know, though. So they can make…arrangements."

Ellis turns to face me. Blinded by the sun behind him, I feel his hair tickle my cheek as he says, "That can wait."

He straightens to take something from his backpack—the flask. Unscrews it.

I draw in my breath, and he says, "Don't worry, I know I'm

driving," then smiles blindingly for an instant, mocking us both, and takes a pull. "That should hold me for a few hours. Or another five minutes. You go back and start searching the cabin. I want to stay here for a bit."

The sun reddens the side of his face—slipping, slipping toward its own bloody reflection in the Pacific—as I give him space to say goodbye to his sister.

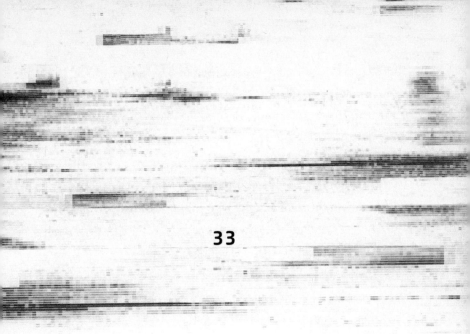

33

Now that the sun has set, the pines around Caroline's cabin blend into purple pools of shadow. As I pass the henhouse, where Lazuli is busy shooing the chickens in for the night, the ocean wind goose pimples my skin. Smells of dung and mealworms bring me back to the ranch.

Simple tasks, iron-clad routines. If I were still there, those skulls might have come to different people, in Texas or New York or Brazil, and never touched the coastal enclave of San Rafael. Rory, Anil, and Emily would be going out tonight, looking forward to the long Labor Day weekend.

A hand on my arm makes me jump—Lazuli. Is she going to tell me to stay away from Caroline's possessions?

"Ellis is coming," I explain, feeling the energy for politeness slipping away from me. "We're going to have one last look, if it's okay—we won't touch anything."

Lazuli has released me, but her eyes stay on mine. "I didn't mean to scare you. Did you know Cl—Caroline very well?"

Something about that gaze makes me go stock-still. *She knows something.* "She babysat me when I was little."

"Can you think of anyone who might want to hurt her?"

My head shakes of its own accord. "No. But she did...well, she hurt herself, when she was younger."

"There's something I didn't want to mention to Ellis just now, but I'm not sure I want him to hear it first from the sheriff, either. That man doesn't have the best bedside manner. Maybe you can tell him when he's ready."

My vision blurs with the effort it takes not to look eager. *Breathe. Just nod.*

"When I first went in there, after I found her, I did open the laptop," Lazuli says. "I don't know what I was expecting—maybe a note. The first thing I saw was an e-mail with a picture attached. The sender was weird—no name, just something with the word 'survivor' in it. But it wasn't in the spam folder."

She wets her lips, her eyes darting up the lawn, where a flash of coppery hair tells me Ellis is approaching. "I'm not sure why I'm telling you this. I really shouldn't be."

"You're telling me," I say, "because the picture was a skull."

Her eyes go mild with shock. "How did you know?"

. . .

Caroline got a skull. Caroline stepped (ran? fell?) off a cliff. We're back at the beginning, and things still make no more sense than they did weeks ago, because we still can't find the server.

I wait to walk the rest of the way with Ellis, while Lazuli returns to her chickens. My stammered explanation didn't make much sense, but she let it ride with the polite unflappability of rich people, and I can't afford to worry about whether she thinks I'm in cahoots with whoever caused Caroline's death.

Someone sent her a skull. Someone is still running the server.

On the steps of the cabin, Ellis pauses to offer me the sweater he's knotted over his shoulders.

"I'm okay. You need it." I fetch my hoodie from the pack, my fingers grazing the smooth, eyeless face of Raggedy Ann. Her presence is weirdly reassuring, but God knows how I'd explain her to Ellis, who's holding the door for me.

Stepping inside, I smell his breath, minty mouthwash and whiskey, and my cheeks flush. There's an almost formal space between us now.

Inside, it's too dark to see much. Ellis finds a lamp, and Caroline's wall of photos appears again, the real setting of the game springing to life. I run my eyes down the row of pictures, looking for anything I've missed, while he wakes his phone and snaps a photo. "I'll image-search that tower. It's weird enough to be a landmark."

"It's not actually a tower." *How do I know?* "It's a furnace, I think. The hole in the roof is a smokestack."

"So maybe they were smelting something? Like a mine?"

"I guess." While Ellis works on his phone, I bend closer to a photo of the log cabin, my whole body going still with the effort of focusing. Why do that spindly porch, those spiny logs, look familiar? The cabin's not part of the game.

Below the photo, barely attached by a yellowed piece of tape, hangs a sheet of notebook paper. I peel it from the wall and find small, crabbed handwriting:

Fear = concentration. Induces hypnotic state. Addictive.

Runes on safe trees = conditioning. Rewards for playing. Locks in hypnotic state.

Level 13 kills player. Vulnerability. Depression. Secondary hallucinations link game death to real trauma.

Skull = hypnotic trigger. Returns player to game. Randoms, keening, rustling = game transfer phenomena.

Could Caroline have experienced it, too—the sounds, the visions? Was this her blueprint for the Glare, or was she struggling to understand it, just like I am?

I show the paper to Ellis. "It's how the Glare works, I think. But what are game transfer phenomena?"

He leans in, frowns. "It's like when you play *Tetris* so much you start seeing the blocks everywhere—on the highway, in the grocery store. Or like that guy who thought *Grand Theft Auto* was telling him to steal cars in real life."

"So the game hypnotizes you. It addicts you. It isolates you. And then, when you can't play anymore, it starts invading your reality. But only when you're triggered." There are no puzzle pieces snapping neatly into place in my mind, only rugged cloudbanks pushed by a desert gale, their meeting points edged with lightning.

"The triggers come from somewhere," Ellis says.

The photo of the cabin draws my eyes like a magnet. As I focus on it again, a second image flashes behind my eyes: *my parents arm in arm in front of a rugged dwelling.*

It was one of the pics I saw when I first explored my online history, the Encyclopedia of Me. Maybe I'm grasping at straws.

Still, my legs go shaky, and I sit down in Caroline's desk chair. "Ellis, could you find an old photo in my mom's Facebook feed? She never bothered to delete her account."

It takes forever and less than a minute for Ellis to hand me his phone.

"Do you mean this one?"

My parents stand entwined in front of a log cabin, her head resting on his shoulder, a mischievous smile on her lips. *Blast from the past!* the caption reads. *Back when we were dating, Mike brought me to this remote corner of the Shasta-Trinity National Forest preserve for some wilderness living. Pure, unadulterated Nature!*

I compare the images side by side. The logs with bark clinging to them; the low-hanging, mossy roof on flimsy posts—it all matches. The only difference is that one image has my parents in it, and the other doesn't.

They vacationed in the Glare, or the inspiration for the Glare. *They* were there, not Caroline.

Mom told Dad the game was Caroline's idea, but Mom has a little habit of censoring her past. Mom designed games. Mom mentored Caroline and gave her games to test. Mom visited the black tower.

Her face in the photo is young and impish, with a hint of something withheld in its expression. What else did she hide from me?

I don't want to say what I'm thinking, don't even want to think it. Maybe Ellis isn't the one who has the most trouble being objective here.

But we'll never know if we don't check it out. Facebook's location tag says *Twin Hills Mine, Shasta County, California.* "Look up Twin Hills Mine on your map," I say.

Ellis has sharp-pointed questions in his eyes, but he lowers his head and starts tapping his phone. "You gonna tell me why?"

"I think it's the place in these photos. When Caroline e-mailed me, she said she thought the server was there."

After staring at the screen for a moment, Ellis reaches for my hand and places the phone in it. There's a new tension in his body, an excitement, and his fingers linger on mine as I gaze at the map.

"Five hours," he says. "We can go tonight."

34

When Erika answers the phone, I can tell she's struggling to keep her voice level. "Where are you?"

Outside, the forests and farms of inland Marin zip past, the foliage clotted with charcoal dusk and only the sky still alight. We're headed for the I-5, which will take us up to Shasta County. Ellis stares straight ahead, his hands steady on the wheel, his long legs drawn up in the small car, and I try not to remember his hand holding mine.

"We're still looking for Mireya." It hurts to lie to her, but we *are* looking for a way to help Mireya. I wouldn't have called if I didn't need to ask what I do next: "She hasn't come home, has she?"

"No. Her mom says she disabled her phone, so they're trying to get in touch with her boyfriend."

Disabled is one word for it. I hope fervently that Mireya is holed up with Anthony, and that she's made him turn his phone off. I try not to remember the blood on her forehead, the whites of her eyes.

"And Dad? Is he home?" I don't look forward to telling him what I suspect about Mom.

"No. He has a last-minute meeting with venture capitalists in San Diego." Erika's voice is rising now, worse than this morning. "I told him I'd look out for you, Hedda. I need you to tell me where you are, and then to come back. It's practically dark out!"

"I can't do that." The quaver in her voice paints the whole picture: her white knuckles as she clutches the phone, the way she blinks a little too fast when she's upset. I should just hang up now, because nothing I say will reassure her, but I can't. "I'm with Ellis, and I swear we'll be back tomorrow. Please just trust me, okay?"

I glance at Ellis as I speak, wondering if he's put things together like I have. My grip tightens on the phone, that treacherous glassy portal to the rest of the world.

"You said you trusted *me* this morning." She's got her voice back under control. Maybe Clint is nearby and she doesn't want to scare him. "So why can't you just tell me?"

Because you won't believe me. "I'm sorry. See you soon, I promise." As I hit the end button and turn off the phone again, something clenches inside me.

"Was that your dad?" Ellis asks.

I shake my head and almost laugh, feeling tears come to my eyes. "No way. That was my stepmom. If it were my dad or mom, I could lie to them, no problem," I go on, something driving me inexorably toward the thing I don't want to talk about, "but with Erika it's different. She doesn't lie to me."

"Yeah, I know what you mean. I never totally forgave my folks for not talking straight to me about Caroline."

"My mom..." And now the thing is between us, immovable as a boulder. "I used to think she *was* straight with me. But she never told me about that place. The national forest."

I'm not explaining myself very well, but Ellis has seen the same clues I have. "Do you think she could have created the Glare?" he asks in a neutral voice. "Maybe you didn't get it from Caroline, after all. Maybe you found it at home."

Staring at the glowing yellow lines in the gathering dark, I remember his reasoning for why Caroline couldn't have been running the server, and relief washes through me. "Mom's been out in Arizona with me for the past ten years. We haven't been apart even a night in all that time. She hasn't been making stealth trips to California."

Unless the server isn't in California. Unless Mom has it stashed somewhere on the ranch along with her secret cell phone. It shouldn't be possible, because I know every inch of that place, but the mother I've seen reflected in Dad's stories isn't the one I know. So many of the things she told him about Caroline may actually have described herself. She could have been someone who liked using games to modify people's behavior. *Control yourself*—it was always about control, wasn't it? She brought me out to the desert to remold me, and when I tried to take control back, her game sucked me in again.

Even now, I taste the craving for the Glare on my tongue,

bitter and tangy and wild. The part of me that loved playing is still in there.

Could Mom have created the Glare to punish kids for being glued to their screens? Or created it and then felt so guilty she wanted nothing to do with the internet for the rest of her life?

"Maybe no one's running the server anymore," Ellis says. "Maybe it's running itself."

"Could it do that?"

"Not without maintenance, if it's out in the middle of nowhere. And I think it is there. Caroline told you to find the place in the picture for a reason."

He sounds so confident, so certain, as if he believes things will fall into logical alignment as soon as we reach that cabin. As if there's a mystery we can solve, a culprit we can drag to the police. And I want to believe he's right, want to feel his fingers clasp mine again, want to stop seeing Anil's terror and the whites of Mireya's eyes.

But more than that, I don't want my mother to be the real monster.

. . .

At about midnight, when it feels like we've been on the freeway forever, I close my eyes and drift into blackness.

I wake to find the car parked, the dashboard display dark. Outside, a tepid greenish floodlight illuminates a gas station canopy. Beyond, the darkness is a plunge into deep space.

Ellis's face appears in the open window. "I just realized I'll kill us both if I don't get coffee. Want anything inside?"

I open the door and stand up, working out kinks in cramped muscles. "I'm coming."

When I woke, for a second, I didn't remember. Not just this impossibly long day—*Caroline, Mireya, Anil, Cheyenne's taunting voice*—and not just yesterday—*blood caked in the ridges of a vinyl seat*—but everything since I came here. For an instant, I was on a trip with Mom through the desert, returning from a birthday dinner in Phoenix. Back when I believed in her.

Now, standing under the fluorescents of a twenty-four-hour mini-mart, choosing between Hazelnut Crème and Burnt Vanilla, I miss the morning slant of light on the desert. I miss the sandy soil under my heels. I miss the manic clucking of the hens and the strange caterpillar pupils of the goats and the routine of chores and the good kind of tired you feel after a day of bending and pushing and hauling.

I miss the librarian and the bank teller and the county fair, and, most of all, I miss Mom. Her tireless presence beside me, weeding or milking or reading aloud. Her steadfastness, her tenderness, her anger, even her exaggerations and unfairness.

How could she? It's a dark web I'm not ready to untangle.

I grab a few stale muffins, pay, and follow Ellis back across the light-smeared asphalt. The air is night cool, spiked with gasoline. A minivan is refueling in the bay beside ours, the others empty.

Something burbles and snaps in my right ear. On a screen attached to the gas pump, a ghostly image of a girl in a striped top cavorts to a pop song. The camera zooms in on the Pepsi in her hand.

I glance away. To my left hovers the faint glow of the

interstate; to my right, the stars shine fiercely above a horizon of shaggy pines.

Ellis is arranging our huge coffees in the cup holders. I don't *hear* the too-familiar vibration of his phone. It slips down my spine and roils inside my gut, a signal bypassing my brain.

And like a fool, I look back at the closest screen.

The girl dancing with the Pepsi is gone. In her place is a skull made of clouds and light. Gaping eye sockets, grinning mouth.

My heart takes a wild leap, and I free-fall, wind whistling in my ears, even as my brain reminds me, *Not real! Blink. Ground yourself.*

I do blink—hard—and visualize dirt and seedlings as I slide into the car, fists clenched, spine rigid. I don't have to glance at the pump to know the skull is gone now. It's not real, only conditioning and suggestion.

"Ellis." It's hard to speak through my tight jaw. "You need to turn your phone all the way—"

I stop short. Ellis sits hunched double, his face hidden against his knees and his fingers wrapped around the wheel, rocking slightly back and forth. A continuous sound comes from deep inside him—a hum? a moan?

"Ellis!" Did the phone affect him, too? But he never played to the end of the game. The greenish light makes his pale fingers seem to glow.

I touch his shoulder, somehow cold even through the sweater. The noise he's making gets louder. "Are you okay?"

The cold intensifies, and I snatch my hand away, at the same time the sound sharpens to a point that hurts my ears. *Keening.*

I lurch away, my head hitting the window so hard I see starbursts, but it's too late. The thing is turning to me.

It has no eyes or nose, and yet it *is* Ellis—a younger Ellis. I recognize the slumped shoulders, the nervous sideways droop of the head. I can almost hear him saying, "I don't want to play that game again!" though all that comes from the gaping hole of his mouth is the keening.

The mouth is lipless. It wears a grin—no, a rictus of pain.

My hand creeps into my pack and closes on the utility knife. "Stop it!" I yell, trying to cut through the sound. "This isn't real."

Where Ellis's eyes should be, jagged slits open—no iris, no pupil, just polished obsidian directing a keen, alien gaze at me. The face is a white mask. The fingers, long as shoelaces, unwind from the steering wheel and reach out clawlike for my shoulder.

I've died like this in the Glare dozens of times (*throttling, strangulation*), and I move on instinct—ripping the knife free of my pack and jabbing at the hand, forcing the distended fingers to release me.

The keening turns to a bray of pain. "Hedda—"

I don't wait to see if he's okay, if there still is a him. I shove open the door and run.

Out of the deadly pool of light, away from the will-o'-the-wisp screens. *Don't turn. Don't look.* The keening goes on, soft but distinct, in the grass, in the woods—everywhere. I run in the dark and toward the dark, my breath coming short and weeds pricking my ankles, till strong hands grip me from behind, yanking me to a stop, and I scream, "No! Get away!"

"It's me." A deep voice, a human voice.

I know Randoms. The hands will wrench me around and

271

lace themselves fast on my throat and push till I have no air left. I clutch the knife, ready to stab it backward into soft flesh, into *something*.

And that same voice says, "If I let you go, will you promise not to run?"

Blink. Remember the soil. *Blink*. Remember him on our lawn, the warmth of his hands.

These hands are warm, too. I nod, my breath coming in sobs, and as the fingers release me, I let the knife go.

I sink down in the grass and breathe the smells of airborne seeds and crisp stalks, of summer dried out and blowing away. I feel it—*him*—sitting beside me, keeping a couple of feet between us. The keening is fading, almost gone.

Ellis's voice says again, "It's me."

"I know." I close my eyes. How will he look if I turn around? He could be Anil, Rory, Mireya, Emily. Anyone who reminds me of the damage I've done.

But I need to act like he's Ellis. Like he's real. "Did I hurt you?"

"Scared the shit out of me." He breathes. "But it's just a scrape. What did you see?"

"Not important." I can't stop seeing that miserable little hunched Random—its hideousness like an accusation, its eyes hungry for me. I don't want him to know.

"Has it gone away yet?"

"I'm not sure." I don't dare turn around, but remembering the warmth of his hand, I say, "You can touch me if you want."

Fingertips on my back, and then the hand spreads itself flat. Five fingers, normal length, and a palm.

"It's my fault." Ellis's voice has a halting, uneven cadence to it. "I unlocked the phone to check my messages. I must have messed up my Do Not Disturb settings."

"It's not your fault."

His head is closer, his chin almost resting on my shoulder, each inhale warm against my ear. *Real. Human.* I reach for the hand that hangs at his side and drape his arm around me, remembering how we stood at sunset.

His chest is solid against my back, his heartbeat a dull resonance. "We'll make it stop."

Will we? "Ellis, I saw a skull without getting a skull text, just triggered by the noise. It's all in my head now."

Ellis rests his chin on the crown of my head. "I know, but you'll get better."

He's so confident I won't be like Caroline or Anil. Never stabbing him in the eye because I think he's a Random, never hurting myself. What power does he have to say I'll get better?

None at all. Just the warmth of his arms and the husky vibration in his voice that makes some clenched part of me unfold.

"Okay," I say, and open my eyes.

We sit without speaking, me staring off into the darkness and feeling him without seeing him, my finger on the steady pulse in his wrist. Sooner or later, I'll turn around. I'll trust him to be real.

Ellis exhales and shifts, his breath on my hair. Abruptly the weight of him against me becomes *so* real I'm afraid to budge, almost afraid to think, and I have to break the silence with the first stupid thing that comes to mind: "Did you really bag Jerusha Pierce?"

"'Scuse me?"

"Anil said so." It's *beyond* stupid, and I laugh weakly, but it's all good, I need to focus on anything but how physically close we are, and how much closer my body seems to want to be, and how recently I looked at him and saw a Random.

His lips graze my ear. "No. I did not. And now I want you to turn around."

I twist in his arms, eyes closed. Knowing this is ridiculous, a waste of time, and best-case scenario I'll end up one more girl clinging to him in the Encyclopedia of Ellis, just like Mireya hinted long ago at the barbecue.

Worst-case scenario, he still isn't him.

The first kiss is so light I barely feel it, a slight press of the lips. Then he catches my bottom lip between his and releases it, and hair tickles the tip of my nose as he says, "Open your eyes."

It's hard to find breath to speak. "Not yet."

"It's just me." Laughter gurgles in his throat. "The one who was too chicken to play to the end."

"You're not—"

Before I can finish, his mouth opens, his tongue darting between my lips. As he pulls back I open my eyes, feeling a flood of warmth in my chest, too, like the time I drank from his flask.

I don't see a Random. Just the curve of Ellis's cheekbone, barely visible in the dark, and the glint of an eye. I creep my fingers around his waist, under his sweater and T-shirt, to feel the human skin. I reach for his face—

And he disentangles himself from me and stands up, offering a hand to hoist me to my feet. "We should get back on the road."

Walking back to the car, I still feel his mouth on mine, the tickle of late-night stubble. "Did you do that just to…bring me back?"

"Of course." Ellis doesn't look at me, but his tone still has that gentle laughter in it. "Because making out right now would be weird and inappropriate, right?"

I buckle up, still too aware of every move he makes—adjusting the rearview, flicking the hair out of his eyes. Remembering the burnt-coffee taste of his mouth and the weight of his sweater as I peeled it away from his waist. "I guess."

"Too much heavy life shit going on. One of us would end up exploiting the other one's fragile emotional state. Let's never speak of it again." He hits the ignition button. "Hedda, I'm kidding."

"Oh!" And for the first few miles, all the way to the entrance ramp, I say nothing.

He asked me what I saw back there, and now I feel wrong about not telling him. But how do you tell someone, *You're my greatest fail? After everything that's happened, daring you to play is still what I'm most ashamed of?*

When we're on the freeway, he clasps my hand where it rests on my thigh. "When I said the desert misses you, I was actually thinking…I'd like to visit you in the desert. With no distractions. Just us and all that open space."

"I'd like that, too." My voice is small and dry. "Though there'd also be goats."

He chuckles and releases my hand, but I still feel his grip.

"Your phone's off now, right?" I ask.

And then we laugh—an electric, semi-hysterical laughter that leaves us weak-limbed—till the silence of the road takes over again.

35

When the wheels hit dirt, I open my eyes to a sea of evergreens.

The sun has just risen. We're on the brink of a hill, walls of forest on either side, every needle seething with reflected light. As I watch silvery feathers of cloud float in the sky, it's easy to forget everything that happened in the dark.

Not that I necessarily want to forget all of it.

"Almost there," Ellis says, and guzzles the last of my mega-coffee.

"Do you want to sleep for a few hours? You've been up all night."

He shakes his head. "Got the old adrenaline pumping, couldn't sleep if I tried. Let's just go check it out. Maybe it'll be another dead end."

"Maybe not."

I imagine the source of the Glare close by, hidden everywhere and nowhere, a forest of wonders primed to fascinate and terrify. It doesn't feel evil. It feels as incapable of moral choice as an engine gasket, and maybe that's worse.

I don't know if I'll ever get the Randoms out of my head, whether we smash the server or not. But when Ellis meets my eyes, it's like he's running his hand down my bare spine, and something inside me flexes and expands.

If only I'd listened to him when we were six. If only I hadn't been so obsessed with impressing Mom and Dad. But for me, the only way to *have* parents was to impress them.

A few miles along the dirt road, Ellis says, "I think we're going to have to walk from here."

A hundred yards ahead looms a ten-foot chain-link fence with a padlocked gate. "This is private land?" I ask. "I thought it was a forest preserve. A campground or something."

"We're on the very edge of the preserve. The roads probably stop once you get in there."

This road continues on the other side of the fence, winding through yellow grass until it disappears behind a wooded hill. Ellis parks in a dirt pullout, and we grab our packs and lock the doors. "Connectivity this far out must cost a mint," he says. "If somebody is running that server from here, they have a satellite hookup."

"So we're trespassing?"

"Probably. You chicken?"

"No!" Then I see his grin and realize he's teasing.

"I was worried there for a minute." He jabs a toe in the fence and scales it easily, then straddles the top and extends a hand. Two-thirds of the way up, I wobble, and he catches hold of my waist. "It's okay, you're good."

I let him steady me and survey the landscape, trying not to think too much about his fingers grazing my bare skin. There it is—off to the right, hulking above the trees.

"The tower! I mean, the smokestack."

Suddenly Ellis's hands on my waist could be anyone's hands. The world slides under me, as if I'm a fixed figure on a scrolling backdrop. Everything reorients itself around the square black tower—oak, pines, spruce, grass patches, road, pale blue sky, us. I know where I am because I've been here before—not in real life, but inside the game.

Ellis is staring in a different direction. "That's a camera."

I follow his gaze to a small black plastic cube affixed to a gatepost. "You think someone's watching us?"

"Motion activates it, and they probably monitor it on their phone. If they're bothering to. You okay?"

I nod, and he removes his hand. My heart canters with fear and excitement as I jump down on the other side. *They could know we're here. They who?* The drop takes my breath away, and my head spins, fatigue overwhelming the haze of mini-mart coffee. I can still see the very top of the tower.

On the ground beside me, Ellis peers at his phone, safely in airplane mode; he's filled it with photos of the images we found in Caroline's cabin. "If the tower's due north, the cabin could be just over that hill."

"This whole place is part of the game." I look where he's pointing, at a trail leading up a slope toothy with rock ledges.

Reality. Stay in it. "I mean, this place *inspired* the game. I died on that hill once. A Random hid in a cranny under a ledge."

Ellis doesn't seem as spooked as I am, but then, he didn't play as much. "Let's go that way. If we're looking for a server, just from a logistics standpoint, I'm gonna say the cabin is a better bet than that ruined tower or smokestack or whatever."

I can't argue with that, much as I long to explore the tower, so I follow him up the hill where tall pines churn like surf. Sharp-spined cones crunch under our feet.

A cone rolls at my feet. A rustle to my left, and I turn, Glare-gun raised, but the attack comes from above—a flash of white, an impossibly long arm jerking me sideways. The screen judders and turns to a negative image, then blacks out.

"Hedda!"

I look up into his blue eyes, shaking off the memory. "Don't you remember this place?"

"Sort of." He slips his hand in mine—warm, with a steady pulse at the base of his thumb. "I think I prefer the version without things trying to kill me."

As the trail winds up and around the rock ledges, we break into single file, staying close enough for me to smell the sweat that darkens the collar of his T-shirt. The sun is getting hotter, and I pull off my hoodie, too.

What if we were out here for a hike and a picnic—on a date, like my parents all those years ago? Would the birdsong still seem unusually muted? When Dad brought Mom here, did he sense a darkness inside her, or did that come later?

"We should approach carefully," Ellis says. "Just in case—you know, in case someone's here and they saw us on the cameras."

"I know." The deciduous trees are speckled with red, just as they were in my dream. Each step takes us over mats of dead leaves that crackle underfoot.

Crackling, rustling, slithering. Them.

A hollow rap against a trunk makes me whirl, but it's only a woodpecker. The Glare tugs at me, more memories pressing in.

The Glare is a forest. The Glare is a labyrinth. It's alive with glowing eyes, sentient sounds, eager fronds that reach out and stroke my hand. It's a dead forest of ones and zeroes, a place we can all experience, but where we'll always be alone. I see now how artfully the game designer re-created this landscape, weaving details into a tapestry, and yes, that feels like Mom, who notices beauty even in the desert.

I try to focus on things the digital world can't replicate: the rich, gritty smell of decaying leaves. The mushy give of the path under my feet, firming as we climb the rocky spine. The width of Ellis's strides—the strides of a young, fearless athlete who's not scared of the Glare, not like when he was six. Not as scared as he should be.

I tell myself I'm not scared, either. Maybe we'll find someone in that cabin, but for now there's only us and the woodpecker and the muted songs of other birds undisturbed by civilization.

"How are we going to get rid of the server?" I ask.

"Got some tools from the trunk." Ellis pats his pack. "Hammer should do it."

He can't have forgotten what he saw so vividly illustrated last night: Destroying the server will stop the texts, but it won't make me stop seeing Randoms. For those of us who've already been conditioned, it may be too late.

It should be so easy to control something that's all in your head.

"There!"

We've reached the brow of the hill, where silvery grass trembles across a small clearing. Beyond, the cabin hunches in a grove of scrubby pines.

True to the photo, it's smaller and rougher than the cabin where Caroline lived. Bark streaks the logs. Close enough to see the porch and the white satellite dish on the roof, I imagine Mom and Dad standing there, arm in arm.

Ellis pulls me away from the path. "Let's go around the sides first."

We split up and case the cabin, though the place feels profoundly empty. A generator purrs from a shed against the back wall. Peering into a bleary window, I'm trying to make sense of the dimness inside when a splintery impact makes the frame shudder.

I freeze, heart racing, my shirt damp against my back. *Where are the safe trees? Are they coming?*

But it's just Ellis bashing in the door with a hefty tree branch.

"I thought we were going to approach carefully," I say as a whole rotten board rips free, sending him staggering inside.

He says between pants, "Didn't see anybody, and there's no road up here anyway, just the trail."

Sure enough, there's no one in the cabin, which consists of a single room and a rickety loft. One corner holds a sleeping bag on an air mattress; another, a camping table covered with cans, kitchen implements, and half-empty water jugs.

No sink, but polarized outlets and a dangling lamp make it

clear the place is wired. On an orange crate beside the makeshift bed, someone's left a glass of cloudy water and a paperback called *Knights of the Moons of Triton.*

Someone was here, not long ago. Their outline is pressed into the air mattress. Their lips touched the gummy rim of the glass; their fingers leafed through the book. They spent the night here, reading before bed—far from everyone, alone in their private realm. With their server?

Something protrudes from under the bed, and I bend to find a thin silver laptop plastered with stickers. *Question Authority,* names that are probably bands. I reach for it, but stop at the sight of a dark, smudgy fingerprint.

Rising, I nearly trip over a plastic bag lying on its side. The drawstring that closes it is loose, and clothes spill from the opening: a T-shirt and sweatpants covered with brown stains.

Red brown. I stare down at the stiffened fabric, my pulse suddenly thundering in my ears, seeing Rory in the car again.

"Shit!" Ellis says.

I jump, but he's not seeing what I am. He's up in the loft, face to the wall.

Sweat beading under my shirt, I climb the wobbly ladder and find him staring at a spot under the eaves. On the pine boards is a dustless rectangle the size of a small chest.

"The server. It was right here—see that outlet? They took it away."

"You think they…" I still feel weak from the discovery of the laptop and clothes; it's hard to focus on anything else. "Because they saw us on the camera?"

"No, we just got here. Maybe they know things are closing

in on them—too many dead people. Or maybe they were just redecorating. Let's look for other buildings."

"The tower." I try to get my breathing under control. *Too many dead people.* If I show Ellis the bloody clothes, will he insist on leaving immediately? Finding the police?

That might be the rational thing to do, but we can't leave yet. We need to see the tower.

We'll just keep on being careful.

Ellis reaches for my hand. "You okay?"

I nod. *It can wait.* "The tower next."

36

The tower stands alone in virgin forest.

Chasing its silhouette on the horizon, we scramble down the far side of the hill, cross a field of grass and scrub oak, climb another slope. The trees close in almost immediately, their mossy trunks damp to the touch. Leaf litter lies spongy on the ground, each step bringing scents of vegetal decay.

I remember my dream of leaves swirling as the Randoms dragged Rory underground. Something clammy brushes my face, and I bat it away—a scarlet maple leaf.

And a voice in my head keeps saying, *Get to the tower. Get to the next level. Of course you can do it, you're not scared—keep playing.*

When I was six, the Glare must have been every kind of

exciting—Christmas and birthdays, carnivals and amusement parks, promises of *more, better, bigger, soon*. A secret between Mom and Caroline, something I craved because I was excluded. Every unbearable anticipation, every sleepless night, every reason to keep living.

We pass an oak that could fit three of me inside its base. No rune on the massive trunk (*there should be*), but someone has carved words there: *The only winning move is not to play*.

And that feels oddly right, too.

"Hedda!" Ellis calls, ahead of me.

A last bend brings me into a clearing, and here's the tower. I stand still, drinking it in—less like a tower now and more like the base of a giant, rough-hewn chimney, narrowing as it rises. Each of its four faces has a bricked-in archway at the base. The only actual way inside is a person-sized hole where the bricks have crumbled.

The hole is half-blocked by dirt and trash—rusty cans, yellowed newspapers, silverware. I kneel on the junk pile and clamber gingerly toward the opening, hoping for a glimpse inside. There's no magical power source in there, of course, but—

One of my hands sinks through loose dirt and closes on something hard and right-angled. I yank my fingers free, dislodging the object—a small framed photo.

A boy beside a lake with a fishing pole. *Dad*.

What's this doing here? It should be at home in Dad's study, just as this forest and tower should only exist on screens. Everything telescopes, dreamlike, as I flip the photo over and see a childish scrawl: *Ur pathetic*.

And in that instant, I see all the things I overlooked, all the evidence I didn't put together.

His favorite quote on the tree. His childhood photo. His calm voice telling me Caroline created the Glare. And the same voice saying, *Sometimes you have to turn your back on the old demons and rise above the bullshit, Hedda.*

Demons. Randoms.

"Hedda!" Ellis calls, louder. Warning.

I scramble up, stuff the photo in my hoodie, and join him. A few paces past the tower, in a muddy clearing, a new-looking Ford F-150 is parked with a black canopy drawn tightly over the bed. The open tailgate offers a glimpse of shiny plastic and metal—electronics.

"The server," I say, at the same time Ellis says, "Shit."

Dad steps out from behind the truck, wearing faded jeans and a flannel shirt.

I feel my heartbeats space out, my breaths, my blinks, as he walks unhurriedly toward us. Above, two crows wheel upward in a chaos of shiny wings.

Ellis already has the hammer out of his pack, ready to smash the server; sun flares silver on the handle. His face is frozen in puzzlement.

"Hedda! What on earth?" Dad's own face shows jovial surprise, but the expression is paper-thin. He walks like someone who hasn't slept in days. "What brings you out here?"

"What brings *you*?" I keep my voice neutral. *You're supposed to be in San Diego.*

Dad detours to open the cab. "I own the place. This used to be my grandpa Frank's property, and now Erika's hell-bent on selling it, so I came to have a chat with a real-estate agent. She didn't tell you?"

Because she didn't know. He told Erika one lie, and now he's telling me another. "We came from Bolinas," I say, emphasizing the name.

"Stunning place. Great beaches." The smile is forced, as if he knows perfectly well who's in Bolinas—or was.

Ellis sees it, too. Hoarse with suspicion, he asks, "What's in the truck?"

Dad glances at Ellis as if noticing him for the first time. "Equipment. Doing a little moving from one office to another. You're the Westover boy, aren't you?"

Ellis edges toward Dad. Warning bells ring in my head: *He's not thinking. He's going to do something reckless.*

"I'm surprised you don't know my name, Mr. Vikdal," Ellis says. "I mean, you've been telling Hedda *all* about my sister."

Dad's eyes flick to me. "I didn't know Caroline well, I'm afraid. My wife did."

"Are you sure of that, Dad?" I remember the drawing of the skull Caroline did, the one Ellis showed me in the yard night before last. Seen from the corner of my eye, it looked like a man's face.

His.

More and more pieces are fitting into place. The night Mom fired Caroline as a babysitter, she said, she found her at the computer in Dad's study. Caroline may have been Mom's intern, but Dad could have been her real mentor.

My oblivious, cerebral, above-it-all father shouldn't have anything to do with a half-mythical game that kids dare each other

287

to play in dark rooms. With blood under fingernails and wild runs off cliffs and rulers stabbed in eyes. But here he is.

"She was going to tell on you, wasn't she?" Ellis's voice is raw. "So you had to get rid of her."

Dad's eyes go flat, as if his sociable exterior is a rubber band that's been stretched to the snapping point. But when he turns to me, he sounds helpless, almost plaintive: "Hedda, what's going on? What's the matter? Is it what happened with your poor friend the other day?"

We're back in our old roles, me a problem he's trying to solve. But the land we stand on, the trees around us, the tower—they all testify against him.

"*You* made the Glare," I say.

"Oh, Hedda, not the Glare again. Whatever your mother says, a game can't hurt you."

"You know it can." He has to, or he wouldn't be lying. He wouldn't have loaded his equipment into that truck. His eyes wouldn't have that sickly, exhausted sheen. "We're going to turn it off before it hurts anyone else."

Dad's hazel eyes flit from me to Ellis. "I'm so sorry you have to see us like this," he says. "The thing is, Hedda suffers from certain...phobias."

My face burns. "It's not just me!"

But Dad keeps speaking to Ellis in that awful reasonable tone, as if he's decided Ellis is the saner one: "I don't know what she's told you, but I blame myself for not addressing the problem sooner. Maybe we can go home and do that now. Would you mind putting down the hammer?"

Ellis tucks the hammer behind his back like a little boy who's been caught at something. "Is that the game server?" he asks, gesturing at the truck bed.

"I have a couple of servers in there. But this story of the Glare..." Dad glances between us in that plaintive way again. "Hedda, I feel to blame. I knew Jane was unstable. I never should have—"

My nails jab into my palms. "My friends are dead."

"And I'm so sorry."

He *looks* sorry, and for an instant I almost believe there's no deadly game, only turmoil in my head, *off-kilter* and fractured memories and guilt and confusion.

Then Ellis grabs my hand and says, "Your whole damn property is a life-sized version of the game that made my sister hurt herself. I've played it. I know."

Dad goes very still. "Hedda, has he been drinking?"

"No."

I squeeze Ellis's hand, and he goes on, his voice gaining strength, "And then you took on a persona and went on message boards and taunted people and dared them to play. *You're* L13Survivor, aren't you?"

"I have no idea—"

"My sister wouldn't have done that, and she wasn't a survivor anyway. There are no survivors of level thirteen. Did you push her off that cliff?"

Without giving Dad time to deny it, he yanks me toward the truck bed. "Let's get this done."

While Ellis is reaching for a handhold on the tailgate, Dad

comes at us faster than I've ever seen him move before, and the patronizing mask on his face is gone like it never existed. He has no expression at all.

Something silver in Dad's hand arcs through the air and goes *thwap*, jerking Ellis's head to the side. Ellis crumples to his knees.

37

"**N**o!" I grab the silver thing—a baseball bat—and try to wrest it away.

Dad pushes the fat end at me like a battering ram, hitting me right below the collarbone. The impact knocks the breath from my lungs and spreads outward in ripples of pain, vibrating from my toes to the roots of my hair.

When I can breathe again, I'm slumped against the side of the truck beside Ellis, looking into the barrel of a handgun.

Dad's expression is focused, his stance easy. He's like a different person. "Snap out of it!" he says.

I raise my hands, each heartbeat splintering the world in two. There's blood in Ellis's hair, trickling down his cheek, and the sight sends prickles down my legs.

Ellis moves—crawling, reaching for the hammer in the grass. I stretch out, too, trying to nudge it closer.

Dad's booted foot kicks the hammer away. With a grating click, he cocks the gun and aims it at Ellis, who collapses with a dull moan.

I breathe shallowly around the crater of pain in my chest, my brain still telling me this is *Dad*. He's a man of words, not violence. I just need to explain. But something deeper, pulsing in my throat, says there's no point.

And I realize why Caroline didn't tell me who was running the server. She assumed I knew who created the game.

"*You* gave Caroline the Glare." Now I understand why I was always so eager to play. My universe revolved around Mom, but Dad was the elusive star on the horizon.

The Glare is Dad's private place, an extension of his mind. He populated it with memories and movie quotes and his own childhood terrors. Where else would I go to understand him? To make him love me?

Mom would have warned me if she'd known. But she was so wrapped up in her theories about evil screens reprogramming brains that she failed to notice the reprogrammer in her own house. And I kept my shameful secret—that I'd tried to win the game of Dad and failed—until the desert buried it, and I kept it even from myself.

Dad is looking down at Ellis in a way so blank it scares me.

"I tried," he says. "Honestly, Hedda, I thought you were more levelheaded than your mother. But you had to dig out that address and start passing it around."

"I didn't know!" From the corner of my eye, I see Ellis stagger to his feet.

Dad sees, too. He swings the bat.

"Don't!"

The bat halts inches from Ellis's temple. His ragged breaths mingle with mine as I step between them, trying to believe Dad won't hit me again. He doesn't want to hurt me.

"You don't understand." My voice comes out jagged. "All you need to do is turn off the server, and it stops."

"He doesn't give a shit," Ellis says. "He *wants* to hurt people; he probably gets off on it—"

Dad sidesteps and snaps the bat down on Ellis's shoulder, his arm remorseless as a pendulum. Ellis gasps. My wild rush at Dad tears a scream from my throat, and I don't remember the gun until he's knocked me backward into the grass.

I force myself upright to see Dad whack Ellis a second time on the shoulder and press the gun to his forehead. To me he says, "Go in the truck and get the backpack."

Ellis curls up on the ground, arms shielding his head. I step toward him, but Dad says, "Do it."

He speaks softly, like we're playing chess again and he's ordering me to concentrate. Sobbing breaths burst from my lungs as I hobble to the truck and get the pack.

Dad's right; none of this would have happened without me. I found the Glare, I gave it to Mireya, I dragged Ellis here. It's my fault he's bleeding.

All this time I spent trying to impress my father, and I can't even reason with him. I can't do anything.

The sky is still blindingly blue above. The pine and spruce

press close around us with their clean, resinous odor. Dad wipes sweat from his face with the hand holding the bat. His eyes are slick. "There's a rope in there. Get it."

I rummage in the backpack—sweatshirt, flashlight, water bottle—and he says sharply, "Just the rope. You're in this now, understand?"

"No. I don't." I ease the nylon rope out, keeping an eye on both of them. Ellis is clutching his wounded shoulder, and his bangs are matted with blood; he doesn't look in any shape to run.

"I gave the kid a chance!" Dad emphasizes each word in a pained way, jabbing the bat in Ellis's direction. "His sister, too—I only went to Bolinas to sound her out, but she wasn't reasonable. She was going to call some tech blogger and try to make him believe her story. And your little friend with the pink hair thought he was going to publish some kind of viral exposé. Thought I'd just *let* him tell everybody I put that game online. He was bugging me for a 'comment,' if you can believe that."

"You *did* fucking kill my sister," Ellis spits out.

While I say, "Rory? You mean Rory?"

I remember the laptop in the cabin. The bloody clothes.

Dad just says, "Tie his hands. Tight."

He kicks Ellis in the side, but there's no venom in his voice as he goes on. "Your friend came to see me with a kitchen knife, Hedda. When I triggered him, he grabbed it. Went for me." He wipes sweat from his forehead. "He was primed for violence. I acted in self-defense."

The rope goes slippery in my fingers. "You triggered Rory? With a skull text?"

"I can't control how it affects people." Now he sounds

self-righteous. "I never meant it to work that way—you think I can program monsters into people's heads? The prototype didn't go beyond level thirteen. The skulls were an in-joke."

"A *joke*?"

"A goof on all those urban legends. Back then, when Caroline told me she was seeing things, I thought it was just her. I didn't make the connection to what happened to you until I checked my server log. It *shouldn't* work, Hedda. It only works because people believe it. The things people see when they get the text that says *Ur pathetic*—none of that's real."

"I know that." I remember the disappearing image. "But how—"

"I don't know!" His hair's sticking up from his forehead, his eyes wild. "They see those words and that skull, and they imagine whatever made them feel the most pathetic, I guess. Or at least Caroline did. It's like they *need* to see it."

I shake my head, my mouth going dry. "Why would they need to see something that hurts them?" *Why would you write* Ur pathetic *on a photo of yourself?*

"If I could answer that question…" For a moment his face shows a ghastly clash of expressions: guilt, remorse, incredulity, disgust. Then nothing. "You know better than I do. Tie him tight, and I promise I won't hurt him."

I squat beside Ellis and reach for his wrists, close enough to feel him trembling.

"Go," he whispers. "Run."

"No!" I turn to Dad. "You know this is wrong—you just said so. You don't want to do it. Why—"

A clap splits the air. I turn just in time to see a strip of bark

295

from the fir behind us go flying like shrapnel. The trunk bears a new wound, pale and oozing, inches above our heads.

Tendrils of smoke bleed from the barrel of Dad's gun. "That's the one useful thing I learned from Grandpa Frank," he says.

My fingers feel swollen and alien as I loop the rope around Ellis's wrists. He's clenching his fists, and I know that's smart; when he relaxes, so will the rope.

This is a game, just like chess, just like the Glare. We need to beat him.

"You don't want to hurt us," I say. "Why can't you just stop the game?"

"Hedda." It comes out in a sigh, as if my name hurts him. "What do you think happens if I shut down the server?"

I keep winding rope around Ellis's wrists, as loosely as I dare. "People stop dying."

"People who were warned. Why do you think I post those messages as L13Survivor? To give them a fair chance."

"No, to tempt them." I lob each word at him. "*You* put the game online in the first place."

Dad crosses his arms and stares at tire treads in the mud, the gun still cocked in our direction. "I hoped you'd understand."

"Understand what?"

"Without *that*"—Dad points the gun at the truck bed—"this whole life vanishes. No house, no Tesla, no college for you. No new contracts for me, no healthy bank balance. No career, no respect, no family. Just nightmares."

"But your nightmares went away."

The trees press around us, and I see my father as a small boy wandering these woods, finding his grandfather inside the black tower. Begging Grandpa Frank to stop waving the shotgun at monsters that weren't there. Waking in terror from a dream in which those monsters surrounded him.

"They went away," Dad says, "after I put the Glare online."

I want to laugh, but he looks dead serious. "The Glare keeps your nightmares away?"

"It contains them." When he says "them," his eyes flit over my head, around the clearing.

He believes it. He's scared.

I start to move, but the gun snaps back to me. "Double knot. Your part's almost done."

I knot the rope with tingling fingers. "So you're saying, if we smash the server, your nightmares come back?"

Dad's eyes keep scanning the woods. "You wouldn't remember, Hedda. But before the Glare, I was working like a dog, racking up debt, waking up screaming at night, trying to convince your mom and everybody else I wasn't an inch from needing to be institutionalized. Those words the Glare sends to everybody, *Ur pathetic*—those were the words I kept hearing in my head, just like I had since I was a kid. *You're pathetic. You'll never amount to anything.* I had to get those words *out* of my head, so I put them in the game, just a little taunting message, and then—"

"It worked." He sent his shame to other people, passed it on like a virus, so it wasn't just his anymore. He wasn't alone. He was connected.

He nods. "That server let me sleep at night, and when I was awake and working, all my ideas were gold. I was free—finally. Isn't that what you've always wanted—freedom? To get off that goddamn ranch and be your own person?"

Yes. But not this way. "Whatever happens, I'm going to tell people. You know that. I have to."

"Don't be dramatic." Dad clears his throat; his voice is weakening. "No one would believe you, and you won't get any more skulls—I've made sure of that. We'll decondition you, and you'll be fine, as soon as..."

Something thuds beside me—the bat. Dad has dropped it to take out his phone.

"Forgive me," he says. "One last time. I'd rather you not be around for this part."

Ellis sucks in a breath. "He's crazy. He's going to—"

The phone buzzes.

"—kill me."

Ellis's fingers have mine in a death grip, but it's too late. My eyes go to the screen like moths to a flame, and I look straight into the empty eye sockets of the skull.

And the forest comes alive.

38

First, the keening. Far off to my left, then to my right, creeping closer.

In the woods, something rustles. Crackles. Slithers. White flashes high in a ponderosa pine.

I turn just in time to spot something dashing from a hemlock thicket to the big spruce. My mouth goes dry as I see pendulous arms helping it move, legs bending the wrong way.

I have no Glare-gun. *I'm going to die.*

The sharp scent of pines has turned rusty as blood. I'm on my feet, everything pulsing, every inch of skin a target. This is their hunting ground. This is their game, and I'm in it.

A voice echoes faintly in my head: *He's going to kill me.*

Ellis said that about Dad, and it makes way too much sense,

but where is Ellis? Where's Dad? Sunlight has turned the whole clearing to pearly haze, the truck only an outline.

I turn the way we came and see nothing but Randoms.

It's like the corridor at school, except instead of jostling in all directions, they come straight at me, pouring up the hill like an invading army, wave after wave. They move like snakes, bodies shaping themselves fluidly to the terrain. And instead of talking and laughing, they're keening.

A hundred or more, their eyeless heads drawing a bead on me, their long-toed feet catching boughs and swinging. Keening and keening.

I can't move. Can't breathe. An icy wind gusts toward me. In the glowing mass, I see a face that looks like Anil's—and then his likeness flows to the next Random and the next, moving across them like a wave. Behind the keening, a distant roar begins.

Is this what happened to Anil when he ran outside? Did they come for him?

The thought releases me, and I run for the tower, the only safe place, aiming for that jagged wedge of blackness where the foundation has crumbled. I need to go low, to crawl—

I'll be back, Ellis. I can't die like Anil did.

I fought back in the game—how do I fight back here? Where's my ammunition?

The tunnel smells of slow decay, of subterranean concrete, of ancient fires. I flounder into the heap of junk, dragging myself on my elbows through liquor bottles, Mason jars, mold-spotted greeting cards, all glued into a semi-solid mass by leafmeal and moist dirt.

Something ice-cold grabs my ankle.

Not real. I kick out viciously with my free leg, my head swimming. *I'm fighting with myself.*

Then I'm past the junk and sitting upright in the center of the tower, panting, in sunlight again. I don't remember the cold fingers loosening and releasing me, only kicking and kicking. I double over and catch my breath, then roll on my back and gaze up at the opening in the smokestack.

Blue sky is filmed over with luminous clouds. As I watch, they drift into the shape of a familiar face. Not the skull this time, but the creator. The one it all belongs to.

My father gazes down, his cloud features frozen in a kind yet patronizing expression, as if we're still playing chess. He's with me in this safe place, watching over me, guarding me from the things outside.

It only works because people believe it.

I close my eyes and feel the tower press around me, and beyond it, the rest of the Glare.

His voice was the voice in my head, the one that made me keep playing. He was the Glare, and the Glare was him. The Glare never ignored me. It never forgot me. It always offered what I needed, and by the time I realized there was no way to win, it was too late.

I'm dead in the game. I died when I was six. I shouldn't be here at all.

Never mind, keep playing, my father says in a voice that vibrates deep in my bones, in my blood vessels, through my cell walls and into the coded strings of protein that make up my DNA, so close to his—because we, too, are just code in the end, though we think we're more.

Recharge. Keep playing.

A hectic pulse begins to beat in my head. *I gave the kid a chance,* it says. *I gave him a chance.*

Ellis has lost his chance, and Dad has Ellis, which means I have to get out of here and find them before—

The black walls of the smokestack pulse, shiny from the sunlight above. *Stay. You're safe here.*

But I can't stay, because it's exactly what he wants. I force myself to hands and knees again and crawl toward the opening.

If I stay here in the tower, Dad will return to the truck without a word about what happened to Ellis, and he'll set up his server in the cabin again, and he'll drive me home, and he'll expect me to keep my mouth shut because I don't want to go back to the desert and milk goats, because I like living in a beautiful house and riding in a beautiful car, and who would ever believe me, anyway?

He couldn't control Caroline, Rory, or Ellis, but he thinks he can control me. I haven't given him any reason to think he can't.

The junk pile is harder to scale from this side. I navigate its hillocks and hollows, tin and glass pricking my knees, and something jabs me in the gut—the framed photo I stuck in my hoodie.

Pulling it out, I realize I'm looking at the whole image. The one on Dad's desk was cut in two, leaving Dad alone, but now I see the face of the person who stands with a possessive hand on Dad's shoulder.

An old man—Grandpa Frank? He smiles, twisted and manic. The eye sockets are hollow, the cheeks too gaunt. It's the face of a skull.

The same skull I saw last night at the gas station, on my phone, on the plane.

Grandpa Frank is the skull, and Dad's hunched shoulders tell me he fears him, hates him. Enough to slice him out of the photo, enough to haul his possessions out of the cabin and dump them here where they'd never see daylight.

What did he tell me when I asked about the photo? *Sometimes we think that by cutting the worst things out of our lives, just severing them, we can get past them. It's a sort of magical thinking.*

I understand that too well.

I unzip my pack and slip the dirt-encrusted photo inside. If he can use magical thinking as a weapon, so can I.

It only works because people believe it.

When my fingers meet Raggedy Ann's soft face, it's like a chemical reaction—suddenly I'm lifting her out and pressing her to my chest. Still holding her, I scrabble the last inches outside.

39

The air shudders with my heartbeat. I can see the truck, see that Dad and Ellis are gone, but the circle of trees and sky keeps pulsing, strobing.

Flash: nothing there. Flash: something white, and I need cover, I need safety.

A rune glows on the trunk of the tree Dad used to demonstrate his shooting prowess. I bolt to it and hug it tight.

Five seconds. The forest continues to strobe, and with every other beat, Randoms creep toward me—from high in the trees, from underground. The keening intensifies.

I force myself to focus on the world outside the Glare. They must have left on foot. The trail we took here leads on, uphill.

The keening vibrates in the tree trunks, in my bones. It covers me like water, layer on layer, and I have to make an island in my brain long enough to decide that Dad didn't take Ellis back to the cabin. For what he needs to do, he went deeper into the woods, deep enough to drown the sound.

The keening stops all at once.

And still clutching my doll, my talisman, I run.

A moving furrow of leaves blocks my path. I leap right over it (*not real*), dash around the truck, and bend to snatch the bat from the spot where Dad left it. With it in one hand and Ann in the other, I head up the path, tasting iron.

Leaves slither. White shapes vault from tree to tree.

Here in these desolate woods, Grandpa Frank saw aliens. Monsters haunted Dad's dreams. The trail keeps getting steeper. I trip over a sapling and come down hard, my jaws jammed together by the impact. The bat starts rolling down the slope, and I catch it and go on, waiting for the moment when cold fingers will close on my ankle again.

But they seem to be hanging back. As if they're waiting for something.

At some point I drop Ann to get a better grip on the bat. Leaves crackle where she lands, whirling and flurrying, but I can't stop.

A few more gasping strides, and I'm cresting the hill. Below, a short, piney downslope ends at a sheer drop-off. The momentum carries me straight toward Dad, who's dragging Ellis down the incline.

Dragging, because Ellis is trudging along, hurt but alive, and when I see that, I get my second wind. At the bottom of the cliff grow tall, shimmering maples; their crowns fill the sky.

I was almost too late.

Needles slide under my sneakers. I scrabble for footing on the steep slope, tightening my grip on the bat, and come to a stop right above them. Ellis's head whips around.

"I smashed your server," I say, breathless. "It's gone. Can't you feel it?"

Dad turns, too, but there's only glowing white where his face should be.

For a sickening instant, I stand frozen, facing a Random wearing my father's clothes. Under the shiny, pixelated skin, the outlines of his face are crying, straining, as if he's trapped inside.

Yet he speaks in a calm voice: "You didn't smash anything. You know better."

I say, "It's gone, so there's no point in hurting anybody else. Let him go."

As I raise the bat, the Dad-Random presses the barrel of his gun against Ellis's cheek. "Don't move, Hedda."

The wind rises. The bat freezes in midair. I have to make him believe just long enough to lose his focus.

"I smashed it because I love you." I drop the bat and reach into my pack and pull out the stained, dirty photo of Dad in the clawlike grip of Grandpa Frank. I thrust it so close he can't turn away. "I bet *he* loved you, too."

My father laughs. His face is his face again—pale, sweaty skin and hazel eyes and glasses. "Never," he says. "He knew I was...pathetic."

He stares at the photo like it's the funniest thing he's ever seen. When he opens his mouth again, no words come out.

Now, while he's distracted. But as I bend to grab the bat, Dad's laugh turns to a moan. He lowers the gun and tears the photo from my hand.

"You *did* smash it," he says.

Ellis yanks himself free, stumbling straight into me, while Dad staggers backward, down the slope, eyes still glued to the image. The amusement on his face has twisted into shock, and then into horror. The moan rises again in his throat.

"Run!" Ellis yells.

I don't run. I can't even move, only watch as Dad's head darts like he hears something behind him. Back the other way, and then he cranes his neck to scan the treetops. I can't see anything that isn't there, can't hear anything but the sound he's making, but I know exactly what he sees and hears.

Rustling. Slithering. Keening. Fleeting white shapes in the trees.

He thinks I smashed the server. He thinks Grandpa Frank's monsters are coming for him.

And because he believes it, they are.

My father jerks backward as if a rope has yanked his ankle. He drops the photo and nearly drops the gun, then regains his footing and turns in a wobbly circle, aiming it wildly. I duck—but he's not aiming at us, not even seeing us. *There? There? Where are they?*

Magical thinking. Dad's nightmares are immune to bats and bullets. They are everywhere.

Ellis shields me with his body as my father breaks into a flailing run along the edge of the cliff—only to halt and turn in a circle again, cradling the gun against his chest. He is distinctly keening now.

"The hell?" Ellis whispers, as I say, "He doesn't see us anymore."

And then the nightmares fall on my father.

The gun claps. We both duck, and when we raise our heads again, he's down like a tree in a gale. He rolls and thrashes in the pine needles, his hands clawing desperately, trying to rip invisible fingers from his neck. His glasses go flying.

Another gunshot, and I press my hands to my eyes. The sounds of struggling stop abruptly.

I hear a choked sob or gasp that could be any one of us—a small sound, a pleading sound. Then silence, and I lower my hands, but I don't look down.

Ellis moves first.

When he lets me go, I sink to my knees. My muscles have gone watery, and it takes all my effort to keep my gaze on him as he approaches the edge.

"What?" I ask when he doesn't move.

Ellis keeps looking down. Shakes his head.

After what feels like hours, I walk closer to the edge and look, too. Dad lies on his side with his arms contorted against his chest as if he's still fending off an invisible assailant, and his temple—

Blood pools under his head, in his hair. I look away.

He seems naked without his glasses. I look around for them, wanting to prop them back on his nose, but Ellis says, "Don't touch anything. They'll need to see exactly how it happened."

Ellis is the one who leans close and checks for a pulse. I wait for him, feeling the tree against my back, sturdy and strong. I let my mind go blank.

The photo lies in the dirt, facedown, saying *Ur pathetic* over and over. I don't pick it up.

40

On the way back down the hill, I discover Raggedy Ann. She is mud-stained, and her right arm and left leg have been ripped from her body.

I tuck her in the crook of my arm. *It's okay. It's okay.* The missing limbs are nowhere to be found.

. . .

We smash the server into dozens of pieces, and then hundreds, using Ellis's hammer. Irritated by the noise, crows caw and fly off in a scuffle of wings.

I wish it had exploded. I wish it had fought back. But it's only a machine.

Who were the original Randoms? Aliens escaped from a

military base? Kids who tormented Dad at school, or frat bros who mocked him in college, or girls who wouldn't date him? It doesn't matter. When the nightmares stopped, he thought he'd escaped, but they were still there waiting for him, the instant he thought his server was gone.

The instant he saw his own version of the skull.

The sun is past the zenith now, the tower standing stark against the blue. I keep expecting Dad to limp down the trail toward us, carrying his gun.

I've told Ellis about the bloody clothes and the laptop in the cabin. They should help bolster the story we'll tell.

"Could you have a concussion?" I ask. "He hit you hard."

"Not dizzy yet."

My mind keeps slipping back to the top of that cliff, like the memory is something I need to steady myself. I'm there, standing in the golden-lime-green light that sifts through the maples, when Ellis says, "Nobody would believe us if we told them everything. You know that?"

"I know."

. . .

Blink, and we're in the Prius again, jolting back up the dirt road toward the highway. Silver feathers of cloud linger above the pines.

"Here's the story," I say. "After our friends died, and you learned about Caroline, we needed to get away, so we came here. We found the stuff in the cabin. We met Dad and started asking questions. And he...well, he ran away from us, and we couldn't stop him. When we caught up with him, it was over."

"And the server?"

"We found it like that." I feel so tired I can hardly speak. "He must have smashed it himself."

Ellis is nodding. "I found my sister online, and I dragged you to Bolinas. And after I found out she was dead, because I'm an irresponsible drunkard, instead of informing my parents, I ran off to Shasta County with you."

"They'll never figure out he killed her, though." The words feel alien in my mouth. "He did push her off that cliff, didn't he?" He sent her a skull, too, but maybe triggering her didn't work and he had to do the job the old-fashioned way.

"Probably." Ellis stares straight ahead at the road. "But it's not like it matters if we pin that on him, right? Not now."

"Still," I say, "Caroline deserves for people to know what really happened to her. She tried to warn me."

Blink, and the I-5 spools out before us like a dappled gray river, yellow lines stretching to infinity. I close my eyes and see the lime-green light of the spot where my father rests in the Glare. Are the Randoms still there, or did they go with him?

. . .

When I turn on my phone, approaching San Rafael, things become real again—the reflective signs, the clouds, the gash on Ellis's temple.

"We'll have to explain that," I say, but don't hear the answer, because text after text from Erika is scrolling down my screen.

Please call and tell me you're okay.

I mean it.

Then, from this morning: *Please, please call.*

Please answer.

Several hours later, around the time we left Dad's property: *Mireya's here. Seems ok, but scared. Wants to see you.*

The next text, from forty minutes ago, is the one that makes me sit up straight, nerves alight and stomach churning: *This is Mireya. You need to come home and help me find yr dad. He made the Glare, and Rory figured it out. Some kind of signature in the code he sent me. Turning all phones off now.*

So Mireya figured it out, too. When the cops find Dad on that clifftop, they'll think they know exactly what happened—that he couldn't run from his own guilt, however they choose to understand it.

But that's not what matters now. Mireya needs to know she's no longer in danger. "Ellis," I say, "step on it."

41

Our street looks the same. The sun is lowering, its late glow catching in the cottonwoods as they ripple in the bay breeze, leaves showing their silvery undersides.

Ellis pulls into our driveway, and I slide out before he can stop the car, the seat belt alert dinging. "Wait!" he yells.

I'm already pounding up the front steps, my breath catching with the sudden exertion after so many hours of forced immobility, because I know who's in there.

My brother, who showed me how to ride the waves. Erika, who sat with me in the grass of the dark backyard. Two people who just lost a family member because of me and don't know it yet.

And Mireya, who brought me to school with her, who shared

the story of her own distant dad with me. If she hurts Clint or Erika, if she hurts herself, if anyone's hurt—

The key turns, and I throw open the door to find Clint stretched on the living room rug, adding a piece to a Lego skyscraper.

He squirms when I try to hug him, relief bringing tears to my eyes, and says in a tense, adult voice, "They're in there."

I wish I could hold tight to him and tell him everything, because whenever and however he hears, this is going to rip his world in two. Sometimes it's the absent parent who becomes the lodestar of your life, because you can imagine him however you want him to be.

From the kitchen, Erika's strained voice calls, "Hedda?"

I have no weapon to meet Mireya if she comes at me the way she did last time. But she won't, will she? The conditioning can't last. With Ellis close behind me, I tiptoe from hardwood to dingy pink tile, bracing myself.

Erika and Mireya sit on opposite sides of the kitchen table with a pot of tea between them. Steam in the air reddens their cheeks.

Their eyes meet mine—Erika's nervous, Mireya's raw and red—and I know no one here is seeing Randoms. Not right now. Erika says, "Thank God you're okay," but in a flat voice, and she doesn't get up.

Mireya says, "We've been waiting."

"We need to talk. It's *all right*." I try to send her the full message with my eyes, reluctant to say it in front of Erika, because Ellis is right about no one believing us. *No more skulls.*

"Erika, I—I was up in Shasta County. Dad was there. Something happened."

Erika is staring at me. "Is it true, then?"

"What?"

"Your dad killed Rory," Mireya blurts out. Her forehead is washed but not bandaged, covered with short dark gashes.

I expect Erika to protest, but she only says in a small, emotionless voice, "When your father was drunk once, he told me he'd written a piece of code that could make people see things that weren't there. He said it was his greatest achievement, and he only got rid of it because he was afraid it had hurt you. He said it was the hardest decision of his life." Her gaze moves from me to Mireya. "I didn't take him seriously. I should have, shouldn't I?"

"It's over now," I say.

The tension in Erika's jaw shows me this isn't over for her. She thinks Dad will come back to sit in this kitchen, maybe tonight, and she'll have to decide whether to repeat everything Mireya said about the Glare or let it go.

She doesn't know his grandfather and the Randoms have got him, unsafe and unsound.

"Hedda," Ellis calls from the living room.

There's too much to say, and shrinking time to say it in. "Erika, I—"

The doorbell rings, an abrasive chirp.

Erika jumps to her feet. She glances at Mireya as if expecting her to bar the way, but Mireya shrugs.

Erika goes to the door. "Oh!" I hear her say, startled. "We weren't expecting you."

316

And then a familiar voice, a voice that brings back ten years of patient hard work under desert skies, says, "I got Hedda's letter."

I sink onto the chair that Erika vacated, feeling the last ounce of resistance bleed out of me. "Mom, I'm in here."

42

Mom comes with us to the police station. She sits beside me the whole time we talk with Detective Lu and two of her colleagues. Her eyes flash whenever she gets near a screen, but she doesn't say anything.

It's a bizarre story—so much death in it, so close together. We can't explain the motive for Dad hurting Rory, so we don't try, hoping that whatever is on his laptop will fill in some blanks.

Detective Lu asks Ellis and me the same questions, over and over. Her eyes remain wary, but right before she lets us go home, she makes a call to the sheriff of Shasta County and asks him to send two deputies to Dad's property.

Ellis goes home to his parents, and we go back to the gabled house behind the cottonwoods. Mom is quieter than I've ever known her. She makes tea for Erika and heats leftovers. Right before dinner, the detective calls and speaks to Erika. We eat in silence while Clint plays a game in his room, and then Erika nearly chokes on a bite, her eyes full, and says, "I have to tell him," and gets up and goes upstairs.

Which leaves Mom and me alone.

Here we are in the kitchen with the dingy pink tiles, where I tried to cut words on my arm to stop the Randoms from coming. In the beautiful home where she raised me until everything went wrong.

I face her across the table. Her black hair is down and combed, and she wears makeup and a turquoise sweater, something she'd never do on the ranch, and she looks younger. Softer.

I feel guilty now for thinking she created the Glare, but it's true she tried to sever herself from parts of her life, just like Dad did. "You came because of my letter," I say. "Because I told you I'm not afraid of the Glare anymore."

It feels like ten years ago that I wrote that letter—so proud of myself for shaking off childhood fears.

Mom nods, and her jaw tightens, making her look more like the mom I know.

"You just left your sick friend?"

She shakes her head. "My friend's estranged sister decided not to be estranged from her after all. They're having a long visit."

Everything about her expression says, *And you do need me here, right? Look what happened. I told you so.*

Normally that look would send bolts of hot rage through me, but I'm not capable of holding bolts of hot rage today. Every time I close my eyes, I see the canopy of trees below Dad's resting place.

Still, there's something I have to point out. "You didn't even call. Why?"

"I knew what you'd say."

"You didn't want me to be prepared. You figured you'd just show up and drag me back to the ranch, and I'd be too freaked out to say no."

Mom contemplates the tabletop, letting me win the stare-off. "Does it matter what I was planning when I left?"

She's right. Things have changed, and I won't have much choice about going back with her now.

With one eye on her, I pull out my phone and turn it on. (*Don't buzz. Please.*) I draft a message to Ellis.

When I glance up again, Mom's glaring with the force of a cyclone—nostrils flaring, leaning forward in her chair as if she hopes to wrest the phone from my hand by sheer brainpower.

But she doesn't actually reach for it.

I switch the phone into airplane mode. I put the phone down.

And then I get up and fold her in my arms, shocked by how small and brittle she feels for the first time in my life. She stiffens for an instant, but then she wraps her own arms around me and holds tight.

So fierce. So determined to protect me, though she hasn't known how to do that for a while.

"It's okay, Mom," I say, rubbing her shuddering back. "I'm okay. You don't have to worry anymore."

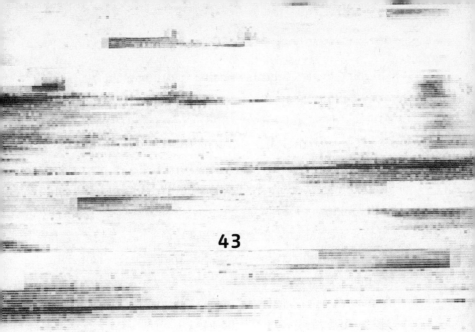

43

The goats seem to like Ellis. He rubs their foreheads and even lets two bored adolescent kids chase him around the barn.

"Careful," I say, "or they'll try to make you stay here forever."

"Maybe I wouldn't mind."

"You've never been here when it's a hundred and fifty degrees." I load him down with a bucket of hen feed and draw a gallon of water. "Or alone all winter with nobody but a middle-aged technophobe for company."

Both of us glance toward the house, where Mom is busy stirring gravy and mashing sweet potatoes for Thanksgiving dinner. When I told her Ellis would be driving out for a visit, she took it surprisingly well; she's even been making civil conversation with him. But then, a teenage boy in the house could never be as disturbing to her as the unwelcome guest I brought back with me from California: my phone.

Once a day I turn it on to exchange e-mail with Ellis, Mireya, Clint, and Erika, and sometimes to talk with them. The rest of the time, I hide it in a rotating roster of places, just in case Mom gets ideas. So far, she hasn't found it, or maybe she isn't looking.

Maybe she's started to accept that I, too, have a line to the outside world. And maybe she's glad to know she was half-right: Something did reprogram my brain.

Someone.

"But you're okay, right?" Ellis asks. "I mean, you don't feel as alone as you used to?"

I remember what Dad warned me would be the result of smashing the server: no California, no college. I feel my jaw stiffen. "I can take it. Just not forever."

"You'll get into Cal next year. No worries."

I *will* go to college, and it can't come soon enough. With some of the money from Dad's estate, I take community college courses in town twice a week now. They give me a chance to go online and to see other human faces, and each time I return to the ranch—on my own now, with my license and my own beater car—I don't feel as much like I'm going to Siberia.

Outside the barn, November sunlight falls soft on our faces, reflected off the vast stretches of yellow- and red-brown. Ellis thinks it's cool how barren it is out here—easy for him to say, having lived in Marin all his life.

I can't pretend I don't miss it.

The chickens cluck up a racket, milling around our calves, and I remember how I named them all: Agatha and Dorothea and Judy and Noreen. My friends.

"I'll be back in the summer," I say, showing Ellis where to pour the feed. "Erika says I can watch Clint while she's working." *And you'll be right next door.*

Down by the creek, the cottonwoods have yellowed, and the dry air has a bite to it. Wedding Cake Mesa looms red on the horizon.

"I saw Erika just before I left," Ellis says, watching the hens scramble for feed. "She said she's thinking about selling the house and moving to a condo."

Erika's hinted as much to me, but the news still hits hard. I turn away, snapping the water bottle into its stand. "I love that house. But I know it's expensive."

Dad's warning wasn't just talk. With him gone—*say it, dead*—Erika is struggling with debts and property taxes and private school tuition. It doesn't help that everyone thinks Dad shot himself because he stabbed Rory in the hatchback, and that he stabbed Rory because Rory found out Dad was giving away software on the Dark Web that contained code that belonged contractually to Sinnestauschen Labs, code that Caroline stole and passed to Dad for his own game.

At least, that's how the cops and reporters understand it, and it's the only story anyone's likely to believe. As for what *exactly* happened on the Dark Web—well, it's called the Dark Web for a reason.

I don't want to think Dad planned Rory's murder. I want to

think he triggered Rory and stabbed him, as he claimed, in self-defense. But what difference does it make?

Sometimes, during the long desert nights, I have a waking dream in which a neighbor sees Dad get into Rory's hatchback, and he's arrested that same day. He never drives out to Bolinas to push Caroline off the cliff. He never drives to Shasta to move the server. We smash it, and he goes to jail and helps other inmates learn basic computer skills.

And every time I visit him, he reminds me I'm the one who brought the Glare back home. He tells me about his unbearable nightmares and the words "You're pathetic" he can't expel from his head.

"Hey." Ellis touches my elbow. "You doing okay?"

"It's just so weird having you here. Like you belong to a different part of my life, a different world."

He picks up the empty feed bucket. "You're coming back to California."

"I hope so. It's just, well—if I do come back, I don't know if I'll be ready."

Ellis's brows pull down. "Because of phones? Do you still get triggered?"

I shake my head too quickly. "I think that's over. It's just different out here. Want to go see if the table's set?"

I don't tell him what I'm thinking: that Dad never escaped the place he grew up or the fears that lived in him those summers in Grandpa Frank's cabin. No amount of magical thinking could sever him from his past; no amount of code could rewrite it.

Emily, Rory, Anil, Mireya, me—we all had past "fails" we

were ashamed of. We tried to click away from them, but the Glare brought them back. And hearing a phone buzz still sets something vibrating deep inside me like a residual organ.

We walk to the house, the sky striped the color of a bruise, and maybe Ellis can tell what I'm thinking about, because he takes my hand.

. . .

After all the leftovers have been stowed in the fridge and the dishes have been hand-washed, we take a walk up the ridge in the dark. I could find the way blindfolded, and Ellis insists he doesn't need a flashlight if I don't.

"Don't risk your neck just for fun," I warn him.

"I can't watch the game out here. I gotta entertain myself somehow."

Way up, where there's a view of the valley for miles, we spread out a blanket, then arrange three candles among the crags and light them. Rory, Anil, Caroline. Emily's out of the hospital and getting better every day, just like Mireya and me.

The flames waver fluidly in the darkness, casting ghostly reflections against the glass holders, but they can't drown the brilliance of the stars.

I hesitate a moment, then pull out Raggedy Ann and prop her up a safe distance from the candles. She has new eyes now, but I haven't replaced her limbs, and I wonder sometimes where they are and who has them.

As Ellis stretches out on the blanket, and I lean against

him—tentatively, because we haven't really started touching again yet—his phone buzzes. I feel it against my hip.

Look at me, the phone says, like always. *Look, look, look, look.*

I hold my breath, not daring to turn and look at Ellis. My shoulders go rigid, my eyes scanning the crags around us and the ragged line between the mesa and the stars.

They are there. They must be. I always know when they're there.

But I see nothing. I hear nothing.

"Hedda." Ellis's hands creep round my waist, pulling me back into the shelter of his body, like they did that night at the gas station. "It's okay. Nothing's there."

Does he know how close I came to hurting him that night?

I try to relax into his arms. "I'm fine."

If I reached under his jacket and grabbed his phone right now, if I activated the camera and peered through it into the darkness, what would I see?

The desert pitch-black feels different now, dense with unseen presences. The candles that honor the dead keep dipping and pulsing, and Ellis's breath is warm on my neck.

He thinks the game's over, but I know Dad's out there somewhere, still playing. It was his choice, after all, to make it unwinnable.

So I'll keep playing, too—just not his game.

"Do you have the flask?" I whisper.

Ellis shakes his head. "I'm cutting back."

"Good." I feel guilty for asking, and that opens a deeper pool of guilt in my chest, and for an instant I think I might drown.

The flames keep flickering, and Ellis's fingertips press my bare skin. Slowly the warmth of his flesh, the soft gusting of his breath, bring me back to myself.

Far away, in the empty rooms and alleyways of my mind, I still hear the keening.

ACKNOWLEDGMENTS

This story took a while to decide how it needed to be told, and I'm grateful for all the help I received along the way. My agent, Jessica Sinsheimer, kept me on track with grace, patience, honesty, and no qualms about suggesting I kill off more characters. Hannah Allaman provided brilliant editorial guidance as the story moved toward its final form, while Laura Schreiber was invaluable at the earlier stages. Thank you so much to everyone on the Hyperion team for your support and for the gorgeous presentation of this book.

Rachel Carter and Dayna Lorentz weathered turbulent brainstorming sessions, read way too many drafts, and offered brutal frankness when I needed it. Nicole Lesperance and Jennifer Mason-Black contributed incisive feedback and emotional support, as did Pat Esden, Vikki Ciaffone, and Aimee Picchi.

Andrew Kozma, who knows way more about gaming than I do, generously helped me add a layer of authenticity.

Thank you to the Sweet Sixteens and Absolute Write for the community, to my coworkers for the understanding, to Harvey Sollberger for always being ready to discuss ideas, and most of all to Sophie Quest and Eva Sollberger for the steadfast conversation and commiseration, year in and year out. Finally, thank you to my readers. Writing is about trying to make a connection, and without you, I would be like Hedda in the desert, reaching out and getting no signal.